This story moved my heart on a deep level. It is eye-opening, gritty, challenging, and hopeful.

> — LAURA A. GRACE, AUTHOR OF DEAR AUTHOR: LETTERS FROM A BOOKISH FANGIRL

Would I, a non Christian, be able to understand? to relate? Well yes ... yes I did, not only understand, but I also enjoyed it SO very much!

> — OVI, GOODREADS

Allison handles each theme and character with grace and gentleness, while never shying away from the truth, leaving the reader with a story that will stick with them long after they finish the last page.

> — NOVEL-TEA READS

Wow. Just wow ... Well written. Relatable. Captivating. I will definitely recommend this to friends. I actually plan to pass my copy of this novel along to my mom and ask her to do the same after she has read it.

> — OF BOOKS & PORTKEYS

Living Water

Allison Wells

MONSTER IVY
PUBLISHING

For My Husband, the one and only man in my life.

Chapter One

PAPARAZZI

*I*f you had told the high school version of me what my life would look like by the time I was in my forties, I would have laughed in your face. There are so many times I would have found a redo button handy. But, life happens and we just have to get through it.

One thing I knew for sure—I never wanted to be infamous. I don't know anyone who would want that. I never wanted to be famous or well-known, either. I didn't want people to know who I was as I walked through a door. There's too much baggage that comes with that. Too much responsibility. I did my best in high school to not even stand out. I just wanted to get through life as unscathed as possible and live a nice, normal life.

Didn't everybody want to be a household name? My family thought so. My father was a senator who found ways to put himself in the spotlight every chance he could. My sweet Momma was more concerned with appearances than reality, preening when she knew a camera would be around. And my sisters, all three of them, would have killed to be a topic in the tabloids. They relished the limelight and felt they deserved every pat on the back they could get.

Not me. I would much rather watch the news than be the news. I always felt that way.

Being noticed meant being exposed and I never wanted to be exposed. Being exposed meant people could see through you, make snap judgments and those could affect the rest of your life. Like my grandparents. My grandfather had also been a senator and when a scandal broke out about him in the 1960s, my poor grandmother had a heart attack and died. My father was only twelve years old, his sister only six. The media chewed my family up and spit them out and it killed my grandmother. I was convinced my entire childhood that my sweet mother might suffer the same fate if my dad got mixed up in something.

Even at school, I didn't like it when teachers called on me. I liked it even less when the paparazzi tracked us down for a candid, unsuspecting photo. Who would like that? Didn't these people know that their actions could have deadly consequences?

It was in my junior year of high school when my father, South Carolina senator Dennis DePrivé, voted down some big education reform bill. It would seem like that was the wrong choice, because the world and everyone in it went crazy, bashing him left and right. Or, at least that was how it seemed to me. His name, and the name of his family, was dragged through the mud. I worried about my mother's health.

After that big vote, he had come back home to spend a few days with us in South Carolina and let the dust settle. Little did we all know that the paparazzi would trail him all over Columbia. I certainly had no idea photographers would be waiting for me near my car after school on a

Tuesday afternoon, wanting to snap photo after photo of the senator's poor, under-educated daughter.

A male voice bellowed at me. "Roxie! Roxie, look over here!"

I jumped, nearly tripped, and dropped all my books. Heavy paper-bag clad books spilled and slid on the unforgiving gravel of the parking lot. I had not been looking toward my car, but instead watching the guy I liked, Josh, head for his own truck, guitar slung over his shoulder like the true star he was.

Now I was faced with three men hovering near my car, all with cameras for heads, as their faces were completely obscured. The sound of camera shutters ricocheted through my head.

"Ms. DePrivé, what do you think of your father's decision to keep schools in the dark ages? Don't you think he, and your school, should join the rest of the world in the '90s? What will happen at the turn of the century?"

"Do you feel like you're being deprived of a quality education?"

I hated it when people asked me questions I had no way of answering. I was a teenager. I didn't know what my dad did at his job. And how many teenagers are interested in both their father's jobs and politics?

With the cameras in front of them, I had no way of knowing who had asked what. Not that it mattered. Tears began to sting my eyelids as I searched the ground for my scattered belongings. I didn't want my backside exposed for them to take photos of that, so I tried to turn so that the men were at my side.

I didn't reply to them. I couldn't—I honestly had no idea what they were talking about. My father spent most of his time in Washington, D. C. and only came home a few days each month and on holidays. I didn't ask what his politics and policies were any more than he asked how my life was going.

I quickly gathered my things, threw them into the passenger seat and slid behind the wheel of my old Monte Carlo. With the door closed, the photographers got bolder and snuck closer to my window. I yanked the scrunchie from my hair and pulled mousy brown locks in front of my face before I hit the gas and peeled out, hoping I kicked up enough dust to choke the intruding men. The photographers ran after the car a few steps before giving up the chase. They got what they had come for.

The next morning, I was horrified to see my dad reading the paper with my face splashed across the front page. The headline announced, "Senator DePrivé Denies Daughter Chance of Top Education." I did not appreciate waking up to the candid front page photo of me dropping my things. My lackluster ponytail was flying in all different directions, I had a zit the size of Mount Rushmore on my forehead, and I was mid-surprise so my mouth was agape.

Despite the headline and photo displayed across the front of The State, then the Washington Post, and who knows what other newspapers, my father held no sympathy for me and my plight. He only shook his head and cursed the journalists who would do anything for a story, including stake out a high school parking lot. My mother reminded him it was my face on the front page.

"Margaret, it may be Roxie's face, but it's about me. I just wanted to come home and relax a little. Is that too much to ask? They're just using her to sell their blasted lies. Maybe I need a press conference." He shook his head and slammed the paper down on the dining room table next to his orange juice.

A look of compassion crossed my mother's face as she sat next to my father. "Dennis, poor Roxie…"

A vein throbbed on his temple as he snapped at her before she could finish. "Poor Roxie nothing. She's fine." He looked up from the paper and gestured toward me standing in the kitchen. "See? She's fine. Hand me the phone, Margaret, let me call my publicist."

My mother never spoke up against my father. Margaret DePrivé was a proper Southern wife with her husband at the head of the family. His word was law and she would never go against him. I knew that well enough.

"Roxie, this is why having your hair and makeup done is always important. You just never know," Mom said, shaking her head as she got the phone for my father.

It was always about appearances for Momma. She always said looking good equaled feeling good and being good. I didn't know if I prescribed to that idea, but it has been ingrained in me and my sisters from childhood. They were always ready for a camera to leap out at them and begin an impromptu photoshoot. Meanwhile, I was the ugly duckling back in the corner, but I was happier that way.

My shoulders slumped as my mother once again gave me a look of pity. I didn't want her pity. I wanted to disappear. I grabbed my backpack and lunch and went to school, wishing I could wear a sack over my head. Maybe then they wouldn't mock me.

Thankfully my schoolmates didn't read the paper, so they didn't see my unflattering photo. That or they didn't realize the girl in the paper was me, the quiet girl at the back of every classroom. I was still completely unknown to Josh Keene, a fellow junior who everybody knew. A few teachers gave me expressions of concern throughout the day, but they didn't say anything outright. I think if it hadn't been for the DePrivé name, they would have never known it was me.

I only knew a handful of people at school and really only had one friend, Jessica Pinner. She had indeed seen the offending picture of me. She shook her head at me and told me she was sorry. At least she didn't treat me like a child or try to explain the intrusion of privacy away. I managed to make it through the day in one piece.

That evening my sister Lori had a different take on my photo in the paper. Lori was only a year older than me, but she was attending the Governor's School of the Arts for her senior year of high school. She was constantly busy with horseback riding, volunteering at a homeless shelter, and being a Girl Scout. When she called that night she had been quick to voice her jealousy over my being in the paper.

"Rox, geez you're lame. You always get the attention and you never actually do anything. Meanwhile, I'm like Mother Theresa over here and nobody notices," she whined.

"What do you mean, I always get the attention?" We were always in the news in some fashion or another because Dad was always up to something. We were often photographed with him or as a family without anyone being better paparazzi fodder than someone else.

I could visualize my sister shaking her head at me, her honey-blonde hair moving ever so slightly, blue eyes gleaming, pink lips forming a pout. "You don't understand the plight of a middle child. Shelly and Jenny are always pictured as future senators or First Ladies, and you're the adorable baby who has always been told to look cute. I'm just stuck in the middle with never a comment thrown my way. Remember that Thanksgiving article in Southern Home? You were front and center in the picture, even though I was wearing that gorgeous fuchsia dress. Shelly and Jenny were quoted. I was like the redheaded stepchild."

Shaking my head, I felt the hot tears form in my eyes. "I was ten when that article came out. It was years ago, Lori."

"It doesn't matter. It's always about you. I dress as bright and loud as I can so people will actually see me, and instead I'm hidden away at this school, and you end up in the paper. You and your outdated clothes from last year."

I couldn't believe my sister would want to trade places with me in this instance. "Did you see the picture? I looked like a freak. It was awful," I reminded her.

She thought a moment, then quipped, "You know what they say, 'No publicity is bad publicity.'"

Exasperated, I threw my free hand up in the air. "I don't want any publicity. I just want to go about my life and not have anyone or anything interfere."

With a sigh, my sister clucked at me the way our mother had. "Well, you know, Roxie, the story was really about Dad. Not you."

I knew. Everybody seemed intent on reminding me. Why did they always think I would forget these things? No, I didn't want the attention, but I knew how it worked. I knew how to play the game between my family and the media.

After that, I started to wear my long, straight hair down over my face more. Maybe if nobody could recognize me, I wouldn't show up in any more newspapers. I also asked the school to transfer my parking spot to one in the front corner of the student lot. At least then I could scout for paparazzi before getting to my car. A marked police car also sat in the teacher lot across from ours and watched as school dismissed every day.

I'd always done my best to blend into the crowd, but I did so even more after that incident. I kept to neutral colors like black, khaki, and blue. My shirts were oversized and baggy, so I hid in them. It helped that it was in fashion to wear baggy clothes. Nothing bright like Lori. Nothing edgy like Jenny or tailored like Shelly. I didn't want to be caught off guard again.

The plus side to my new incognito look and parking spot was that I could blend into my surroundings and watch Josh go to his own truck just a few spots down from mine. He drove a 1984 Chevy pick-up. It had been painted bright orange and it stood out just as much as he did. It would be the most uncool car in the world if he wasn't the one driving it. Not like the hand-me-down 1992 gray compact Honda I drove around. It faded from memory, much like I did.

But I would sit in my car, turn on the Cranberries, and watch Josh stride to his car. He would carefully place his guitar inside, rev the engine, and drive off without a care in the world.

I would have never known then that Josh Keene would be the first man I would walk down an aisle and promise my forever to.

Chapter Two

WHAT'S LOVE GOT TO DO WITH IT?

My senior year of high school wasn't that much different from the previous three years. Nobody knew me, I got decent grades, my social life was pretty non-existent. I hung out with Jessica from time to time, but her parents had made her get a job. She was mortified to be working at the mall with all those typical kids, but she fit right in with the crowd at Spencer's where she sold novelty items and crude T-shirts.

My father made me apply to the University of South Carolina. I hid the acceptance letter from him, which wasn't so easy since he had lost the election and was home all the time now. But I had stuffed it in my backpack and hid it in the outside trash can. He'd figure out I wasn't going eventually.

Not that I had any plans. Did I need to have my life figured out by the time I graduated? According to my parents, I certainly did. I needed a life plan at seventeen years old. I told them I would figure it out. Didn't I want to be a lawyer or at least go to school to get my Mrs.? No.

Paying for school just to end up married was not my goal in life.

I relayed this to Jessica and her boyfriend, Brian. They were going to college together down at the beach.

"Who's typical now?" I asked, jokingly.

"It's not typical, actually. It's quite rare for romantic partners to travel to the same college." Jessica had an answer for everything.

They soon left me alone, and I ate lunch while doing some math homework outside. I was at a long table, but there were groups at all the tables around me, including Josh Keene and his groupies.

My crush on Josh had only gotten stronger. He was a sensitive man wrapped up in a rock star image. He cried when Kurt Cobain died, and complained when Green Day became a bunch of sell-outs more interested in money than the music. He never went anywhere without his guitar, and even though it wasn't supposed to be in classrooms, our teachers never said anything to him. I always wondered if they were in awe of him or if they just didn't care.

He was handsome to boot. With his blond hair hanging loosely over his face and piercing blue eyes, he had the look of a surfer, but he had never been surfing as far as I knew. We lived two hours from the beach. He was tall and skinny, wearing baggy jeans and flannel shirts. It worked for him. Josh was hard not to notice. I tried not to notice him for four years.

Where I was wholly unremarkable, Josh was the opposite. He wanted to be noticed and he was noticed. Josh was gregarious. A social butterfly. He knew everyone and everyone knew him. Lunch every day was spent sitting on one of those long faux-wood tables, strumming out chords with a crowd of people around him. Usually girls. Usually girls who were willing to let him get to at least second base. But even the guys liked hanging out with him. But Josh – Josh really didn't care what people thought as long as he got to play his music.

Looking back, I should have kept this in mind. Music was Josh's life, and nothing else would measure up.

On this day, his usual entourage was around him. Girls wearing wide-legged jeans and too-tight crop tops, guys who wore the same hairstyle as him and called everyone "Dude." His song of choice was the popular Green Day song "When I Come Around." It was one of my MTV favorites, so I sang along quietly. I sat alone, my head buried in my work.

Apparently, my accompaniment didn't go unnoticed by Josh, because the music stopped, and he slowly sauntered over to me. I didn't notice at first, not until his shadow came over my notebook. I knew it was him right away. I looked up, feeling the rush of burn on my cheeks. His bleach blond hair fell over his baby blue eyes. His smile made the hairs on the back of my neck stand. It was electric.

"You were singing," he said simply. He slid into the seat next to mine at the plastic patio table. I could smell CK One on him and I willed myself not to inhale too deeply. Had I been singing that loud? I didn't think I had been.

I looked around to see if anyone was watching him talk to me. Sure enough, several pairs of eyes were trained on us. I could feel my stomach flip flop at the attention.

Blushing even more, I admitted, "Yeah. It's catchy. I have the CD." Then I added, "I'm sorry if I disrupted you." I folded my arms in front of me as a buffer between us. My pencil stabbed me, but I didn't flinch.

His long, lanky fingers pushed hair behind his ear. "Nah, man. I mean, that was great. You have a great voice." Then he snapped his fingers like he had a brilliant idea. "You should sing with me."

My eyes widened at his suggestion. Josh Keene wanted me to sing with him? To my knowledge, he had never invited anyone to sing with him. His band was solidly established around town, but as far as I knew, none of his bandmates contributed their voices to the music.

The heat on my cheeks flamed and must have scorched my throat because I couldn't speak at all. I licked my lips and swallowed hard. Was I going to swallow my tongue? Pass out?

"Sing with me," he requested again. Those eyes were hypnotic.

"No, no, I can't," I stammered with nervous laughter. Was he playing a cruel joke on me? Was I on that hidden camera show?

I quickly glanced around. Nobody seemed to be mocking me. There were no cameras flashing. What had drawn him over to me, I wondered. I wore a pale purple T-shirt and blue jeans. My hair was pulled back into a long ponytail; nothing about me screamed for attention.

"Yeah, listen, you have an awesome voice," he told me, catching my eye and smiling. He looked genuine and his expression was inviting.

"Really?" I croaked.

"Yeah. Roxie, right?"

I could only nod. He knew my name.

"You interested, Roxie?"

Josh Keene knew my name.

Unsure what else to say, I nodded. "Sure." I looked into his eyes and smiled, hoping there wasn't any school-lunch lasagna stuck in my teeth. "Any time." I tightened my arms around my middle, almost willing myself to pull away from him.

Josh tore a piece of paper from my notebook and grabbed the pencil from my white-knuckled fingers. He wrote down an address. "This is where I live. Come by tomorrow morning around eleven, and we can jam in my garage." Taking the paper from him, I managed to agree. He stood, guitar in hand, winked at me, and walked away, his hair bobbing as he went.

I sat dumbfounded for a few minutes. Josh Keene knew my name. And he wanted me, of all people, to come to his house and sing with him. I pulled my ponytail around my neck to cover the redness while I willed my skin color to come back to normal.

The stares from those sitting nearby didn't abate. I could feel their eyes boring into me. I could hear their whispers behind my back. *Who is she? What did Josh say to her? Does she even go to school here?* The color stayed in my cheeks and I felt overheated. I needed to get back inside to cooler air and away from prying eyes.

Closing my math book, I looked at the address he had given me. I should crumple it up and forget the whole thing. Maybe the joke was when I showed up tomorrow. If I went to Josh's house, the kids at school would talk. I didn't want that. But then again, I would do just about anything to hear Josh say my name again. A name he already knew.

I looked at the address again. It wasn't too far from my house. I smiled and stood up. And I almost tripped over the bench legs as I started to walk away. My immediate thought was to see who was watching, but I held still, took a deep breath, and scurried inside. I, who always wanted to go unnoticed, was noticed by Josh Keene. The feeling was terrifying and exhilarating.

At the end of the school day, my friend Jessica found me. Her heavily lined eyes and babydoll dress created a strange juxtaposition of styles. She fell in step beside me as I walked to my car.

"Rumor is you're going for a make-out session at Josh Keene's tomorrow," she said, her voice low.

"Who told you that?" I pulled her close.

"Oh, everyone is talking about it. Mandy A. and Mandy L. are very unhappy. And Kevin wondered if you were new." Jessica rolled her eyes.

"Believe it or not, Jess, he invited me to come sing with him." Hours later, I was still unsure I had heard him correctly.

"He knew who you were?"

I stopped in front of my car as other kids walked by, talking and laughing. "He knew my name."

"I want a full report," Jessica said, her black-rimmed eyes crinkling up as she smiled.

I couldn't stop the blush from creeping up my neck if I wanted to. I only nodded and turned, fumbling with the keys to my ancient car, glad the days of photographers chasing me were behind me since my dad was back to civilian life. Jessica went off to her own car down the same row.

The next morning I arrived at the address promptly at eleven. Then I realized he probably wasn't used to people being on time and I didn't want to look like a geek, so I waited five minutes before going up to the door. The house was a brick tri-level with pastel blue curtains in the windows. A cheery looking white, wooden bunny leftover from Easter greeted me at the top of the stairs.

I checked my reflection in the door glass. I had taken great pains to look like I had made no effort at all. I wore my light brown hair loose around my shoulders. I had moussed it so it looked like I hadn't actually brushed it. I wore shorts that were a little too short and an oversized T-shirt that almost completely covered the shorts. A scrunchy sat on my left wrist with my watch. It had taken me forty-five minutes to decide on that outfit earlier in the morning. Now I was second-guessing it.

I knocked anyway. A beautiful woman opened the door. She reminded me of Princess Diana, full of grace and poise. She even was styled like her with a flowery dress that looked like something from a royalty-only catalog. Her blond hair was pulled back in a slick bun, but a few curly tendrils had been strategically pulled from their confines.

She smiled at me, tipped her head to the side, and asked, "May I help you?"

Timidly, I replied, "Hi. I'm here to see Josh." I couldn't even look at her. I wasn't even sure if she heard me. I cleared my throat, but then thought it wasn't ladylike. I pushed my hair behind my ears, suddenly feeling like I wasn't good enough standing before the princess-like Mrs. Keene.

"Sure, come on in, sweetie," she said, holding the door open. "What is your name? I'll tell him you're here."

"Roxie," I said. "Roxie DePrivé."

She held out her hand and I shook it. "Nice to meet you, Roxie. I'm Grace Keene, Josh's mother. Hang on, I'll find him for you."

And that was the first time I met my first mother-in-law.

Of course, I had no idea at the time. I guess it's common not to realize exactly who someone will be in your life until after you've met them.

I also had no idea that Josh would sweep me off my feet and turn me into the Yoko Ono of his band, The JORDS. In case you were wondering, JORDS stands for the band members' first names – Josh, Owen, Rich, David, and Stephen. It wasn't exactly creative. But the ORDS members of the group thought I had come to ruin everything.

Josh had me start singing with the group. It seems he thought The JORDS needed a female element but neglected to tell his friends about it. That first jam session wasn't quite as private as I thought it would be; I was there to rehearse with the band as a female vocalist. I was flattered. The other guys – not so much.

Rich and Stephen left the band within two weeks when Josh wouldn't get rid of me. I tried to get them to stay, repeatedly. I told them time and again that I did not want to be a famous singer, I only wanted to listen. Josh, though, Josh was convinced I could make it big. Josh thought I had a magical voice. He called me his muse. And if you've ever been a teenage girl, you know that when a guy calls you his muse, you stick around, because that is the ultimate compliment.

A month or so later, David left to join another band. And after graduation, Owen packed up and moved away to start college early. So it was just Josh and I. We would rehearse songs every other day in the garage. Well, he would sing, I would listen. He convinced me to sing every so often. Then we would make out. His mother would knock and bring in cookies and sodas, never speaking, only smiling.

And one day, about a week after I turned eighteen and two weeks after we graduated, Josh asked me to marry him. Sort of. We had been dating all of six weeks.

"We should get married. We'll be like Kurt and Courtney," he said as he flipped through a magazine. I didn't want to remind him that Kurt Cobain was dead and Courtney Love looked like a heroin addict.

"Not funny, Josh," I said as I flipped through a magazine of my own. I dog-eared a page with an outfit I liked.

He sat up and tossed his reading material aside. "I mean it, Roxie. Billie Armstrong, man, you know he said, 'Our passion is our strength.' I think we could be a music power couple. They'll make an MTV special about us as high school sweethearts."

"Seriously? You're not joking?" I dropped the magazine and wiped my suddenly sweaty palms on my legs. My heart picked up its rhythm.

"Why not? Let's do it." It was his way of being romantic, and that was his proposal.

My momma always said to follow your heart. And I was certain my heart was here, where there was a boy totally infatuated with me. No other boy had ever paid me attention. Who wouldn't want to marry that?

I emphatically said yes.

My parents emphatically said no.

"He's a shiftless piece of trash," Daddy said. His face turned red as he shook his head side to side.

"No, Daddy, he has a lot of potential. He's going to be a famous musician one day," I pleaded. "And I'm eighteen," I added for emphasis. That meant I was an adult, did it not?

In hindsight, this was not the best argument of my life.

"How will you pay the bills until then? And what if he never makes it? Do you know how many people head to a major city to make it big and wind up dead in a dumpster?"

"Dennis, really," Momma said. "Don't scare her."

He looked at my mother, the vein on his temple throbbing and his brows scrunched up behind his glasses. "I want to scare her, Margaret. This is a terrible idea and I cannot support it. Roxanne, I forbid you to marry this kid. You are the daughter of a senator. The youngest of four unmarried daughters, I remind you. And this kid? He's a punk. I know his father. He's a coward!"

The words "ex-senator" nearly crossed my lips, but I didn't dare utter them. I crossed my arms in front of me with the anxiety building. This was not going well. Didn't they see I was an adult now? I had graduated from high school. I didn't have big scholarships like my sisters had. I hadn't even wanted to apply to college. What else did I have going for me?

Daddy continued, "Margaret, you have spoiled her. She has no motivation. No aspirations. This is your doing." He took off his glasses and pointed them at my mother, who simply folded her arms and stared back.

But she didn't speak against him. She never did.

"Daddy, please, we're in love," I tried again. Surely he wouldn't stop me if I was in love. Didn't love conquer all things?

"Roxanne, you can't even begin to imagine what love is," he said, rubbing his temples.

"Your father is right, Roxanne. It takes a lot of time and devotion to know what love is," Mom said, patting my shoulders as she gave me a look that said I would never understand.

A deep breath fortified me. I could stand up for myself. "Devotion—"

But Daddy cut me off. "The answer is no. DePrivé girls do not marry shiftless bums. You girls are made of quality stock. You'd be a pretty girl if you just tried, Roxanne. If you marry him, I *will* cut you out of this family."

That was that. When I opened my mouth to speak again, my mother raised her eyebrows and shook her head. I was not allowed to speak against him again.

Instead I said, "Fine. Nevermind. We won't get married,

Daddy. It was a silly idea. I need to go, okay? I'm going to spend the night with Jessica." Defeated, I hung my head low. I turned and went to my room and packed a bag. Neither of my parents followed me.

Except I didn't go to Jessica's. I went to Josh's house, which thankfully was only a few blocks from my own. And then we got into his orange pick-up truck and drove the forty-five minutes from Lexington to the courthouse in Saluda County and applied for a marriage license.

"In South Carolina, there's a twenty-four-hour waiting period," we were told by a gruff woman with a droll voice as she reached across her desk to hand us some forms. The rolls of her stomach prevented her from reaching all the way to us. I had to stand to stretch across to them. "Fill these out, sign the bottom, hand 'em back over, and then you can get married as soon as tomorrow. Do you have an Officiant?"

"A what?" Josh asked. He raked his hands through his blond hair.

"Officiant," she repeated. "A minister? Rabbi? Someone to pronounce you man and wife?" We both shook our heads. The woman nodded and grabbed another form. "And fill this one out and Judge Holder can do it for you. I think he's got some openings tomorrow for such a happy occasion."

She did not smile at all when she said 'happy occasion.'

We sat down at a little table on the other side of the confined office and filled out the papers. Or, rather, I filled them out, even Josh's side, because he didn't like to write. It might cramp his guitar-playing hand, he said. He almost loathed to sign his name at the bottom.

"But Josh, just think, when you're famous one day you'll have to sign your autograph for all your fans," I pointed out. He had no problem signing his name after that. It was shortly after that he perfected his Josh Keene scroll. I was already being wifely and I beamed with pride.

After we left the courthouse, we realized we would need wedding bands. We headed to the local Kmart with twenty dollars between us to see what we could find. Two simple, silver-plated bands sat near each other in a garish white case. One size six for me, one size ten for him. They were each eight dollars. We bought them and Josh put them in his jeans pocket until they would be put on our fingers the next day.

We went back to his house after that since we had to wait until the next day for Judge Holder to marry us. But when Josh asked his mom if I could stay she said no, because it wasn't right for us to sleep under the same roof unmarried, and Jesus would not approve. Neither, she reminded us, would she or my parents. I still had not met Josh's father. We didn't tell her we were planning to get married the next day.

So I took my bag and walked the ten blocks to Jessica's house. I didn't tell her anything about our plans or the rings. Nobody else understood, why would she? We watched an old movie on cable, flipped through her magazines, and fell asleep in the wee hours of the morning.

The next morning I went through my bag to find something to wear for my wedding day. It was not quite how I had planned. I always thought I would get married in a white wedding gown with poofy sleeves and a big veil. But, I realized, that didn't matter. What mattered was that I was about to marry Josh. I fished my nicest dress from my bag – a flowy knee-length blue dress with spaghetti straps. It would have to do. I borrowed Jessica's curling iron and curled up my hair as fancy as I could.

At about one in the afternoon, Josh pulled up to Jessica's

house and honked the horn. I ran out, slung my bag onto
the floorboard, and buckled up. He hit the gas, burning
rubber as he went. As he drove, I imagined our married life.
He could be in the magazines, and I would be happy to
support him. Or maybe we would get regular jobs and work
our way up the ladder. One day, he could be a professional
musician.

Again, we found ourselves at the courthouse in Saluda.
This time we got to stand before the judge. Judge Holder
was a nice man. His dark hair was going gray at the temples
and for some reason, he reminded me of the principal from
Saved by the Bell.

"Alright now," he said as he looked over our forms. "Roxanne and Joshua. You're both pretty young to be getting
married. Are you sure you know what you're doing?"

Josh smiled and worked his charm. "Of course, sir. We're
going to be the next Kurt and Courtney."

"Who?" The judge arched his eyebrow. Clearly, he wasn't
up on the current '90s music.

I smiled. "Think Sonny and Cher." My mom had loved
them when she was a kid, she had said.

The judge just chuckled a little. Then he looked at me.
"And your parents know you're doing this?"

"Yes," I said, doing my best to look him in the eye. It
wasn't a lie. I had told them we wanted to get married.

"And they didn't want to be here?" I could tell he was
fishing for information, but he knew there was nothing he
could do. We were both the legal age and did not need our
parents' permission or approval.

I could only nod as I blinked back tears. I looked away
and picked lint from my dress. Josh was completely void of
reaction.

With a final nod, he had us stand before him to recite

our vows. "Joshua, please repeat after me," he commanded. "I, Joshua Alexander Keene, take you, Roxanne Leigh DePrivé, to be my wife. To love, honor, and cherish her all the days of my life."

Josh looked at me and smiled. His sparkling blue eyes were all I could see as he recited the words.

I was sure I was completely in love as Josh spoke his vows. Somehow, I had managed to catch and marry one of the most popular boys from school. Now I was becoming a woman and a wife.

"Do you have a ring for her?" Judge Holder smiled and raised an eyebrow again.

"Oh, yeah," Josh said with a laugh. He reached his hand into his jeans. The same jeans he had worn the day before. He produced the two rings, a tic tac, and some lint. He flicked the lint to the ground, popped the tic tac in his mouth, and gave the rings to the man before us. Judge Holder shook his head and grimaced.

He gave Josh the smaller ring. "Place this on the third finger of her left hand and say, 'With this ring, I thee wed.'"

Josh crammed the ring onto my finger so hard I nearly yelped. But I held it in. My finger was red and throbbing, but the ring was on. Josh again repeated what the judge had told him to say.

The judge turned a sympathetic smile to me. "Now, Roxanne, please repeat after me. I, Roxanne Leigh DePrivé, take Joshua Alexander Keene to be my husband. To love, honor, and cherish him all the days of my life."

I looked at Josh. This was to be my world from here on out. We would be married today, Josh would make a career of playing his guitar soon, and then we would have plenty of money. After that, the children would come. I could see it all flashing like a crystal ball before my eyes. I eagerly repeated the vows of marriage.

The judge then handed me the other ring. I tenderly slid it onto Josh's ring finger. "With this ring, I thee wed," I said before the judge could instruct me. He nodded in approval. I beamed in response.

I stared into Josh's eyes as the judge said a few words that I completely missed. His eyes were so clear, like gazing into perfect blue pools. I would get to look at these eyes forever. Could I have been any luckier?

"Marriage is not something to be taken lightly. This is a life-long commitment. I now declare you husband and wife," Judge Holder said, clapping his little book shut. "You may kiss your bride."

Josh raised his eyebrows at me and took me into his arms, his calloused fingers rubbed over my back. I felt his mouth come over mine. It was like I had always imagined it. That is, until I felt like he was shoving his tongue down my throat. I gently pushed away before the judge could be offended and straightened my dress.

"Congrats, kids," Judge Holder said with a sigh, unclipping his blue tie. Then he looked at me and asked, "Hey, are you any relation to Senator DePrivé?"

I blanched. "No, who's he?" My heart pounded in my chest. I did not think about all the people who knew my dad's name.

But the judge just shook his head and waved the thought away. "Let me take a picture for you," he said with a weak smile.

He produced a Polaroid camera from a shelf and pushed the shutter button before either of us had a chance to pose. The picture popped out, and the judge handed it to me. I waved it around, waiting for it to develop and dry. A minute later, I had a half-blurry picture of me looking surprised, Josh's arm tight around my waist, and him wiping his chin on his sleeve.

This would be the only pictorial evidence of my first wedding.

Chapter Three

HOPELESS ROMANTIC

*T*he gruff woman from the day before handed me a copy of the marriage license. I had no idea we needed a license to be married. I wasn't sure if I had to keep it with me at all times and I was afraid to ask, so it stayed in my wallet from then on out. If needed, I had proof I was married to Josh Keene.

"Let's go, babe," Josh said. He took my hand and led me out to his car. With the engine started, Josh looked at me. "Mrs. Keene, what do you want to do now?"

I giggled. Mrs. Keene? That was me? "I'm Roxie Keene now," I said with a blush.

Fun fact I did not know back then: You have to go to the Social Security Administration building with your birth certificate and marriage license to get your name changed. Since I didn't know this, my name was never actually changed from Roxie DePrivé to Roxie Keene.

Josh nodded. "Roxie Keene." A smile crept over his face. "Sounds like a rock star. Let's head to Seattle!"

"Seattle? Isn't that a little far away? We might need to stay here until we have money. It takes a lot of gas to get to

Seattle," I reminded him. Besides, now that we were married, I wanted to see if my parents would change their minds.

"Well, Seattle is the hot music scene. Everything's coming from Seattle, you know. We can play gigs to pay our way west," Josh said.

For some reason, I thought once he had a wedding ring on his finger, he would magically morph from a wanna-be rocker to a responsible adult. I felt like that change had happened in me. Now I wanted us to find real jobs, find a place to live, drink coffee, and read the newspaper every day. That's what adults did. But Josh didn't suddenly become an adult. Maybe, I thought, the change would be more gradual for him. 'Boys will be boys' right? I would give it time. I was a patient person and I loved him.

"My momma always says to take things one step at a time. Let's go tell our parents we got married," I said with a level head.

Josh agreed.

As we drove, I practiced in my head what we would say to our parents. I would tell my father that we were in love, we were legally married with a signed license and everything. My father loved nothing more than the law, so that was the best approach, I thought.

We stopped at my parents' house first. That was a bad idea.

My mother sat on the couch reading a book. When she looked up and saw me with Josh, she shook her head. Immediately her eyes darted to my left hand. She was no fool.

"Roxanne, do not tell me what I think you're going to tell me." The book was discarded, and she stood.

Shoulders back and chin up, I puffed myself up as much as I could. "Momma, Josh and I got married this afternoon."

"What do you mean you got married?" My mom yelled. She paced the floor, lighting a cigarette, the smoke billowed around her blond hair. "Your father is going to kill you!" She looked at me. Then she looked at Josh. "No. He's going to kill you," she said pointing a finger at him.

It was then my dad's truck pulled into the driveway. It was silent inside until he walked through the door. "Who's truck is that outside, Margaret?" Then he saw Josh. "Roxanne."

"Dennis, she's lost her mind," Mom shrieked, lifting my hand for him to see my wedding ring. "She went off and got married! Married!" Mom paced again and lit a new cigarette, forgetting about the one she had burning away in the ashtray on the table.

Dad's face grew red and a vein on his forehead became prominent. This was becoming a permanent look for him. "You what? Are you serious? Do you know what this could do to me?"

My father, the former senator, everyone. Dennis DePrivé, upholder of tradition, values, and the good people of South Carolina. And anything that didn't fit into that mold – like a rebellious teenage daughter – was tossed aside. My older siblings had learned that. Apparently, I was not as quick of a learner as I had thought.

"Daddy, I..."

"No, Roxie," he said as he balled his hands into fists. "Don't you know what this will do to my reputation? My business? Don't you know how this will look? You're not pregnant are you?" The whole room stopped, my mother looked like she might pass out.

I was shocked. I wasn't that stupid. I hadn't let Josh get that far yet. I shook my head.

"Thank God. Then we can erase this," he said. "We can get this annulled before anyone else finds out. Give me the Rolodex, Margaret. I'll call Walter Traddler, the attorney. He owes me one anyway. Roxanne, what judge in his right mind would marry two kids? I will have his head."

I looked to Josh who stood back away from me. His face was pale, his blond hair covering his left eye. The right eye was glazed over, like a deer in headlights. Shouldn't he be by my side, defending my honor? It looked like I would have to do it all myself.

"No, Daddy," I said. My voice was soft and shaky, my shoulders now hunched over, but I still spoke. "We love each other. We're going to be together. I'm eighteen, you can't do anything about this." I hadn't been able to meet my father's gaze, but for once I put myself before my father's career.

He stopped me. "Well, Roxanne, there is one thing I can do. Get out. You're not welcome here anymore."

Rushing to my side, Momma spoke up, "Dennis, now, really?" Her hands squeezed my shoulders.

"No, Margaret," he said, shaking his fist in the air, "I won't have it. We told her not to do it. And I won't have a daughter married to a lazy bum like this. They can both leave, and you can call the attorney to change our wills and take her out of them."

Tears swam in my eyes. This was not how it was supposed to happen. They were supposed to realize they had been wrong and be happy for me. "Daddy?" I squeaked out.

"Not anymore," he said as he opened the front door and held it open. He motioned for us to leave.

"Momma?" I looked to her to do something. Anything.

"Not a word, Margaret," Dad warned. Mom leaned against a wall and put her head in her hands, smoke billowing around her. She would not speak against him.

Josh didn't need any more prompting. He quickly took my hand and led me out the door. "I hope it goes better with my parents," was all he said as he burned rubber away from the house. I used the hem of my dress to wipe my tears.

Josh's dad traveled for his job. I don't think I ever found out exactly what he did. But his mother, the princess look-a-like, took the news somewhat better than my own.

"You got married?" She sat across from us in their living room. We were sitting on a plush deep burgundy couch. Grace Keene was perched on a cream-colored high backed chair, her own back straight as an arrow. Her smile never faltered, but I could tell this was not what she was expecting to hear from her son.

"Yeah, Mom, we did," Josh said with a smile and a nod. For as prim as his mother was, Josh was just as relaxed. His legs were stretched out in front of him, his shoulders rested on the back of the couch.

I, for my part, found myself mirroring my new mother-in-law. I wanted her to like me. I needed her to like me. Accept me. And I was scared. Incredibly scared.

She looked at me and blinked several times. "Are you in a family way, dear?"

Why did people keep thinking I was pregnant? I shook my head.

My mother-in-law released a sigh of relief. "Wonderful. So long as you didn't sin. You didn't sin did you, Joshua?"

"No, Mom," he said with a half-laugh. "We wanted to be married, so we got married. We're going to be a famous rock couple. It's gonna be awesome. We'll play to sold-out arenas across the world."

Grace blinked a few more times and nodded before asking, "Where will you be living until you sell out those arenas, Joshua? Because you can't stay here."

"But, Mom," he started to whine. It truly was a whine, I was taken aback. It sounded like something from a five-year-old who was told he couldn't have a cookie.

Grace stood. "No, Joshua," she said, closing her eyes. "If you're old enough to get married, you're old enough to make it on your own. Find a job. Find a place to live. I love you, but this is a tough-love situation. And besides, it's a terrible example to set for your younger siblings. You are, however, invited to church and Sunday supper every week. You, too, Roxanna."

I didn't correct her on getting my name wrong. I was too dumbfounded. But in my head I was shouting, "*It's Roxie! Roxie Keene! I'm one of you now.*"

We left after that. Josh had hoped we could live in his room. With the giant poster of Green Day's Dookie album cover on the wall. Now that wasn't happening. It was our wedding night and we had nowhere to go. We were homeless. With no jobs and no money. I realized we had not thought things through thoroughly.

"Josh? Where will we go?" I asked meekly. I folded my arms in that self-conscious way. A chill unlike anything I had ever experienced crept up my spine and spread throughout my body.

"Don't worry, babe, I have a plan," he said gazing into my eyes. He placed his hand on my cheek, melting my heart. "I will take care of you."

I nodded. What else could a girl do? I was smitten, and he said he would take care of me. We sped off in the orange truck, and I wondered if we would be spending our wedding night sleeping in the truck bed under the stars.

We arrived at a beautiful whitewashed house right around sunset. It was nestled on a vast lot overlooking Lake Murray in one of the ritziest neighborhoods I had ever encountered. It was the prettiest house I had ever seen at that point in my life. Josh parked in the driveway and got out of the car, ignoring me as he strode to the door.

"Adam? Are you in there? Open up!" He knocked loudly.

I got out of the car and ran up to him. "Who's Adam?"

How was I to know at that point the role Adam would come to play in my life?

"Adam's Adam," was all he replied to me, but he continued to shout. "Adam! Are you here? I need a pillow, man!" He banged on the door some more.

It creaked open and a man with red hair and a red goatee greeted us. He smiled wide at my new groom and they shook hands. "Josh! Hey, man!" He glanced at me, "And who is this?"

Josh smiled and pulled me close, "This is my wife as of this afternoon. Roxie. She has the voice of an angel, man. But listen, we need a place to crash, my mom's kind of steamed. Do you mind?"

Adam's eyes glinted, thinking. But then he nodded and ran his fingers through his beard. "Newlyweds, huh? Congrats, Joshie. Yeah, that's fine. I've got the perfect room for you two lovebirds! Come on in," he turned and walked into the house.

It was every bit as luxurious on the inside as it was on the outside. Lush furniture in muted neutral tones welcomed us. Little pops of color like yellow and turquoise here and there kept catching my eye. The art of the walls looked like it belonged in a museum; it was really modern. I wanted to stop and study them, but I kept walking with Josh. Adam even had giant, wall-sized television.

Adam stopped in the living room in front of an over-stuffed coffee-colored couch and turned to me, "Roxie, was it? I'm Adam Joyce. Welcome to my home."

I looked at him finally and thought he didn't look too much older than me. Maybe in his mid-twenties. He was tall and trim with fiery red hair and a smattering of freckles. Adam Joyce did not seem bothered by us showing up unannounced, begging for a room.

How did he have a home like this? Was this his parents' home? "What a beautiful place," I commented.

"It's a rental, but I'm renting to own. I've lived here for about a year now. I'm actually a real estate agent," he said with a hearty laugh. "And it helps the image to have one of the most gorgeous homes on Lake Murray." He clapped his hands together. "Let me show you around. I owe Josh, so you can stay as long as you like. Please make yourselves at home."

"I think I'll just sit for a few minutes, if you don't mind, Josh. I'm a little overwhelmed," I admitted. I sat on the couch and sighed. "You two go ahead. I need a minute to breathe after everything."

The two took off to see what Adam called his "play room." This was not the wedding night I dreamt of at all. Nothing about this day was as I had envisioned it, but I knew life was not a fairy tale. I would make the most of it.

Noting my growling stomach, I got up in search of the kitchen and found it in the next room. I discovered a bowl of fruit on the counter, and Adam had said to make myself at home, so I grabbed an apple and bit into it. By the time I finished, Josh and Adam had come looking for me.

"Sorry," Josh said sheepishly. I only smiled, not sure

what to say as my frustrations were already high. I didn't want to get angry at him on our wedding day.

"Let me show you to your room," Adam said with a wink towards Josh. He walked down a long hallway and motioned to a door as we passed. "This is the bathroom you can use. It also connects into this bedroom here." He pushed open the next door. "You can have this room for a while until you get on your feet."

The room continued with the muted color theme. Pale yellow curtains hung over the window with a matching bed set on a queen-sized bed. A white wood dresser and mirror stood opposite the bed. It was a lovely room.

"Let me go get our bags, Rox," Josh said. He gave me a peck on the cheek and disappeared.

I was left alone in the room with Adam who looked as awkward as I felt. "Thanks for letting us stay," I managed to say. I felt so nervous alone with him. "This is kind of embarrassing, having nowhere to go."

"Don't mention it," he said with a wave of his hand. I could see the freckles on his knuckles stretched all the way up his arm and disappeared under his shirt sleeve. "I can't imagine what you've gone through today. Getting married, and then getting the boot. Josh told me all about it."

"Yeah," I answered and wrapped my arms around my stomach. "My parents kicked us out. My dad disowned me. And Josh's mom said we couldn't stay there either. I guess we didn't think too far ahead."

"Are you okay?" He took a step closer to me, but retreated when he saw me flinch.

"Yes, of course," I said, fighting the tears that threatened to spring forward. The events of the day were catching up with me. "This is really nice of you."

Adam smiled. "No big deal. Josh is a great guy, I hope you'll be happy together. And like I said, I owe him."

I wanted to ask how they met, but Josh came back with our bags. He hefted them onto the bed and turned to look at us. "All right, then. Thanks, Adam." When Adam didn't move, Josh cleared his throat.

Adam's eyes widened. "Right! Wedding night. Goodnight, you two. Help yourself to the kitchen." He looked from Josh to me. I didn't like the look he gave—I felt like he was looking right through me or something. He left then, closing the bedroom door behind him.

I suddenly had bigger concerns than the look on the face of a man I had just met. This was my wedding night, and I had no experience with boys beyond a few kisses. I had no idea what Josh's love life was before me, to be honest, but I didn't care. I loved him. I was nervous and excited and so many other emotions I could have never described. But nerves definitely took over.

"Do you want something to eat, Josh?" I asked as I took a step toward the door. I was stalling. There was no reason to rush, was there?

The look on his face answered for him. "Nope."

I blushed wildly as he came toward me and swept me up into his arms. I giggled and put my arms around his neck. Pushing nerves aside, I kissed my husband as he gently placed me onto the bed.

Once we fell asleep, we slept soundly till well into the next day. When I glanced at the nightstand clock, it said it was past eleven in the morning. I rolled over and faced Josh, who was still sleeping. Feeling my stomach rumble, I thought I had better get up and find something to eat. Perhaps I would make brunch for my groom. But then I remembered this was not my house, nor my kitchen.

Quietly, I got out of bed and searched through my bag. I found my toiletries and padded into the bathroom to brush my teeth and wash up. I looked in the mirror, searching to see if I had suddenly become a woman overnight. I looked just as I had the day before, and as I had a few weeks prior when I graduated from high school. My face was still youthful, my hair was still light brown, my eyes were still the deep brown they had always been.

Still in my pajamas, my hair in a messy ponytail, I made my way to the kitchen. With no sign of our host, relief came in the form of a long exhale. All little girls love to play make believe, and this was like a giant game of it. I was married and in a gorgeous home.

I tapped my fingers on the countertop for a moment, questioning if I should grab an apple or if I should actually try to make food. With another grumble from my middle, I decided on making food. I opened the fridge, hoping to find something more than beer and was pleasantly surprised at how well-stocked Adam's fridge was. I took out eggs, mushrooms, and cheese. I could make omelets for everyone easily enough. With a little searching, I found a mixing bowl and a large pan and set to work.

I didn't hear Adam when he came through the door and into the kitchen. But when I looked up and saw him staring at me, I jumped and screamed, nearly toppling the omelet bowl over.

"I'm sorry, Roxie," Adam said with a small smile. "I did not mean to frighten you." He looked like he had just come in from a workout. His T-shirt was wet around his neck and he wore track pants that matched. His red hair looked more vibrant with a gleam of sweat over it.

With my chest heaving, I closed my eyes for a moment.

"That's okay, I just wasn't expecting you," I said. "I hope it's okay that I'm in here. I thought I would make omelets."

"Wow, a beautiful girl who can cook, huh?" Adam flashed a pure-white smile at me. "Please help yourself to anything you can find. Make yourself at home."

I smiled, "I love to cook. It is one of the few things I can do without ruining everything." Realizing I was still in night clothes, I quickly turned my back to Adam. "And I'm not too sure about being pretty." I poured the egg mixture into the pan and listened to the sizzle. The smell wafted up to my nose; it smelled heavenly.

"I didn't say pretty, I said beautiful," he corrected. Adam moved behind me and pulled plates down from a cabinet. Then he got close to me, too close, making me realize I was wearing little more than a tank top and short shorts. I could feel the heat radiating from his body. Then he reached around me and opened a drawer, revealing the silverware.

"'Scuse me," he said. His hand brushed my back as it went past me. I didn't like the way it felt. It was almost like it was intentional. "Sorry," he said, again flashing that smile.

It was then that Josh came into the kitchen, his hair disheveled, wearing a white tank top and pajama pants. He yawned and stretched before taking a seat at the bar. I was smitten with my new groom. "What's going on here?"

Adam answered, "I came in from my run and Roxie here was making us all breakfast."

I smiled, feeling a little nervous. This was the first meal I cooked for my new husband. I hoped he liked it. "I made omelets," I said with pride. I wanted him to be proud of me, too.

Josh scratched his head. "Whatever," he said. "I'm starving and ready to eat."

My ego felt a little deflated after that. I plated the eggs

and passed one to Josh. I gave another to Adam before taking the last plate for myself. We ate in silence.

When Adam excused himself, I turned to Josh. "What are we going to do today? It's our honeymoon! And we need a place to live." I searched his face for any ideas.

"We can live here for now. Let's give it a few days, then we can look for jobs. There are some clubs in Cola I'll apply at. Maybe I can deejay or something until we have some money saved up. Besides, we won't be here long. A few months, and we can head out west," he said as he stood.

"What about me? What am I supposed to do?"

Josh kissed me on the forehead. "You be my muse. Maybe you can get some gigs at one of the clubs. We'll go out on Friday, go to a few clubs, meet some people. We'll see if any of them are looking to hire a guitar player or need a deejay. And you can sing. You know, Greene's does a karaoke night. Maybe a talent scout will discover you."

I nearly laughed, but then realized he was serious. "You want me to sing karaoke for a living? You know that doesn't pay. How will I make money?"

Smiling, Josh winked at me. "You worry too much. We'll figure it out, Rox. And like you said, it's our honeymoon. Let's just enjoy today." And with that, he took me by the hand and led me back to the bedroom where we stayed for the rest of the day.

Chapter Four

THE GLORY OF LOVE

That week turned into several. We were still living with Adam. Josh was still hitting up the clubs in Columbia, seeing if any visiting band needed a guitarist either for the night or permanently. None did. After Josh had practically pushed me on stage for one night of karaoke at Greene's, I asked the manager if they were looking for help, and they hired me on the spot to be a waitress.

Gina, the girl who trained me, said the fewer clothes I wore, the better my tips would be. She modeled herself after the hip-hop group TLC and even looked like the one called Chilli with bronzed skin and tight curls. She wore baggy pants and skin-tight, cropped shirts. Many of the male patrons would wag their eyebrows at her or whistle. A few tried to get handsy, she had told me, but she knew how to avoid that and gave me pointers.

She was right. After a few weeks of jeans and blouses, I slowly changed to short skirts and revealed more cleavage than I ever would have normally. I had become a poser. I wasn't comfortable, but the tips I brought home tripled, and we needed the money. My look was modeled after Gwen

Stefani and the Spice Girls. Not that I liked the Spice Girls, but dressing like them meant I carried more money home in my pockets. If my father hadn't already kicked me out, he would have for these clothes. It was embarrassing, sure, but I was making money.

Occasionally, people we knew from high school would come in for karaoke night, and I could see them trying to place me. Once I began dating Josh, this shrinking violet had become something of a bird of paradise. My name was whispered by every teenager in town. I'm sure the rushed wedding had caused tongues to wag as well. And now here I was, dressed like a Spice Girl, serving beer. I sighed at the thought.

Josh still did not have a steady job. He played here and there for little pay. But no club would put him on a regular rotation, and no band wanted to bring him on as a guitarist or singer. Josh remained upbeat and optimistic. And he constantly talked about picking up and working our way west, first to Nashville and winding up in Seattle. He was convinced he would make it big in Seattle. He wasn't seeing that the scene was changing again, and Seattle was becoming a has-been music town. Nevertheless, I was supportive. It was my duty as his wife, and I would do anything for Josh.

Of course, the only married couple I really knew were my parents. My mother always supported my father and always did what he said. She knew how to dress and act the part, so I did the same. My mother was the epitome of a senator's wife. So I became the epitome of a musician's wife.

I had called my mom twice and both times she barely spoke, her voice strained. She only asked if I was okay and taken care of. Not once did she invite me over or ask where I was living. She did, however, offer to have my sister bring my clothes to wherever I was. I spoke to Lori more frequently and had seen her a handful of times. She was attending classes at the University of South Carolina, and while she didn't agree with my getting married, she still tried to talk to Mom and Dad about forgiving me and welcoming me home.

After three months of working non-stop at Greene's, and not quite four months after our wedding day, I nervously bought a pregnancy test from the drug store. I paced the floor of our borrowed room, sweating and nauseous. I was waiting for Josh to get home and I kept reading and rereading the instructions. I wasn't sure where he was, but he wasn't home and I needed him.

Marriage had taught me that the perfect life I thought I would get did not magically happen. We didn't have a home of our own. We didn't make a ton of money. And I had no idea where my husband was—how could I raise and keep track of a baby? How had Momma done it when she was a young mother? How did she keep going when my father was always on the road? Would she talk to me if I called to ask?

When Josh finally did return, I quickly pulled him into our room. But he was chomping at the bit to talk to me as well, jumping from one foot to the next, rubbing his palms on his thighs.

"I have something to tell you," we both blurted out at the same time.

"Mine is big," he said with a huge smile.

"So is mine," I said quietly. I took hold of his hand, placed it on my flat stomach, and blurted it out. "I might be pregnant."

"What do you mean?" The smile was gone, replaced with a grim, straight lip. His hand released mine as if it was on fire. He blinked several times. Hadn't he heard what I said?

"I mean, I might be having a baby, Josh. We might be having a baby," I said, half nervous, half excited. I wrapped my arms around my middle the way I always did. Partly for warmth from the October chill, partly from nerves.

He looked around the room and sat down, his face almost expressionless. "This would change everything," he said.

I laughed. "Yes, it would."

He shook his head. "Wait, aren't you on the pill or something? Coach O'Brien said all girls were on the pill."

The smile from my nervous laugh quickly morphed to a scowl. "What? Why would he tell you that? Girls can only be on the pill if they have a prescription for it and pay for it. I have no prescription and no money for it. You know that."

He ran his fingers through his bleached-out locks. "Are you serious? I thought they handed that stuff out like condoms. I thought we were good."

"Well, I didn't see you with condoms," I countered.

"Because I thought you had it under control!" He was shouting and I was shaking.

With a calming breath, I tried again. "Listen, Josh, I know we're young, and I'm not even sure, but—"

He raised his eyebrows. "Not sure? Well, how do you get sure?" He licked his lips nervously. "I mean, how can you find out?"

Sensing that his nerves were not out of potential excitement like mine, I frowned. "I take a test, Josh. I had to buy this thing on my own, so I was waiting for you – my husband – so we can do this together." I picked the box up from where it sat on our bed and showed him. "It only takes a few minutes for results," I said, my voice flat.

Wasn't he supposed to be excited? I know we weren't really ready, but we could get ready. We could find a place to stay, and he could get a job. There had to be some amount of excitement in him, right?

"Go take it." His voice was high and strained. It was more of a command than anything else.

With a huff, I went to the adjoining bathroom and ripped the box open. I read the instructions carefully once again. It seemed simple enough. Pee on the stick and wait to see if the window turned blue. Blue meant I was pregnant. Not blue, not pregnant. I did as the instructions told me.

Josh banged on the door immediately, and I heard his head thud against the wood. "Well?"

"It's not done yet," I snapped at him.

This was not how it was supposed to go. We were married. This was the next step for us. Marriage, then children. Josh didn't seem to understand that. I knew it would have been nice to have our lives in better order, but perhaps this would give him the push needed to actually do these things. Maybe he would finally start to grow up.

Within a few moments, it became clear. The test did not turn blue. I was not pregnant after all. I expected to be disappointed with the results, but instead I felt relieved. True, I was not ready to be a mother yet, but I would have welcomed a child anyway. I was more relieved that nothing was tying me to Josh eternally, aside from the ring I wore on my hand.

Perhaps I should have paid more attention to that feeling. Maybe it would have saved me at least a little time and effort.

I exited the bathroom and shook my head. "Negative," was all I said.

Josh had never looked so thrilled in the time I had

known him. "Oh, thank you! Dodged a bullet there!" He picked me up and spun me around.

Now I was angry. "Josh—"

He interrupted me again. "Oh! Roxie, I almost forgot. I talked to the manager of the Blasted Lemons, and he said a new band was being formed in Nashville. They're holding open auditions next month, and he thinks I'd be perfect for it. I got a real shot at this, Rox!"

I shook my head as I paced before him. "Josh, how would we get to Nashville within a month? We don't have that kind of money."

Josh had a gleam in his eye. "Oh, Roxie, we can do it. Me and you, baby. We'll be an instant hit in Nashville. I may not be a country singer, but I can start at the bottom. It's all about the music, right?"

Now I understood why having a baby was not on his radar. His dreams of becoming a musical sensation were at bat. Would I ever come first? His enthusiasm was contagious, however, and when he didn't jump up and say "sike," I sighed. "I guess, look into train tickets. I'll see how much we have saved up. Could we sell the truck?"

"Aw, Rox, you're the best," he said. He grabbed me in his arms and kissed me hard. When he let go, I nearly fell over. He raced out of the room to call the train station.

I knew exactly how much money we had saved up. I had six hundred eighty-seven dollars in my toiletry bag, where I kept the money. I did my best to buy groceries for us and Adam, and I insisted on paying Adam a weekly rent, though he usually slipped it back under our door when we weren't home. I would just hide it somewhere in the house. It wasn't much, but I felt we needed to pay him for his hospitality.

Worn out from the emotions of the past few minutes, I lay on the bed and closed my eyes. What a nerve-wracking day. I was almost asleep when I heard a knock on the still-open door.

"Roxie? I'm sorry, I didn't realize you were sleeping," Adam said, his head through the door.

I opened one eye. "It's alright, Adam," I said. I opened the other eye and sat up. "Do you need something?"

He came into the room wearing a three-piece suit, something I had never seen him wear before. He was quite dashing and almost looked like a prince from a fairy tale. My heart raced at the sight of him looking so handsome. Why would it do that? I blinked a few times, reminding my eyes this was Adam, not Josh.

Seeing that I noticed his clothing, he spun around and posed. "Like it?" He never asked me for fashion advice, especially since his regular uniform was a polo shirt and khakis. This was a well-made, tailored suit.

"You look nice," I said, swallowing hard. "What's the occasion?"

"That's why I am here," he said. "I have a meeting tomorrow with a huge broker. This could make or break me, Rox. He wants a dinner meeting, and he's bringing his wife. I need someone to take. Would you mind?"

I shook my head, confused, "Are you asking me out on a date? Can you not find someone not already married?"

He smiled. He had a dazzling smile. "It's not a date. I need someone, a lady, who can hold a conversation with the wife while I attempt to sweet talk this broker. Think Pretty Woman."

I chortled. "So you want an escort? You're not improving things."

Adam's already ruddy cheeks flamed. "No, no, that's now what I meant. I just need someone to go with me. Like Julia Roberts did for Richard Gere's real estate deal."

His blush was contagious as I felt my own cheeks redden. "You need me to be Julia Roberts? I'm definitely no Fly Girl."

He sat on the edge of the bed a good foot from me. "Whatever, doll face, you have the look. That girl next door thing that's so popular right now. You're wonderful to talk to, and you're smart. And I know you were raised knowing all that etiquette stuff."

"Yeah, I do know all the forks at a place setting and stuff," I replied with a laugh. Charm school had been an awkward breeze a few years earlier.

Adam continued. "Besides, I've seen what you wear to work. Those tight skirts, the belly-baring tops. No guy could resist you."

At that moment, I wasn't sure Adam could resist me, despite my cut-off jeans and baggy T-shirt. The look in his eyes was pure hunger. I'd been more and more uncomfortable around him as time had gone on, but now I worried not just over his feelings but my own. I was trying harder and harder to remind myself that I was married to someone else. I could not be attracted to Adam, no matter how handsome and charming and funny he might be.

I shot up, putting the bed between us. I needed a barrier from him . "Oh, no, Adam. I don't think I'm right for the job," I stammered. I wrapped my arms around my middle, trying to cover myself up. If I tried hard enough, maybe I could become invisible one more time.

"I'll pay," he said. "Five-hundred dollars if this works out as I expect."

I choked on a gasp.

"Pay for what?" Josh asked. He had impeccable timing. I let out a deep, shaky breath.

Adam turned to him. "I asked Roxanne here to be my

assistant tomorrow at a big meeting I have with a broker. Pays top dollar. I just need her to look pretty for me and talk nice to the wife."

Josh pumped his fist. "Oh yeah! We're in!" When I started to protest, he held up his hand. "Now, babe, we can use this. This is our Nashville money, Roxie. We can start out on our own."

The idea of getting away from Adam Joyce was all I needed to hear. If one evening looking pretty on his arm could get me away from the thoughts I was having, I was all for it.

"All right," I said with a sigh. "What time?"

"Be ready at six o'clock," Adam said. He pointed to Josh and me as if to thank us and backed out of the doorway.

"Rox, that's awesome. That's our ticket to Nashville, babe," Josh said, bounding onto the bed. "I added it up. Train tickets, plus food, a cheap motel for a few nights, and of course, new clothes, will be about five-hundred dollars."

"That's almost all our money, Josh," I said, worried.

"Not if Adam pays you. He said that would be five-hundred for you right there. It won't touch what we have saved."

I frowned. "What *I* have saved," I corrected. Josh hadn't earned any of that money. "Anyway, you're right. I guess it's time to start packing. I'm definitely ready to get out of this house."

Again, he twirled me around and kissed me soundly. "Oh, Roxie, I love this. You and me, baby. We're going to make it."

"I love you, too," I said with excitement. Josh's enthusiasm was so infectious, I found myself wanting what he wanted. I wanted his dreams to come true. I kissed him then, deep and soulful, lost in the emotion he stirred up.

It wasn't until later that I realized Josh hadn't said he loved me. He had said he loved this. This, the life of a struggling musician. Of giving up everything to follow his dreams. How little did I realize just how much he was willing to give up.

The next day at six o'clock I was ready to accompany Adam to his dinner meeting. I glanced in the mirror one more time. My hair was parted in the middle and smoothed down with loose curls at the ends. I wore a shimmery dark purple slip dress with spaghetti straps. It was the fanciest thing I owned. I paired it with a baby blue cardigan my sister had dropped off for me with my things a few weeks before. My chunky black heels and makeup completed the look.

Josh had already disappeared, which was typical for him. He often left as the sun began to descend and didn't return home until after midnight. It was frustrating for me, but I was at the point where I didn't mind anymore. I was alone to read, play in the kitchen, or work, which was usually the case.

There was a knock at my door and I told Adam it was open. I grabbed my purse and ran a quick coat of dark lip gloss over my lips as he came in. He let out a low whistle as he looked me over. I blushed several shades of pink.

"You're a knockout, Rox. Thank you so much for agreeing to do this for me," he said. "It will be quite simple, just join in the conversation when you can, and smile a lot."

I fidgeted with my dress. "Are you sure? I am not exactly the smartest person in the world, Adam. And I'm the opposite of a social butterfly."

"Enjoy the food, talk where you can. You know all the polite society stuff. Don't worry about anything else, okay? I hear this guy's wife likes to cook just like you do. You can talk about recipes." Adam held his hand out, inviting me to go ahead of him. I could only nod, ready to get the night over with, and have the money promised in my stash.

We went to a dockside restaurant that was much fancier than I had expected. It was called The Marshall and it boasted cream and blue decor with a wall of windows facing the water. The staff wore all black, with their noses in the air. Nothing like I would wear at Greene's.

Adam introduced me to John and Binny Sweeney. The two guys clapped hands heartily and shook before John introduced his wife to Adam and myself. Adam kissed her hand. John did the same when he was introduced to me. I was thankful at that moment I had grown up the daughter of a senator. I knew all about these formal introductions and knew how to play the part well. We sat at a prime table overlooking the water.

I marveled at the menu, looking at dishes I had only read about in the occasional cooking magazine I picked up. Thankfully, the woman I was there to converse with was a food aficionado, just as Adam had said. We poured over the menu together, commenting on all the amazing dishes.

She was a pleasant woman in her late 30s with bleach-blonde hair and red lipstick. She looked more like she would be friends with my mother than me. Her accent was thick, and she sounded like she was from Charleston. Her husband was trying to impress Adam just as hard as Adam was trying to impress him. They were happy to let us talk recipes while they talked real estate jargon I certainly didn't understand.

Binny told me all her favorite spices to use and the cookbooks she had in her arsenal. I told her about a recipe for chicken marsala I had recently tried out of a local magazine. It was so nice to talk with someone who had a similar interest, and it made me miss my mother. Unlike my mother, Binny was willing to speak with me, instead of at me. I was excited to order my first-ever duck confit, and Binny promised I could taste her scallops.

The two men talked, more or less ignoring us, but I didn't mind. I hadn't seen much of my friends lately, and I really missed my mom. Binny filled in the role of both for an evening. Add to that the most amazing meal I had ever eaten, and it was a nearly perfect evening.

As we finished, Binny looked from Adam to me and asked quietly, "So, how long have you two been together?"

I sat up straight, suddenly embarrassed. "Oh, um, we're not ... we're not a couple," I stammered, trying not to look in Adam's direction. "He's just a friend."

Binny smiled languidly and leaned in to me. She brought her manicured hand up to her cheek and said with her Charlestonian drawl, "Oh, honey, you may not be a couple now, but he has been looking at you all night like a man who knows what he wants. And that, darling, is you. Mark my words. Bat those eyelashes, honey, and he's putty in your hands."

I fought the urge to look over to Adam. He had been looking at me all night? I was floored. I could only smile weakly at Binny as I nervously spun the wedding band Josh had given me on my finger. I guess the other rings I wore didn't make this one look matrimonial.

I didn't tell Binny I was already married to someone else. Instead, I changed the subject back to food, asking if she had any recipes I might try myself.

We parted ways with John and Binny, and I tuned Adam out as he talked about their deal. My mind wandered while I nodded absently. I thought about what Binny had said and about Josh. Had we really been married four months? I thought back to when we had started dating. It really wasn't all that long ago, now that I thought about it. What had I been thinking?

Truth be told, I had known Josh only a few weeks longer than I had known Adam. Sure, I knew *of* Josh much longer, but we had never spoken until he approached me that day at lunch.

But Josh and I were married, and I understood that commitment. And I loved him, despite his flaws. He wasn't perfect, but then, neither was Kurt Cobain. Or Sonny Bono. Or the Captain, I assumed. How did Courtney, Cher, and Tennille handle their musician men?

Adam looked over to me as we pulled into the driveway of his stunning home. "Earth to Roxie. You've been so quiet. Everything okay?"

I blinked and looked over to him, then quickly away. "Yes, sorry. I think that food was too rich for me. I am stuffed and tired. I think it's time for bed."

We got out of his truck and walked up to the door. Josh's truck was parked off to the side. I was surprised that he wasn't at a local club, trying to get on stage with some band or another. I mustered up the spirit to be happy to see my husband. Truthfully, though, I only wanted to sleep.

Inside, I laid my purse on the table and slipped off my shoes. I couldn't get Binny's words out of my mind. Adam had been looking at me all night. Like a man who knew what he wanted. To say I was uncomfortable with his attention was an understatement. And I knew I wasn't a girl that others would find attractive. My family had taken great pains in telling me I could be pretty if I tried. I mean, I was pear-shaped, my hair was nondescript, and I had the occasional break out. Sure, I could pile on the make-up and make myself presentable, but I did not see myself the way

Adam seemed to. And he was friends with Josh. I wasn't used to so much male attention.

I went to my room to change clothes. Josh was there, headphones over his ears, listening to music, CDs strewn all over the bed. When he saw me, he smiled and took the headphones off.

"Hey, Rox. You are smoking!" He stood and kissed me hard. Too hard. His clothes smelled like cigarettes and nightclubs.

I pushed away. "Ugh, I'm tired, Josh. And I feel overly made up."

"You look like a star," he said. "Ready for her own album, her own music video, her own number one hit!" His surfer hair hung over his eyes. I had found that so adorable not long ago. Now I just wanted him to cut it out. And maybe trim his hair.

"That's your dream, Josh." I sat down, feeling like he simply didn't understand me. Frustration mounted as it was clear I was not allowed to have my own dreams. "It's always your dream."

His smile faded. "Our dream, Rox. It's our dream. We can do this together, the rock star and the senator's daughter." He took my hand in his and looked into my eyes. "Isn't this our dream?"

What was that? He had never referred to me as the senator's daughter before. Was that an angle he was playing with? A hardcore musician and the straight-laced daughter of a politician? My eyes lost their focus as I considered his choice of words. How long had he thought of me this way?

"Rox?"

I sighed, snapped from my line of thought. Surely it meant nothing.

Once again, I thought of life dreams. I wasn't even sure

what my dreams would be. I had never entertained the thought. I bit my lip. I only ever wanted attention from a guy who liked me for me. Being famous, looking like a Courtney Love wannabe – was never a part of the big picture for me. I wanted his love, not the love of throngs of fans.

Trying to smile, I shook my head. "This is your dream. I want to support you in it, Josh," I said. I touched my hand to his cheek, feeling the slight stubble from a day without shaving. "I want you to be the megastar. I just want to be along for the ride."

He kissed my hand. It was so sweet. I could have melted right there. This was what I wanted. His smile brightened. "How was the meeting?"

"Adam said it went well. I had a great meal and a nice conversation with a woman named Binny," I said.

"Binny? What a stupid name. You look great."

"I look like a Spice Girl at the Grammy's and Binny was wonderfully sweet. She reminded me of my mother," I sneered. "I'm going to change."

"Wait," he said. "Don't change, please. I booked a gig for tonight. A solo performance at O'Hoolihan's. You're not doing anything now, right? Come see me." His smile was lopsided, he was so happy. The hair in his eyes became adorable again.

"Really? Looking all fancy like this?"

Josh took my hands in his. "Just take the sweater off. Please? You'd be an inspiration for me. Remember, you're my muse."

And then he kissed me. It was the best kiss of my eighteen-year-old life. Better than our wedding kiss. He wanted me, truly wanted me. I felt the love in that kiss. I would have done anything in the world for Josh Keene, the first man who ever actually saw me.

I washed my face and reapplied my make-up. I made sure it wasn't as heavy as it had been earlier. But I wanted to look pretty for Josh. I wanted him to be proud to have me on his arm. I knew what celebrity couples looked like, I read People magazine. Even the non-famous one had to be sexy. If I was going to be Josh Keene's wife, I had to look the part of a famous wife. I would do it for him. Like my mother did for my father.

I scowled as Adam accompanied us. He bought champagne, forgetting that Josh and I were not old enough to drink legally. Of course, as made up as I was, I looked much older than my eighteen years. And Josh, who had recently turned nineteen, was given free booze anyway for being a musician. Nobody asked him for identification.

While Josh was backstage, I finally asked Adam how they had met. After living with him for four months, I still did not know. I wasn't sure how it had not come up before.

"Are you serious, Roxie? Josh is my cousin. Like third cousins twice removed or something strange like that. Our great-grandmothers were sisters, I think. I don't know. But at family reunions, he used to trail me like a puppy dog. We've been close since we were young."

Cousins? How had I not known that? Of course they looked nothing alike. At all. They acted nothing alike.

"All this time you have been living with me and didn't know that Josh and I were related?"

I shook my head. "No. When we showed up he only told me, 'Adam is Adam,' and that was it. I had no idea you were related. I guess I didn't know much about Josh when we got married," I admitted. I still didn't, actually.

Adam looked at me seriously. "Why did you two get married so quickly?"

With a sigh, I told him, "It was such a whirlwind."

He leaned in. "Whirlwind?"

Shrugging, I offered a little more information. "I was kind of a loser, hated attention. And then one day Josh was there, asking me to sing with him. He knew my name. I was smitten. He said we should get married, and the next thing I knew, we had exchanged rings in front of a judge, been kicked out of both our parents' houses, and landed on your doorstep."

"All because he knew your name?"

The shock of that statement hit me. It was true. My simple crush had turned into love at first words simply because Josh Keene had known my name when it seemed nobody else did. "Y-yes. I guess so."

Adam only nodded, but then he smiled and patted my hand with his. "That's a little different from what Josh said," he told me.

I could only shrug. It was romantic at the time. Now it just seemed silly.

"Oh, before I forget, here's your pay for today. Thank you again," he said. He slid into the seat next to me, pushing the chair closer to mine. An envelope came to rest on my knee, his hand holding it in place. "It's cash, since I know you keep your money in your room."

"How did you know that?" I felt my body get hot and I couldn't make eye contact with him. Had he gone through our room? Our things?

His hand didn't move off my knee. The envelope was between my skin and his, but I could still feel the heat. "Josh told me. And you always pay for things in cash," he said.

I relaxed a little. While Adam had been a little more attentive than I would have liked, he had never crossed a line. I forced a small smile. Remembering the envelope, I took hold of it. I felt one of Adam's fingers run the length of mine before letting go. I worked hard to ignore the tingle that ran up my spine and the little leap in my heart.

When Josh came on stage, the smoky bar broke into polite applause. He ran his hands through his hair and winked at the crowd. Several women in the audience catcalled and whistled. I didn't mind too much. I knew it was part of the act. And I knew Josh came home with me at the end of the night. He tapped the microphone and raised his hand as if to signal the start of a marathon.

And with a strum of his electric guitar, he began his show. He played his heart out with songs from Weezer, The Offspring, and Screeching Weasel. The passion he had for his music was evident. He was lost in the notes he played and the words he sang. Nobody existed outside his little sphere, not even me.

That was the night I realized I would forever take second place to his first love.

Chapter Five

BYE BYE, LOVE

wo days later, I came home from work to find
Josh was gone. Not just him, but his clothes, too.
The money for our trip to Nashville, all five hundred dollars
of it, was gone as well. It was like Josh had erased himself
from my life. I sat on the bed dumbfounded. Had Josh left
me? Could he do that? And where would I go if he had? I
was living in the home of his cousin. Would my parents take
me back?

Hot and dazed, I fell to the bed and pressed my palms to
my eyes to try to hold back tears. Then I heard footsteps.

"Josh!" I stood suddenly, my heart pounding. The room
spun with the action, and I had to sit back down.

Adam appeared in the doorway. "No, sorry, Roxie," he
said. "He was gone when I got here. He left you a note in the
kitchen." He extended his arm and held out a piece of paper
for me. His face was turned away from me, his red hair
covering his eyes.

I took the paper, even though I was afraid to read it. Did
he hate me? Would he ever come for me? Was this tempo-

rary or permanent? With a deep breath and jittery hands, I opened the paper and read.

Roxie,

I am sorry to do this to you, babe. I found out the guys from Brick Jones Band were heading west toward Tennasee and they offered to take me along. I couldn't pass up the oppurtunaty. It was an imediate kinda thing, you know?

I'll send for you as soon as I can, Rox. Stay with Adam till then. I only took the $500 so you could have the rest to come out here. Maybe in a few weeks. The dream is alive!

— JOSH

I blinked several times. That was it? He was gone? How could he leave without saying goodbye? How could he pick up and leave so quickly without consulting me? And what did he mean by saying he would send for me? He wanted me to join him still? But there were no promises of love and forever. He didn't even say he loved me. I squeezed my eyes until I saw spots in the blackness.

"He just left? Just like that?" I sputtered. I opened my eyes and looked to Adam then, hoping he had answers.

He stood in the doorway, his eyes sad, and his arms folded. He hesitated a moment before stepping into my room.

"He left me a quick note, too. Here." He held out a jaggedly torn piece of paper for me to read.

"Adam, Great oppurtunaty came and I'm heading out. I hope you don't mind Rox crashing with you until I can get her. Thanks man."

"That's it?"

"That was it," he said. "I know it's not what you wanted to happen. But I'm sure he will send word for you to come as soon as he's set up. You know, when he finds a place to live and has a gig or two under his belt."

"I can't stay here," I said, standing. My eyes darted from Adam to the half-empty rack of clothing. "I've overstayed my welcome. I'll see if my parents will take me back." I went to the closet and grabbed my suitcase, flinging it on the bed.

"You can stay, Roxie. You can stay as long as you like," he said quietly, calmly. Adam stuffed his hands in his pockets, his eyes trained on mine. His voice remained steady, his demeanor calm. Maybe Adam really was a gentle soul after all.

I shook my head, unable to stop the tears. "No, that wouldn't be right." I started pulling clothes off hangers and flinging them into the suitcase. My voice shook as I spoke, "I'm a married woman, and I'm not married to you. I have to go."

Adam remained calm. "Have you spoken to your parents since you got married?"

I stopped, hair sticking to the hot tears on my cheek. "Barely," I admitted. "I've tried. I've spoken to my sister, but that's it. She said Dad is still angry, and Mom won't go against him. She's barely said more than hello when I've tried to call." I sat next to my suitcase. "I guess going home isn't a stellar idea. Especially when I tell them Josh just picked up and left. It would be a whole bunch of 'I told you so,' wouldn't it?"

Adam stepped closer and gently pulled the hair from my face. His eyes were kind and full of sympathy. In a quiet voice he said, "So you stay here. It's fine. Besides, who else would cook for me? I've gotten used to your wonderful cooking. We'll work out a deal. You cook and whatever else in exchange for the room."

Attempting a meek smile, I looked at him. "Thank you, Adam. I know it's been kind of strange between us. But I do appreciate you letting me stay. Hopefully it will just be a week or two, and then I'll be completely out of your hair." I watched as Adam took a deep, slow breath. Was I imagining things, or was he trying to resist hugging me?

Suddenly his eyes were brighter, his hair truer, his smile more genuine. My heart raced. I forced it to calm. I turned my face and looked at the crumpled clothes in my arms.

He stepped backward. "Whatever you need, Roxie. Anything." And I believed him. Adam exited the room and left me to ponder my future.

What would I do now? I guess I would take it one day at a time. I hoped Josh would call the next day and tell me where he was. Nashville was about seven hours away, but I wasn't sure if they were stopping somewhere along the way. I realized I wasn't even sure Josh was actually heading to Nashville, he'd only said Tennessee in his misspelled note. He could be on his way anywhere in the world and I had no idea.

I let go of a big sigh. Slowly, I hung my clothes back on the hangers. My suitcase was returned to the bottom of the closet. I trudged to the bathroom and sat on the lid of the toilet, and stared at myself in the mirror. I was still made up for work. More make-up than I liked, short black skirt, tight red top. I shucked my shoes. My feet were aching. I ran my hands through my hair and reasoned with myself.

Surely he would call in the morning. Of course he would. I mean, I was his wife. This was like a business trip, wasn't it? Then, once he was wherever he was going, he would tell me where to go and I would gas up and go to him.

And this would be a minor blip in our path. Of course. I was overreacting, of course. I took a deep breath of resolve. Momma always told me growing up that things would work out no matter if the road was bumpy. This was just a bump. In a few weeks, I would be by my husband's side once again.

Back in the bedroom, I put on my sweatpants and a tank top, ready for bed. But I couldn't sleep. I tossed and turned for a few minutes, but my brain was too wired. I padded out to the kitchen in my bare feet, thinking I would find a midnight snack. Instead, I found Adam.

"Everything okay?" He glanced at me cautiously, like I was a china doll that might break.

"Yeah, I guess," I said with a huff. "I just can't sleep. I thought I would maybe find a snack."

He waved a package of popcorn in the air. "I was going to make this and watch a movie if you want to join me."

"I don't want to interrupt you," I said, though I was eyeing the popcorn. My stomach rumbled a little.

"Nope. I'm just an insomniac who likes midnight movies on cable," he chuckled. "The Goonies is coming on in about 10 minutes."

I smiled. "That's one of my favorite movies," I told him.

"Same." He put the package in the microwave and pushed a few buttons. Within a few seconds, the sounds of kernels popping filled the air, along with the smell of warm butter.

"I always had a crush on Mikey," I admitted. Whatever happened to Sean Astin, I wondered.

"Not Mouth? Or the brother?"

I giggled. "No. Not my type."

"I still have a crush on Andie," Adam said. I giggled again.

The microwave beeped, and the popping stopped.

I decided to ask a bold question. "How come I never see any girls here hanging around you? I would have thought you would be pretty popular."

Adam snickered. "Roxie, you realize I'm a red-headed geek, right? I mean, I work in real estate, and I do pretty well, but I love to play old video games like Zelda and Sonic and watch 80s movies. I haven't had a girlfriend in almost two years."

I hadn't thought of Adam as geeky. I considered him a moment. Sure, his red hair was shockingly bright, and he had a smattering of freckles across his nose, but his eyes were a pretty shade of blue. He was attractive. And his body was incredibly fit. I had seen him go running almost every day in the time I had lived in his house. And who cared if he played video games? He apparently had quite the head for business and was doing well for himself. That made him attractive. Not that I was noticing that or anything. I was happily married.

"Rox?"

Geez. Had I been staring at him? I snapped out of my reverie and shook my head. "Sorry."

"Lost in thought? Thinking about Josh?" He looked at me through thick eyelashes, but quickly turned his attention back to the popcorn.

I nodded. Of course I had been thinking of Josh, I told myself. I definitely was not thinking about the freckles on Adam's forehead and ears, wondering if they ventured down his chest and biceps.

With a sigh, Adam turned and leaned on the counter with one hip. "Listen, Rox, Josh has always been impulsive. You should know that, you got married a few weeks after you started dating. He lives for the moment."

The fact that Adam was right didn't make it sting any

less. "Yeah, I know. But I thought he would live for me at least a little." I wiped a tear from my eye.

"How about a little Goonies to take your mind off everything?" Adam held up a big bowl of popcorn and raised his eyebrows.

"You don't have rocky road do you?" I giggled.

Adam's expression turned to a grimace. "You usually shop these days. I don't think we have any—"

"I was referencing the movie, Adam," I said with a laugh. "When Sloth offers Chunk the rocky road ice cream."

"Well, now I feel like an idiot," he replied. "Does that mean you'll join me?"

Feeling that sleep would not find me easily that night, I agreed. I followed Adam to his self-dubbed playroom, and we settled in for almost two hours of adventure and laughter. He was a perfect gentleman, keeping his distance and keeping his eyes on the screen.

I worked the late shift the next day, so I spent the majority of the morning hovering near the telephone. Thankfully, Adam had a cordless, so I could carry it with me wherever I went. But throughout the morning, the phone was silent. Around noon, Adam called to see if I had heard from Josh. I snapped at him that no I hadn't and to get off the phone. Surely there was a payphone wherever he was. Or maybe he was still on the road.

In my impatience, I scrubbed the kitchen clean. Then my bedroom and the bathroom I used. I was going to start on the rarely used living room, but I had to get myself ready for work. I carried the phone into the bathroom with me in case Josh called while I was in the shower. He didn't. I dressed in a flowy baby-doll dress and put on my make-up.

About half an hour before I had to be at Greene's for my shift the phone rang. I jumped to answer it. "Josh?"

"Hey, Rox. 'Sup?" It was Josh. I did a little dance and felt my heart leap in my chest.

"Josh! Where are you, baby?" I sat, then stood, then sat again. I couldn't hold still.

"Sorry, Roxie. The band offered to take me, but I had to leave right then if I was down. I barely had time to run back home and pack my stuff," Josh said.

I could hear a lot of noise behind him. It sounded like he was in a bar. Then I heard a girl in the background. I wanted to reach through the phone and pull him out of whatever bar he was in where girls were within arm's reach.

"Where are you?" I repeated. "Where are you going?" I tried to hide the anger in my voice.

"Don't freak, Rox," he bellowed into the receiver. "I'm in Atlanta right now."

Atlanta? Atlanta was never in our plans.

"The Brick Jones Band has a weekend gig here tonight and tomorrow. They said I could play with them. Then Sunday we're heading west toward New Orleans."

"New Orleans? That wasn't part of the plan!" I practically screamed into the phone. I was beyond angry. Did he not consider me at all? Apparently not. "What is going on, Josh?"

"Opportunity, Rox. Word is New Orleans is the next happening music scene. I want to be in on the ground level," he said. "Listen, I gotta run. Time's up. I'll call you next week."

"But – Josh!" I cried. Next week?

"What?"

"I love you, Josh," I whispered into the phone. I closed my eyes and choked back a sob. Next week?

"Love you, too, Rox. This is it! Bye!" The phone went dead.

At least he had said he loved me. That was something, right? I felt such a mix of emotions right then. I loved him, I felt that. But I also hated him. I hated that I had never come first for Josh. I had always been an accessory to his music. Could I spend the rest of my life with someone I loved and hated?

I didn't have time to ponder that question because I was running late for work. I would have to think on it later, like Scarlett O'Hara in Gone with the Wind. I would consider my options tomorrow.

ॐ

J did a lot of thinking in that next week. The more time that went by without a word from Josh, the more I felt firm in my decision. I had to end it with him. I needed a man who loved me, not what I could do for his career or how I looked on his arm. But I had no way of getting in touch with Josh, so I had to wait for him to call me.

My only real girlfriend was my co-worker, Gina. I had told her of my plight, and she told me to kick Josh to the curb.

"He's no good, girl, you know it." She picked up a glass and flicked a tap. "A man who loves you wouldn't just up and leave like that." She flicked the tap off again.

My head hung low. "I know, Gina. But he's my husband. We've already made that commitment."

Tray loaded, she hoisted it above her head. "Yeah, but has that poser fulfilled his vows to you? Or has he broken them?"

Had he broken them? We hadn't really gone through the better or worse, though this was definitely a worse version of Josh. We had never been richer, always poorer. And no illnesses had plagued us, thankfully. But that last part. Till death do us part. We were not dead and he had picked up and left. It wasn't like we had planned for him to go first and me to follow later. He had simply vanished into the night.

It was Sunday evening, more than a week since I had heard from Josh, and Christmas was approaching. I found solace in the kitchen. Constantly cooking, making up recipes, and then cleaning it all up. That night, I made a new risotto recipe for Adam to taste. We always had plenty of leftovers, probably since I cooked too much food. I wasn't ready to accept that I was only making food for two. And the man I had married six months ago was not one of the two.

How was it that in the span of six months I had alienated myself from my parents, gotten married, moved in with a complete stranger, and had my husband leave me with said stranger? What had I become? I laughed. If someone told me about a girl with this life, I would have called her a not-too-nice word. I mopped my brow with a paper towel as I stood over a boiling pot.

As I blew a stray strand of brown hair from my eyes, Adam's voice called behind me. "That smells wonderful, Roxie," he said. "I hope you don't mind, I invited someone to dinner."

My eyes widened. Did Adam have a date? I suddenly felt out of place. "I'm sorry, Adam. I'll get out of your hair," I said. "Give me a minute and you'll never know I was here."

An older woman came into the room. She was impeccably dressed in a green pantsuit with heels that matched. Her strawberry blonde hair was cut to her shoulders. For a moment, I thought Adam had suddenly taken an interest in older women.

"Roxanne, this is my mother, Linda Joyce," Adam said, motioning to the woman. "Mom, this is Roxanne."

"I didn't know you had a cook, Adam," she said, eyeing me cautiously.

"Not quite, Mom," he corrected. "Roxie is a friend of mine and a wonder in the kitchen. She cooks for me every so often." He winked at me. He did not mention that I lived here with him. I wouldn't be the one to bring it up.

"Sorry, dear," Mrs. Joyce said to me. She extended a hand toward me, but I shook my head, my hands were gross.

"My apologies," I said. "I'm a bit messy. But it's nice to meet you." I folded my arms in front of my middle to hide my hands.

"Likewise," she said, still not taking her eyes off me. She semi-whispered to Adam, "She's pretty, Adam. And she cooks. Just a friend?"

I felt a blush creep over my cheeks. I avoided looking at Adam, but I knew he was likely also blushing the way most red-heads were prone to do. I busied myself with straightening up, ignoring her comment.

I guess she didn't know I was Josh's wife. Did she even talk to Josh's parents? Did Josh's parents even know he had left? What had he told them?

Finally, Adam spoke. "Can I give you a hand, Roxie?"

Coming back into the moment, I thought and glanced around. "Could you pop the bread in the toaster oven for a minute? It needs to be browned on top, then it's ready," I suggested. He set right to what I had asked. "Actually, aside from that, everything is done. I'll let you two eat in peace and I'll clean up later." I took off the apron I was wearing and hung it on a hook in the corner.

"Why don't you eat with us, Roxie?" Adam suggested. "Mom?"

Mrs. Joyce smiled. "Adam, I'm sure your friend has other things planned for such a lovely evening. Why don't you pay her what you owe and let her be on her way?" Her eyes crinkled with an unnatural smile. She was trying to place me, I knew. Did she know my father? Had she heard of Josh's rushed marriage?

I didn't like how she emphasized the word friend. Or how she implied I was a hired hand.

The phone rang at that moment. I could feel in my core it was Josh. I thought Adam could sense it too because the rings hung between us like a thick blanket. Slowly, Adam went to the phone and answered.

"Hello? Hi, Josh. How are you?" He lifted a finger to his mother to signal that he needed a minute and disappeared behind a corner.

I felt sweaty and anxious all of a sudden. How could I get the phone if Adam's mother had no idea I lived here? "I had better get going," I said, wiping my hands on a towel.

"What about your pay?" she asked, looking at me intently.

I waved my hand in dismissal. "I'll just get it later. It was nice to meet you, Mrs. Joyce." I excused myself and disappeared around the same corner Adam had moments before. He passed me the phone with an apologetic look and I quickly retreated to my room.

"Josh? Is it you?" I sat on the edge of the bed. I could feel my voice catch a little in my throat. A giggle rose up in my throat and my palms were sweaty like the first time I went to his house. Suddenly I wasn't so sure I was going to end things with Josh. All the love I felt for him welled up inside me. I believed in him. I believed in us.

"Yeah, Roxie, it's me," he said. His voice was dark, it held no excitement in talking to me after a week of radio silence.

"Where are you, Josh? Are you in New Orleans?" My heart hammered in my chest. Would he tell me to come right away? I began to look over my closet, mentally packing.

"I'm here in the Big Easy, Rox. It's amazing. Nothing like South Carolina," he said. "But see, babe, things are not happening like I thought."

My smile fell. "What do you mean, Josh? What's happened?"

"Well, Roxie, it's like this," he started. "I don't know if I can make a real go of this with you back there."

Maybe he was going to tell me to come right away. He needed his muse. I stood and went to the closet. "I can pack. I can be there before Christmas!"

"I'm sending you divorce papers, Roxanne," he blurted out.

I gasped. All the air around me disappeared and the closet of clothing in front of me became a black hole.

"You're great, Roxie, but I don't think we're the next Kurt and Courtney. I was so swept up, and, well, I can't make it big with you dragging me down."

Dragging him down? I was dragging him down? I had done nothing but support him. I had supported his music, I had gone to his gigs, and I had worked my tail off and dressed like a tramp to keep him fed while he sang karaoke in dive bars.

"I don't understand, Josh. We're married. We made vows and promises. I've worked hard to support you. You took off with *my* hard-earned money," Anger did not begin to describe how I was feeling. Wasn't I the one who just a few minutes ago was thinking of telling him it was over? And now he had the nerve to tell me?

"You pretty much whored yourself out to Adam for that

money. I saw how you were looking at each other," he hissed.

His words felt like a slap to the face. The blackness I had seen a moment before became red and I felt like an angry bull seeing that red. I was ready to charge full steam ahead and gorge Josh Keene.

"I did that for you, you jerk! I did that so we could leave together. So we could live out your dream – your dream – together. How dare you, Josh?"

His voice was barely above a whisper. "I'm sorry, Rox. The papers should arrive tomorrow. I think it's called an annulment. I talked with my uncle, he's a lawyer."

His uncle was a lawyer? What uncle? He talked to someone I didn't know about how to leave me? I shook my head in disbelief.

"When did you talk to a lawyer, Josh?" I was in shock, my voice barely a whisper. If he had the papers already and had only been gone ten days, he had done this before he left town. When he didn't answer, I repeated myself. This time I demanded, "Josh? When did you talk to this lawyer?"

"Before I left, okay? I'm sorry, Roxanne."

"Yes. Yes, you are," I seethed. "I'll sign them as soon as they come."

"Thanks. You know what Kurt said, 'I'd rather be hated for who I am, than loved for who I am not.'"

The quote made me shake my head. Did he even understand the words? He was the biggest sellout of all. Did Kurt just up and leave Courtney and their little girl? Well, I guess he had in the end. And now Josh was abandoning me, the only one who had encouraged his dream.

"One more question," I demanded. I forced myself to ask. I wasn't sure I wanted the answer, but I had to ask anyway. "Did you ever love me?"

I heard him take a full breath. "I thought I did." Then the line went dead.

I pried the silver ring from my finger and flung it across the room. I cried myself to sleep that night. It was our six-month wedding anniversary.

And that was how my first marriage ended.

Chapter Six

TEARS IN HEAVEN

fter I signed the paperwork to annul my marriage to Josh Keene, Adam focused a lot of time and attention on me. He was very sweet, always smiling and asking how I was doing. He waited to see me every morning before going to his office, and if by chance he had to leave before I got up, he would call me mid-morning to check on me. I could no longer deny that he had feelings for me. I, on the other hand, did my best to ignore the butterflies I felt and the shyness I was suddenly overcome with when he was around. I did not need another man in my life so soon. But he had opened up his home to me and told me to stay. Without anywhere else to go, I obliged, promising to be out of his hair as soon as I could.

In addition to working at Greene's, I enrolled in culinary school. With encouragement from Adam and Gina, I decided to follow my passion, and I felt the most alive when I was creating new dishes. I had applied for several student loans in order to afford the classes, which was daunting, but Adam helped me fill them out. Thankfully, banks were all too eager to loan me money, and the advisors promised me they were easy to pay back in small monthly increments once I graduated and had a job.

Having a dream was a new thing for me. Momma always used to say if my dreams didn't scare me, they weren't big enough. So it had been easier to just not have dreams of my own.

With Josh, I was trying to give him his dream. And now I found I had one. One in which I was actually talented. I relished every class, and between that and work, I was exhausted.

About two months after things with Josh had ended, I received an unexpected call at work. My sister Lori was sobbing as I took the receiver and cradled it between my ear and shoulder.

"Lori? What's wrong? Why are you calling me at work?" I wiped my hands on a towel and tried to cover the receiver so I could hear her.

"Roxie, it's Mom," she said, her voice sounded panicked. "She's had a heart attack. You have to come now. The doctor said there's not much time."

"What? Are you sure?" I stumbled a little. Mom had a heart attack? How was that possible? She wasn't even fifty yet. "I'll be right there, Lori."

I tore off my apron and explained things to Gina. After a tight hug, she told me to go, reminding me to drive carefully as I sprinted through the doors.

I sped to the hospital. The whole way there, I fought to see the road through my tears. What had happened? I was such a terrible daughter to allow myself to be kept away from Mom this long.

I heaved the heavy doors to the hospital open. I hurried to the desk where an older woman in a cardigan sat primly. I didn't even try to catch my breath. "Margaret DePrivé, please."

"Do you know what floor she's on, sweetie?" The woman spoke as if there was no hurry in the world.

"My mother. She had a heart attack. Please, I need to see her." I felt more tears welling up and I could not hold them back.

The woman's pleasant expression turned to one of concern. She picked up the phone and made a call. I paced before her. Could she not hurry? With a nod, she replaced the receiver without a sound.

" Mrs. DePrivé is in room 117. Up one level in this elevator, go left. That's 110, just follow it to 117."

I was already off, not bothering to give her thanks. Momma would want me to go back and tell the woman thank you, but I would do it on my way back out. Right now, I needed to see my mother.

The room was right where I had been told it would be. I burst in to find my father and three sisters gathered around a small frame in a bed, hooked to too many machines.

Dad glared at me but didn't stop me from coming in to see Mom. I sat at her side and took her hand. She had monitors hooked up to her and a tube hooked under her nose and around her ears. Little noises sounded intermittently, letting us know she was still breathing, and her heart was still beating.

"Momma? It's me, Roxie," I said, my chin quivering.

She slowly looked at me, taking effort to focus on my features. "Roxanne? Oh, baby. I missed you," she said as tears formed in her eyes. A jittery hand littered with tubes and tape came to my cheek and caressed it softly.

"I miss you, too, Momma," I said as tears fell down my

cheeks. "Don't worry, you'll be okay." I said it more to reassure myself than her.

She looked beyond me. "Where is that boy you married? Did he not come?"

I looked down and fiddled with Mom's sheets. "Josh is gone, Momma. He left and we got an annulment. It was final just a few weeks ago."

"Why didn't you tell me? Why didn't you call?" she chided. Always my mother; that was Margaret DePrivé.

I was fairly certain she had heard about the annulment before this. Columbia wasn't that big and the Keene's neighborhood was not far from my parents'. Mom and Grace Keene surely shopped in the same stores and shared mutual friends. And the gossips loved to share any kind of bad news around town.

With a shaky breath, she continued her questioning. "Where are you living? Where have you been all this time?"

"I'm staying with a friend, Mom," I said noncommittally. "But don't worry about me. You need to focus on getting better. We have plenty of time to catch up when you get out of here."

I only stayed about thirty minutes before the nurses came through, telling visitors they had to leave. One glance at my father's face told me my time was up. His button-up shirt was wrinkled, his hair was disheveled, his eyes bloodshot and puffy. It was the worst I had ever seen him look. I did not argue. I kissed my mother and told her I would return the next day to see her.

Important moments in your life are rarely realized when you're in them. This was one. It would be the last time I ever saw my mother. How I wished I had known then.

My mother passed away that night when her heart gave out again. Her funeral was scheduled for the following

Monday. My father made it clear that he did not want me at the funeral, but he would allow it because all of the senator's children should be there to mourn their mother. I didn't quibble.

Adam came with me to the funeral. I had told him he needn't join me, but he had insisted. I was so glad to have a friendly face among the crowd. He never left my side the entire time. I had plenty of strange looks from family members who had heard the rumors of my marriage. I guess news of my annulment also traveled fast because those who had the gumption to talk to me asked about this new man in my life. I had a hard time explaining he was just a friend.

When the service was over, my father approached me for the first time. I smoothed out my black skirt and faced him, Adam behind me. My father looked from me to Adam and back again. My arms went in front of me, crossing under my chest as I prepared for his barrage of questions.

"Who is this, Roxanne? This isn't the boy you brought to my house wanting to marry six months ago," he said passively. "Are you bed hopping now?"

Tears stung my eyes and my jaw dropped. Did my father really think so little of me? "No, Daddy. How could you say such a thing?"

Adam stepped forward to protect me but was careful not to touch me, lest it was taken the wrong way. "Mr. DePrivé, I assure you I'm only here for moral support for Roxie. There is nothing between us."

Daddy ignored Adam and wagged a finger at me. "I heard that the bum you married left. Or didn't you know his mother called Margaret after he skipped town? You're not the only one he left a note for, Roxie."

My voice wavered, but I tried to hold my resolve. "You

were right, Dad. I admit it. Josh was a mistake, but it seems you know that's been resolved. We had the marriage annulled." I couldn't look at him.

"You can't erase a marriage, Roxie," he said, his voice full of disappointment. "Annulled or not, you were still married to him. Is that any way for a senator's daughter to act? Your mother was broken-hearted when you got married. And now look where she is!"

A vein bulged on his forehead and there was a sheen of unshed tears in his eyes. He was speaking in pain, I knew, but his verbal assault still stung.

Tears rolled down my cheeks, and I stuttered. "I, I ... Daddy ..."

A voice called my father's name and his expression instantly changed from rage to his public persona, a grieving man. His head swiveled as someone called to him a second time.

I felt an arm around my shoulder. Adam whispered in my ear, "Let's go, Roxie. You don't need to hear this. He's angry about your mom and lashing out at you." He turned my shoulders and led me away from my father and out the door.

In the funeral home's lobby, we ran into my two eldest sisters, Jenny and Shelly, who were talking quietly. Jenny broke away from Shelly and stopped me. "Roxie, really? You married some slacker a few months ago and then bring someone else as a date to mom's funeral? A date? How dare you?" She motioned toward Adam with a look of disgust.

"That's not what this is, Jenny. How could you think of that of me?" I couldn't believe my ears. I couldn't believe my family had all turned on me like this. "When did I stop being your little sister? Don't you know me at all?"

Jenny flipped her long dark hair over her shoulder. "I

know what Dad told me. I know you disrespected him and Mom by marrying some punk musician. Where did he go?" As she spoke, her twin, Shelly, approached us.

"Jen, calm down. This is not the place for this discussion," Shelly said. Finally, a voice of reason.

Hoping that Shelly might be an ally for me, I took her hand in mine and pleaded. "Shelly, please. I'm not here to be disrespectful. She was my mother, too. I miss her. I've been missing her. I made a huge mistake by marrying Josh. I know that. But it's over."

My sister looked sympathetic, but then shot a scrutinizing eye toward Adam.

"Adam is a good friend who came as a favor to me so I'm not alone," I explained.

Shelly, always the peacemaker, extended her hand to Adam. "Shelly DePrivé, I'm sorry for all this." She smiled at him.

Adam took her hand gently and cleared his throat. "Adam Joyce. I understand emotions are high right now. My father passed away a few years ago. I'm sorry for your loss."

"Thank you. How do you know our Roxie? From school?" Shelly stepped closer. Her short bob shook as she moved and she fluttered her eyelashes. Was she flirting with Adam? She had a fiance on the other side of the room.

"We're good friends, that's all. I'm afraid I did not know her in school," Adam admitted. He was several years older than me, even if he had attended the same high school, he would have been too old to know me.

Jenny, upset that her rant at me had been interrupted, spoke up again. "Adam Joyce? Joyce Realty? Is Linda Joyce your mother?" She looked at Adam as if he was a piece of meat.

"Yes. On both. Linda is my mother. Do you know her?"

"I work with her," Jenny said. "We're both on the advisory committee for Hopeful Foundations. I've heard all about you." Jenny nodded a little, seemingly now approving of Adam.

"Well, I know she's really involved in her charity work, and she does love Hopeful Foundations," Adam said. "I'll be sure to let her know I've met you. Jenny, was it?"

"Jenny Dolinghouse," she said. As she motioned to a man behind us she added, "Mike Dolinghouse, mayor of Cayce, is my husband. Surely you've heard of him."

Jenny thought everyone should know her and her husband. She had political aspirations just like our father, and her husband was cut from the same cloth. Mike Dolinghouse wanted to work his way up the political ladder, and marrying Jenny gave him more clout. Jenny was only twenty-five, but Mike was nearly ten years her senior. Their match had been more about advantage than love.

Adam shook his head. "Nope, sorry."

I had to stifle a laugh at his nonchalant response.

For her part, Jenny brushed off the snub and turned back to me. "Well, Roxie, regardless, this is not how to behave. You know the press will be here and you being here so freshly divorced with another man is scandalous."

I had no fight left in me. I just nodded to my sister. The last thing I wanted to do was upset anyone else in my family. Jenny walked away without another word. Shelly gave me an apologetic look and followed Jenny to where Mike and Shelly's fiancé stood waiting.

"Please, let's go," I begged Adam, feeling a tightness in my chest. "I need to get out of here."

"Don't let them talk to you like that, Roxie. Don't let them walk over you," Adam said. I could hear the anger in his voice. "You're worth more than that. And a mistake you made in your past is just that, a mistake. And it's behind you now. They should be willing to look beyond that."

I looked at my sisters. Jenny with her long hair, her professionally tailored suit, and the mayor of a big city on her arm. Shelly checked herself in a compact mirror, swiping under her eyes for any runoff mascara. Her fiancé, Zach Cash, showed his vanity by taking the compact from her and giving himself a thorough glance.

"My family is all about appearances, Adam. I've never been good enough. My grades weren't good enough. My aspirations have never been high enough," I admitted. "I've been one big disappointment."

"Not to me," said a female voice behind me. I turned to see Lori, her black dress wrinkled, her make-up stained from tears. Lori had been Mom's girl, the most like her. "And not to Mom, either, Roxie. She loved you."

My chin quivered and I rushed to her arms. I clung to my sister, the only one who hadn't shut me out completely and judged me harshly. We said nothing, but we held each other for several seconds. I could feel more hot tears falling from her eyes as she sobbed. When she finally let me go, she looked me in the eyes, her dark eyes watery and sad. She smoothed my hair and nodded.

"I'm going to school now," I whispered to her. I didn't get the chance to tell Mom. Telling Lori was almost the same.

"Are you? Where?" She pulled back and looked at me, her sandy colored hair was matted to her face, but she didn't care.

"Culinary school. I'm going to be a chef one day," I said with a feeble smile.

Lori smiled and nodded. "Mom would be so proud of you. You were always a great cook. And I'm happy you found what you want. I know you want to get out of here. Call me soon, okay?" she whispered. She put her forehead to mine the way we did as children.

"I will. Next week?" I managed to croak out. When she nodded I stood straight and took a deep breath. Lori looked from me to Adam and back again. She nodded again as if to approve and then she broke away from me.

Adam took my hand in his. His hand was large, rough in some spots and smooth in others. "Ready?"

"Yeah, let's go." My shoulders shook and he gently pulled me toward him. He did not embrace me, but his shoulder brushed mine, and I felt his meaning. I looked at him. His aqua eyes shone. They spoke volumes.

As we left, I did not glance back at the family who had turned their backs on me. The father who disapproved of every decision I made. The sister who jumped to conclusions with a single glance. The people who only cared about what was on the outside.

My family was torn apart, or at least I had splintered away from them. Fragmented by my decisions and the passing of my mother, the glue that held us all together. Things never went back to the way they had been.

§&

I threw myself into my schooling. I wanted to make my mother proud. She always said following one's heart was the key to happiness. I made friends at the culinary school. People to study with, people to try recipes out on.

As summer approached, a small group of us had become close and they asked me if I wanted to share an apartment with them. I said yes.

Adam wasn't too thrilled I was moving out. I knew he

liked me, and I liked him too, but I still felt like such a failure after Josh. I needed to spend some time as just Roxie. Not someone else and Roxie. Adam assured me he understood and I promised him I would keep in touch and we would still be friends. He had winced when I said 'friends,' though.

My new roommates were Tarek, Erin, and Remi. Tarek was a self-proclaimed hoodlum, but really, he was a soft-spoken man from the wrong side of town. He loved to cook and aspired to open his own soul food restaurant one day. Erin was a sweet, quiet girl with a midwestern accent who said cooking was the only joy in her life after the death of her older brother a few years before. And Remi was a young Frenchman in the US on a student visa who said he wanted to see what the states had to offer. Why he would choose culinary school here versus back home, I never did find out.

In time, the four of us had worked out our rhythm in our little two-bedroom apartment. Erin and I fell into an easy camaraderie, and we both enjoyed spending time together. The guys were nice and never pushy. Tarek had a girlfriend who was in college to become a teacher. Remi was funny, witty, and a pleasure to be around.

Life was becoming a new normal. No more parents, no more Josh Keene. I was becoming my own woman. Finally.

Chapter Seven

A TOUCH OF GARNISH

*I*t took two years of grueling hard work, but I graduated from culinary school in record time. And as it happened, a new restaurant opened right around that time called Pixie's. I was offered the position of saucier. Remi was hired on as the sous-chef, and we both worked under head chef Ulman Tallant, who was also the owner. The work was not easy, and I often left exhausted, but it was deeply gratifying. For some reason, adding pinches of salt and cumin to dishes made me happy, and for that, I was grateful. Chef Tallant had even allowed me to add my own pumpkin spice soup recipe to the menu for the fall, which was a high honor. Remi had one of his dishes on the menu as well. The rest were creations by the chef himself.

One evening as we were getting in Remi's car to head back to our apartment, he looked at me with a studious smile. "*Cherie*, you are finally looking happy." He put his hand to my chin and lifted it. "I have known you two years now, and in all that time, I have not seen you this happy. Now I see it."

The words were sincere and I could only smile and nod

at his notice. "I am happy, Remi. I found something that makes me happy. I feel like things are turning around in my life."

Remi was only a few inches taller than me and had wavy jet black hair that he kept loose around his face unless he was cooking. Then it was pulled into a little ponytail and tucked inside a hairnet. His dark eyes laughed when he spoke, and I loved to listen to his prattle around the apartment, speaking French to his family back home.

"These are good things, Roxie," he said as we made our way down the winding streets toward home. Erin still lived with us and had taken a position at a different restaurant. Tarek was moving out to get married, and Remi would now have the room to himself.

"I, too, have found a sense of purpose with work. And recently, I have found purpose outside the kitchen," he said with a wide grin. When I raised an eyebrow, he nodded, "I have found the lover of my soul, *cherie*. It's a wonderful feeling."

I was happy for Remi, truly. He had become a dear friend and I wished him nothing but happiness. "Oh, Remi, that's wonderful news. Will I get to meet her?"

"Soon, I hope. Since Tarek is moving out to get married, I have asked Becca to move in with me. If it's okay with you and Erin? *Si vous plait*?" He lifted his eyebrows at the question.

I thought for a moment. I was always taught that living together before marriage was a sin, but then so was divorce. And I had not stepped inside a church since I had left home. As a twenty-one-year-old girl, I had no problems with it.

"I think it's a wonderful idea. Have you talked to Erin?"

He shook his head, "*Non*, not yet. I will tonight. I am so

happy we are both happy, Roxie. I think it's, what you call it, about time."

I laughed. I liked seeing my friend so full of joy. It gave me hope for love in the world. "So, tell me all about Becca."

He told me all about the girl of his dreams until we got home. He talked to Erin, who was fine with her moving in as well. Two weeks later, Tarek moved out to get married, and Becca and a few meager belongings moved into our small apartment. She was a sweet girl of about twenty who worked at the mall but had aspirations of becoming a social worker when she could afford college. I liked her instantly.

§.

One bright morning a few weeks later, Remi came into the restaurant mad as a hornet. He was muttering and sputtering what I could only figure were expletives in French.

"What's the matter?" I asked as I chopped peppers across from him. There had been no hint of anger when I had left our apartment an hour before. I wondered what would cause such a change in demeanor so quickly.

"Stupid government," he said before ranting again in French. "My visa has expired. I have to go back to France."

I stopped my knife mid-chop. "Go back? Why? Can't you stay here?" I knew Remi had his own life, but I was asking for purely selfish reasons. Remi had been such a wonderful friend to me. I didn't want to lose him.

"I have tried to extend it, but it's been denied. I will be deported within the week," he said, throwing his hands up in the air. "I don't want to go. I don't want to leave this restaurant and you, *cherie*. And I cannot leave Becca."

I began chopping again, hoping the repetition would

help me think. An idea came to me immediately. "I know! Why don't you and Becca get married?"

Remi's face softened and he looked at me. "Ah, Roxie, I wish it could be. But *est impossible*."

I came around the table we were working on and took his hands. "But why? It would allow you to stay here. And I admit, Remi, I need you. You've been such a great friend to me."

"Roxanne," Remi sighed. "We have not told you and Erin the whole truth. Becca and I are in love, yes. But the reason she moved in so fast is that she is trying to get a divorce from her husband. So we cannot get married because she already is married. He is what you say about Josh – a bum." Remi looked down at his shoes, embarrassed.

"I had no idea," I whispered. "My divorce was over pretty quickly. But we had an annulment. Can't she do that?"

He shook his head. "No, apparently not. I see no way through this. But it kills me to think of leaving Becca. I was going to propose to her and everything. You know, after the divorce was final." He pulled a little ring box from his pocket and showed me a modest, but dazzling, little engagement ring. I shook my head at the shame of it all. Surely there was an answer somehow.

Later that day as we were preparing for dinner, several men in black came to the restaurant asking for Remi. Chef Tallant burst through the kitchen doors from the front room in a tizzy.

"Remi, you need to go. Immigration is here!" Chef Tallant was a hard boss, but he treated his employees like family and he had grown increasingly fond of Remi. He pushed Remi's arm in an effort to slide him out the back door.

"What do you mean immigration is here?" he asked, his

voice high. "I thought I had more time!" Remi looked from Chef to me, his eyes pleading.

Thinking quickly, I stood next to Remi and dug into his pocket. I opened the ring box and put it into his hand and shoved Remi down on his knee. The door burst open and three men in suits stood in the doorway just in time to see my fake excitement at a wedding proposal that had not actually happened.

The men looked at the scene before them. Chef Tallant stood mouth agape. Remi on the floor before me with a ring extended. The rest of the kitchen looked shocked. Hopefully this plan would work.

"What's going on here?" asked the one in front. His eyes narrowed and his mustache twitched.

"Shh," Chef said, waving a hand at the man. "Do not interrupt this beautiful moment." He had caught on immediately.

Remi looked distressed, so I quickly piped up, "Yes, I will marry you!" I grabbed the ring and put it on my finger. I was relieved it fit. I bent down and hugged Remi, helping him back to his feet. Quietly I whispered, "Play along."

Once he understood what I was doing, he jumped into the role. "Oh, *cherie*, I am the happiest man today!"

And he kissed me. It was probably the most dramatic kiss I had ever received in my life; I had to stifle a laugh. Once the moment was over, everyone in the kitchen applauded. Everyone, that is, except for the three uniformed men who had intruded.

"What the devil is going on?" the first one asked again.

"Don't you see? They are in love!" Chef exclaimed, shaking his round body before him. "I will make you the best wedding cake! I will make all the food for your wedding!" He came over to us and kissed us both on the cheek.

"Remi Bonhomme? You will have to come with us," the man with the mustache said. He took two huge steps toward us.

I cozied up to Remi and batted my eyelashes at the men. "You can't take him, we just got engaged!"

"His visa is expired, miss," he said flatly. His mustache twitched the whole time.

Remi held up his hand to stop the man. "I am sorry, I have been trying to get it extended so that Roxanne and I could have a proper wedding." He took my hand in his and brushed his lips against my knuckles ever so slightly. I knew I blushed a deep red. Fake proposal or not, I wasn't dead inside.

"We have been keeping a close watch on you, sir. We have seen you out with a petite redhead, not this woman," the man said, unmoved.

"Apparently you have not kept that close a watch on me. My love, Roxie, and I live together. It is truth we have another female friend and roommate and she does have red hair. And another with blond hair. But it is this vision that has captured my heart. I cannot wait to marry her," he said as he gently caressed my face.

I pressed close to Remi. "We can make it happen soon, my love," I said. I looked into his eyes and conjured up a few tears. "We can do it sooner if it will keep them from tearing us apart."

The smaller man behind the first one spoke up, "Do you think we haven't seen false weddings take place, miss? It's a crime, you know."

I left Remi's side and stepped closer to the three officers. "The only crime here is you trying to prevent a decent, hardworking man from being with the love of his life," I cried. It was the truth, it was just a matter of who that love was. "How do we prove this to be a real wedding and marriage?"

We sat at a table with the three immigration officials for almost an hour, answering questions and trying to convince them that we were in love and that Remi and I couldn't live without each other. They left unconvinced, but they had left without taking Remi with them.

The rest of the night was spent preparing food and tossing wedding ideas back and forth across the kitchen. This would be my second wedding and Remi's first. Even if it was a sham for a friend, I hoped it would be a little fancier than my first.

A random but willing justice of the peace was signed up to perform the ceremony two weeks later. He had raised his eyebrows when I told him I was getting married for a second time and I was only twenty-one years old. But he had agreed to marry us quickly since Remi was facing deportation. He even offered to speak with immigration to testify that Remi and I truly were a couple in love and not hiding anything. I felt terrible for lying to the pastor, but I did love Remi in a completely platonic way.

We passed out handmade invitations for a Sunday after-noon wedding. Remi invited his friends, including Becca, who said she felt jilted that I was marrying Remi. But she also said she was thankful I was willing to put my neck on the line for a friend. I invited Adam, Gina, and my regulars from Greene's. I also put invitations in the mailboxes of my father and Lori.

Lori called about two hours later and asked me what I was doing.

"I'm helping a friend," I said bluntly. No need to lie to my sister.

"But getting married again? You're still so young. Are you in love?"

I didn't answer her question. "Lori, please come."

"I would, Roxie, but I can't," she said. I could feel the pain in her voice, but her rejection wounded me. With that, I hung up. I didn't need to hear any more.

Chapter Eight

LOVE AL DENTE

emi and I were married in a hasty but lavish ceremony. Apparently, Remi had some money put away, and he even offered to buy my dress. It was an ivory sheath dress and the back dipped low. It hadn't been expensive, but it was a real wedding dress. Remi said it showed off my wonderful back. I felt exposed, but I also felt pretty. My hair was done in soft waves down my shoulders, and my makeup was subdued and alluring. I felt extremely feminine, especially considering I was usually covered in food.

Wedding number two may have been a farce at the time, but at least I looked like a bride at this one and had a proper wedding ceremony.

Remi wore a snazzy tuxedo. I thought back to Josh and his dirty blue jeans and the tic tac he had pulled from his pocket. I shook my head to clear the thought. Remi wore his curly hair down around his face, which was most attractive. For a sham wedding, this was much nicer than my real one.

We got married inside the restaurant since it was normally closed on Sundays. We only had about twenty guests, but it was enough. The immigration official with the mustache was also in attendance. He sat in the back and watched with his stern expression the entire afternoon. When Remi kissed me at the end of the ceremony, he pulled me to him and bent me back into the kiss. It was like a scene from a movie. I know I was swept up in the moment. I hoped everyone else was convinced it was real.

Adam Joyce had come to the wedding after I begged him. Even though I confided that it was a marriage of convenience and not love, he was put off. He sat in the back, his arms crossed, a scowl across his face. When the ceremony was over, he had left, disappointment written all over his face. I almost went after him, but I couldn't. Not without giving myself away.

❦

*A*bout a week later, Mr. Graham, the immigration officer, came by the apartment to make sure everything was on the up and up. He was polite but invasive, and I was a nervous wreck. We had quickly moved Becca's things in with Erin and my things in with Remi. It had been a hectic few days, but we got it done.

Alexander Graham carried a little notebook that he seemingly took meticulous notes in with each step. Remi was in the kitchen, preparing a snack for our guest, while I showed him the small space. Of course, he wanted to see the bedroom. I was mortified.

"Mrs. Bonhomme," he began.

I interrupted him. "Actually, Mr. Graham, I decided to keep DePrivé as my last name since I use it professionally. Remi is completely understanding of that." I smiled, knowing this would go into his little book.

It did. "Interesting," he mumbled. He rolled his shoulders back and twitched his mustache.

"Is that a problem, Mr. Graham? You can just call me Roxie, everybody does," I laughed nervously and crossed my arms. I led him down the hall, feeling like I was single-handedly giving Remi deportation papers.

"Speaking of your name, Ms. DePrivé, this is your second marriage." He spoke matter-of-factly. There was no question attached, though. More like he was stating something everyone already knew.

"Yes, it is," I said as calmly as possible. "I regret that my last marriage was an utter failure, but the man I married turned out to be more in love with his guitar than me. Remi was such a help after that. That's how we became friends." I smiled as I opened the bedroom door and allowed Mr. Graham inside. Remembering that Remi and I were supposed to be married in every way, I added, "And then it blossomed into more. He definitely loves me more than his job. I finally feel happy after so much heartache."

Mr. Graham only nodded. He scanned the freshly made bed. I wondered if I should have left it crumpled up to insinuate something had happened there. He pointed to the closet door, and I opened it for him. He poked his head in and wrote again on his paper. Remi's clothes hung opposite my own. His shoes sat in a row next to mine. I hoped Mr. Graham wouldn't check the other bedroom – half my things were still in there.

Wandering into the bathroom, Mr. Graham called out to me, "Does Remi use an electric or manual shaver, Ms. DePrivé?"

I blinked. What an odd question. "He uses a manual one. He says he doesn't trust electric ones to get all the stubble." I stood in the doorway and watched as he looked around. "Does that matter?"

"Tell me about your morning routine," he commanded, ignoring my question. He opened the shower door and peeked inside. I assumed to see if it looked like we both used it. I had put my rose-scented shampoo in that morning to be sure.

I wrapped my arms around my middle again, my light sweater making me feel both too warm and too cold at the same time. "Our morning routine? Well, I guess Remi usually gets up first and showers. I generally go after him."

"You guess?" Mr. Graham asked with a raised eyebrow. He wrote in his notebook.

I tried not to grimace. "It's not like we have a written rule that he goes first, you know? In general, he rises earlier than I do, but occasionally he doesn't." I felt like I was about to break into a sweat. "Then while I'm showering, he brushes his teeth and shaves and whatnot."

"While you're in the shower?"

I felt like I was describing my morning to a pervert. What did he care if Remi was in the bathroom while I was showering? But I knew it was all part of this unwritten test. "Yes. He usually is done when I get out. Then we dress, make coffee, go over our daily plans, and head to work."

"And you still work together?" He came out of the bathroom and carried on straight out of the bedroom.

"Yes, of course," I said, following him, my heels clacking on the floor. I didn't usually wear heels, but I felt they were more domestic in this situation. They made me feel like Donna Reed. I realized later my mother would have worn heels for this type of guest as well.

"So, you're literally together every day?" he asked as if it was a strange thing.

Weren't married people together every day? I mean, they lived together. I would assume that meant they dined together, watched television together, and more. When I was married to Josh, even with our off schedules, I saw him every day.

I suppressed my frustration and put a grin on my face. "Of course. We often drive together to work. We spend time together outside of work. Remi is so easy to get along with, there's never been an issue."

"And after work?" We arrived back in the kitchen where Remi had coffee and biscotti prepared.

Remi kissed my temple. "What about after work?"

"Mr. Graham wants to know what we do after work," I told him. I put a piece of biscotti on a plate and handed it to Mr. Graham. He promptly took a bite.

"We do what all couples do, *monsieur*. We watch television, hang out with our friends," Remi said, taking a dessert for himself.

I took a long drink from my coffee cup. "We usually work so late, our evenings are pretty boring. We often just fall into bed," I said. Remi nodded.

"And what of your roommates?" Mr. Graham had a thousand questions. I was growing weary of them all.

Remi's curls bounced as he began to clean the kitchen some. That was one thing I appreciated about him – he liked the house as clean as I did. I would have to tell Mr. Graham that.

"Erin is a wonderful friend, and we've all lived together for a few years. Becca moved in after our former roommate got married. But right now, we're just into being newly-weds." I shrugged. Then I looked at Remi with what I hoped were loving eyes. "Thank you for cleaning, sweetie. I appreciate it," I said with a smile.

Remi shot me a knowing glance. "It is my pleasure, *cherie*."

More writing went into the notebook Mr. Graham carried. He asked a few more mundane questions before saying Remi's visa would be extended for one year and one year only. Remi and I jumped up and down and danced around the kitchen. Unexpectedly, Remi picked me up and kissed me soundly. I noticed Mr. Graham nod in approval before saying he would get the paperwork processed. We thanked him profusely.

A few weeks later, Erin moved out to live with her own boyfriend. And aside from an occasional check-in with Mr. Graham, I had my own room while the love birds shared theirs. It was a perfect arrangement as far as I could tell.

My friends were wary of the situation. My old manager from Greene's, Gina, who still remained close with me, was sympathetic but didn't like how we could be thrown in jail for the ruse. Adam tried a few times to get me to move back in with him, but I resisted. It would set off alarms with immigration, and I wouldn't do that.

Even after two years, Adam remained a good friend, and while he didn't agree with my marrying Remi, he also did not say anything about it. While I had felt more ready to date in recent months, everything with Remi threw that off-kilter. I realized a little too late into the ploy that I might be jeopardizing things with Adam. But I couldn't go back on my promise to Remi. If nothing else, I was a woman of my word.

*I*t took a year for Becca's divorce to become final. I was never so glad for the annulment Josh had arranged for us. In that year, Remi and I remained married, and it was uneventful. I was twenty-two, was a successful chef-in-training, and led a quiet life.

When Remi's extended visa was about to expire, we were all sitting at the kitchen table discussing what to do. I knew it was coming. Becca was finally free and had always wanted to travel. Remi had purchased a new engagement ring for her and had presented it to her the week before our little pow-wow. It was time.

"Roxie, *cherie*, I want a divorce," Remi said with a twinkle in his eye.

Feigning disbelief I threw myself onto the table, "No, Remi, don't leave me!" We all giggled. "I know it's time. I'm happy I could help you two stay together."

Becca, with her short red hair and warm brown eyes, smiled at me. "You have no idea what this has meant to us. And I can never imagine the sacrifice you have made for us. You put your life on hold so we didn't have to. How can I repay you?"

I put my hand on hers. "Have a happy life, Becca. Get married. Have little French babies who eat baguettes and laugh at bad jokes." I laughed, but my laughter soon turned to tears. I didn't like seeing the concern on my friends' faces, but I couldn't help myself.

Remi came to my side and patted my shoulder. "Rox-anne, what makes you cry now?"

I looked up to him with his angular features and dark hair. He was my husband. This marriage had lasted twice as long as my one to Josh. And now I was letting it go, another failed marriage under my belt. Suddenly none of this seemed like it had been a good idea.

"I'm sorry, Remi. I just ... This is my second marriage. And even though it's not a real one, it's still chalked up as a failure for me," I sobbed.

"I'm so sorry this is causing you pain, Rox," Becca said as she squeezed my hand.

"It's not your fault. Not at all. I knew this day would come, but I liked living in blissful ignorance," I said as I tried to control my tears. They would solve nothing. "Please promise me you'll keep in touch, okay? Send me lots of pictures. And we have email now, we can be in touch in an instant!"

"*Je suis désolé*. I am sorry, *cherie*. You have helped me so much and deserve the world," Remi told me as he hugged me close.

Marriage number two was coming to an end, and I was barely an adult. How grown I thought I had been. How mistaken I was.

A month later, and the divorce papers were filed. Mr. Graham came back and asked a host of questions about why we were leaving the marriage. I told him it was because Remi wanted to move back to France and I did not. And I wanted children and Remi did not. The differences were too great and we decided to split. He asked about shared property. We told him there had been none. The apartment had all our names on the lease, and it would now be left to Becca and me.

The plan was for Remi to leave in October and Becca would follow mid-November on a sightseeing trip to France. Then I would be alone. I would need to find some new roommates, and fast.

Remi sold his car and gave me the proceeds as something of alimony. I had told him I did not want or need it, but he had insisted. I also got to keep my engagement ring. He also confided in me that he came from an aristocratic family and handed me a check as payment for my time.

"I can't take this, Remi," I told him, not even looking at the amount written on it. I did not want payment for anything.

"No, Roxie, *cherie*, it is yours. Please," he said. "You saved me when I needed it. This is the least I could do. Maybe one day, it will save you."

I looked from the envelope to Remi. "What am I supposed to do with it?"

He smiled at me, his black hair glistening in the light. "Promise me you will do something with it. Something wonderful. *Chose de merveilleux!*"

Tucking the envelope in my pocket, I nodded solemnly. The money would be used for something wonderful. I would use the cash from the sale of Remi's car to help pay off the student loans that were piled up on my desk. I also considered selling the ring he had given me, but I figured I had time to make that decision later. The ring was moved to my right hand.

When it came time to take Remi to the airport, Becca couldn't stand to watch the plane take off, so they said their goodbyes in the apartment. They had clung to each other, making promises and staring into each other's eyes. I gave them all the privacy I could as I stood in the doorway, waiting.

I drove Remi to the airport, sad to see him go. I held back my gulps and tears as I parked to walk him in.

"Are you okay, *cherie*?" Remi searched my eyes. What a true friend he was to me.

"Yes, I'm just a little uncertain of what the future holds,"

I tried not to cry and managed to hold back the tears. "What will happen now?"

Remi held me squarely by the shoulders and looked me deep in the eyes. It was like he could see my whole life. "Roxanne DePrivé, I want you to find happiness. True happiness. I know you worry, but it is not healthy for you. You need to find love. True love. And not just with a man. With yourself."

There was no stopping the tears now. I wept. I wailed. I did want to find true love. I did want to become a success and love myself. But with two marriages under my belt, who would ever want me? I had wasted a year of my life so Remi and Becca could play house. I was now a year older, since I had put my own life on hold. And what had I gotten out of it? A few dollars?

It hadn't seemed like much of a sacrifice at the moment, but it ended up causing more distress in my life than I could ever had imagined.

"You are thinking too much now, Roxie," Remi said, ignoring the stares of those around us. "One step at a time. First, you find out how to enjoy life. Then you find someone who makes it even better. Start there. Nothing else."

I nodded and sighed. "I can do that," I whispered.

"Of course you can, *cherie*. Now, it is time for me to go. You will be alright?" He put his jacket on and picked up his carry-on.

"Yes. Thank you, Remi. I will always love you." Tears stained my cheeks and dress, but I didn't care.

"*Je t'iame*, Roxie," he said, kissing my forehead. "I will call you when I land, and then we will talk every week. I will email, too. Becca will be coming out next month, and I am nervous for that! We will both have happy lives, *cherie*. I promise!"

He waved and backed up away from me. I stood in my spot, as if glued there. I watched as he blew me one final kiss and turned to walk away. Before he rounded the corner, he gave me one more big smile, and then he disappeared. I don't know how long I stood there watching the corner, waiting to see if he would come back, but he did not.

A little old woman approached me and patted me on the shoulder. "Was that your boyfriend, dear?" Her Southern accent dripped with sugary sweetness. She wore a floral dress perfectly suited for a Southern grandmother, and I had a sudden urge to ask her for cookies. They would make me feel better.

I looked at her and smiled. "No, ma'am. That was my husband. Ex-husband, actually. He's leaving me to move back to France and marry the woman of his dreams." It was the truth, as ridiculous as it sounded.

I began to laugh. Just a small giggle to begin, but then it grew. The concerned old lady looked quite puzzled before mumbling something and wandering off. I continued to chuckle and soon it became a full belly laugh. I had tears running from my eyes as I hooted on my own, nobody but the old lady knowing the ludicrous situation I now found myself diving into.

Once I began to take deeper breaths and calm down, I decided to get a soda at an airport restaurant. Momma always said a drink would calm the nerves. As I walked in that direction, an older man stopped me. He wore all black and had a cross draped over his neck.

"Repent, my daughter, of your wicked ways," he warned. His steely blue eyes squinted as he waved his hand to stop me.

I recoiled a little at his outburst. "I don't have wicked ways," I assured him. If nothing else, I was a saint for putting my life on hold for the last year so Remi could stay stateside. Wicked ways, indeed.

"We all have wicked ways. The Lord wants you to draw near to him, and not near to the flesh," the man said, raising his arms. His sleeves fell back and revealed spindly, white arms covered with scars. "Repent of your feminine wiles and fleshly sins."

"Shows what you know. I don't have fleshly sins," I retorted, backing up a few steps.

I walked away from the man, but was shaken. I had never slept with anyone but Josh – and we had been married. That wasn't a sin. And even though I had been married to Remi, there was never anything physical between us aside from a few chaste kisses put on for the benefit of the immigration officer. Besides, what had God ever done for me?

The old man had left me in even more of a sour mood than I had been in moments before. I made my way to the airport lounge. I sat at the bar and asked for a root beer, one of my childhood favorites. I was alone again. And at this point in my life, I hated being alone.

After having a little pity party, I left the airport and decided to get the noise my car had been making looked at. I went to the mechanic closest to my apartment and pulled up. A handsome man with blond hair approached me and gave me a thousand-watt smile.

"What can I do for you, miss?" He wiped his hands on a rag that was dirtier than his palms. The irony wasn't lost on me.

"My car is making a chugga-chugga sound. I'm not sure why," I said. I handed him my keys and flopped into a seat.

The mechanic smiled again as he left the waiting room. It would have been infectious had I not been in such a mood. I didn't think Remi's leaving would put me in such a funk. Maybe it was time I started dating again. I mean, yes, I had been married, but really I hadn't dated since ... well ... ever. Josh had been my one and only boyfriend and we had jumped right into a marriage. Maybe I needed to get back in the game, or in the game at all. Maybe I should call Adam, I thought. But there was hesitation in my mind. Didn't he deserve me at my best?

A few minutes later, the man returned with my keys. "It was a loose bolt. A really simple fix," he said. I looked up at him and must have looked pitiful because his brow furrowed and his mouth puckered. "Really, miss, it's nothing to fret over. You look positively depressed."

"It's not the car. My husband, well, ex-husband now, just went back to France to live. He's some sort of duke or some kind of heir to something over there." I laughed. "And here I am with a loose bolt. More than one, it seems." I laughed at my own sad joke.

"Huh?" The mechanic's shirt had "Ray" embroidered on it. I looked at him through the tears in my eyes. He was too handsome to be a Ray.

"Nothing. I'm sorry. The last thing you need is a sad girl crying her eyes out over a French aristocrat she never romantically loved," I said with a half-hearted smile. I took my keys from him. "What do I owe you?"

He shook his head. "You didn't love your husband?"

Wiping my tears with the palm of my hand I admitted, "No. Well, I loved him as a friend. It wasn't romantic. Now I go back to my hovel of an apartment and he goes back to his French estate. And all I got from the deal was a chunk of change. And speaking of change – how much did you say?"

Ray smiled at me. "It's on the house. It seems like you had a rough day. I tell you what, if the noise comes back, you give me a call." He took a business card from the desk and turned it over. He wrote on the back. "Here's my card. And my personal number is on the back. If you ever need anything – anything – call me."

I smiled, despite knowing my eyes were probably red and puffy. "Thank you. I'm Roxie," I said, extending my hand.

The thousand-watt smile emerged again. He was good looking under all the grease. "I'm Ray." He took my hand and slipped me the card with his number on it.

I went back to my car with a giddy smile on my face. Whether I called Ray or not, this was the first time someone had given me their number because they liked me, not because I wore short skirts in the bar or was their temporary muse.

*R*ight before Christmas I called Lori. She hadn't spoken to me since I had told her I would be marrying Remi. I was sure by now she had heard he was gone and I was again divorced. I was sure my father had heard it, too. News traveled quickly and bad news even quicker.

"I don't understand, Roxie," she said over the phone. "How do you keep winding up with these men?"

"You're right, you don't understand, Lori. I was only married to him so he could stay in the country. We never slept together or anything," I assured her.

"I think you've gone crazy, is what I think," she said. I could picture her shaking her head. "And Daddy, too. Everyone thinks you're loony. And you're getting a reputation as a bit of a harlot and man-stealer."

"Are you serious? You don't believe them do you? Lori, come on," I was shocked. People thought I was a harlot? I had never heard such rumors before. Though, rumors rarely reach the ears of those they are about.

"It's not good, Roxanne. I've heard you lure men away

like a siren, that you're a prostitute, all kinds of things. It's not good at all. Listen, I gotta go. Bye." And just like that she hung up. I sat alone in my little apartment, preparing to spend Christmas alone.

I called Adam. He had been a friend to me all this time. Maybe I could spend Christmas with him. And maybe, just maybe I was ready for romance again. I was still young and attractive, wasn't I? I took a deep breath as he answered.

"Adam Joyce," he bellowed into his phone.

"Adam? It's Roxie," I said, trying to sound upbeat. I could hear a commotion in the background.

"Roxie! It's good to hear from you," he said with a laugh. "I heard Remi left. That's too bad."

"Yes, about two months ago," I said. "Listen, I was wondering—"

I stopped when I heard a female voice come through the other end with Adam. "Adam? Come on, I'm waiting." Adam put his hand on the receiver and I didn't hear his response. My heart sank.

"What was that, Roxie?"

"Nevermind, Adam. Merry Christmas," I said, defeated.

"You, too, Rox!" Then the line went dead. Adam had found someone. He had pined after me for almost three years and now ... Well, there was no point in dwelling on it. That would be a turning point in my life, my not dwelling on Adam.

I went for a walk through town to clear my head. I felt so alone, even more so as Christmas rapidly approached. I would not exchange gifts with anyone that year. I had no friends, not even a family to claim me. Would anyone notice or care if I wasn't around anymore? Everyone had a life but me. Everyone had a purpose but me. I walked down to the river and stood overlooking it, my arms folded to keep warm, when I heard someone say my name.

"Roxie? Your boyfriend went back to Italy, right?"

I looked up and came face to face with Ray, his shirt still stained with car grease. He shook my hand and I noticed his blackened nails, but I realized I didn't mind. It showed he was a hardworking man. His eyes sparkled as they looked upon me. I felt like he was actually seeing Roxie. Not the senator's daughter or a way to stay in the country. I hungered for the feeling that someone saw me for who I was and not for what I could do for them. I wasn't sure how he had found me, but I was glad to see a smiling face.

"Yes, that's right. Well, he went back to France, but that's me." I giggled and wrapped my arms around my middle as was my habit. "Ray, right?"

"That would be right," he said with a smile. "No more noises from the car, I guess?"

I shook my head, "Nope. Runs wonderfully."

"That's too bad. I was hoping you would bring it back in. Or maybe give me a call." He looked away, but he smiled wide. He had a dimple I hadn't noticed before under all the grease. He was a truly attractive man, and it made me blush.

"You busy? Want to grab a beer?" He motioned towards the downtown area. I nodded and he led me to a little place a few blocks from where we were and bought me a beer.

We talked for hours. He was divorced himself; his wife, Misty, had left him a year before. He had no children but liked the idea of them. He has been working as a mechanic for ten years and loved cars. He was a down-home country boy, and I appreciated that. He seemed to understand me in a way that Josh and certainly Remi never had.

We exchanged numbers again, and Ray asked if he could take me on a proper date soon. I agreed. Ray was sweet, a little shy even. He was respectful to everyone around him. I found myself smiling more and laughing. His dark eyes were captivating, and I thought I could stare into them for a long time. We even spent Christmas together. I didn't feel lonely anymore.

It was a whirlwind romance. I clung so hard to the idea that Ray understood where I was in life. We were both divorced, both hardened. We talked about our heartache and how we could help each other heal.

A few months later, Ray proposed to me, and I surprised even myself when I accepted. I excitedly called Gina, who had become my closest girlfriend. She seemed excited for me, but it was hard to tell. I emailed Remi and Becca. Remi said he knew love would find me soon.

I called my sister, as I always did. We hadn't spoken in months. "Lori, please understand," I pleaded.

"What is there to understand? What would Mom say? You want to get married for a third time? You're only twenty-five! Really, Roxie. Think of someone other than yourself," she chided before hanging up.

Finally, I called Adam. I hadn't spoken to him since the call before Christmas. He answered quickly. "Hi, Adam. It's me, Roxie."

"Roxie! Where have you been, doll face?" I pictured his bright eyes and vivid red hair. Adam was a good friend. He had treated me well since I showed up on his doorstep, newly wed and homeless.

I asked him what had been new. He didn't mention any girlfriend. Maybe they had broken up already. I told him about Ray. Then I told him we were getting married.

"Married? Roxie are you sure? What about—you hardly know him," Adam protested.

"I knew Josh this long before we got married," I argued.

That didn't help my case, and I winced. "I'm older now. I know what I want. And he's divorced, too. Ray understands me."

"Why rush, though? Come on, Rox, it's only been a few months since Remi left."

"It's been over six months since he left. And even then, we were never romantically involved, Adam. I haven't been with a man in almost four years." I laughed.

"And this is the man you want to be with? Ray is the man for you?" I could hear the doubt in his voice, and maybe, maybe just a hint of disappointment.

I thought for a moment. Ray made me smile. He wanted me. He understood me. And he was there. Nobody else filled those shoes.

"Yes, Adam. I think so," I whispered. I was trying desperately to believe my own words.

"Roxie, doll face, do you love him?"

What was love anyway? Having things in common? Being attracted to someone? I was sure I had no idea. But I felt good when I was with Ray. Wasn't that enough?

"Rox?"

"Yes," I blurted out, my agitation growing. "Of course I love him."

Of course I knew what love was. This would be my third marriage, after all. Then again, maybe I was as clueless as they come.

Adam wasn't convinced. His silence was deafening and I could practically feel him shaking his head as he cradled the receiver with his ear. I don't know if he wanted me for himself or if he just didn't want me with anyone else. Regardless, when we hung up, I felt worse than I had after talking to Lori.

≈

a justice of the peace married us on a Monday afternoon in June. It was simple, just Ray and I. I bought a cream-colored dress at Sears, and he wore his Sunday suit. It wasn't fancy, but Ray wasn't fancy. He was a blue-collar worker, and I understood that. I left my apartment and moved into a small house with Ray. It wasn't much bigger than my apartment had been, but he owned it and I was excited to have a small yard. I thought I might be able to have a garden in which to grow fresh herbs and tomatoes.

Ray was a wonderful and attentive husband for a few weeks, gentle and loving. But after those first few weeks, he began to change. It was slow, but noticeable. He began to come home later and later each day. He had been supportive of my still working, but then suddenly, he didn't like the idea of me being around others at all. He asked me to quit, and I refused. He fumed but said nothing else.

When he began coming home drunk a few nights a week, I started to wonder what was going on. Momma would have said the blinders were taken off my eyes. I realized Ray was not the kindred spirit I thought he was. But I had to make this marriage work. I couldn't have another failed marriage under my belt. I tried talking to him about what was going on, but he ignored me or said there was no problem. So I began to ignore the problem myself.

One morning we woke up, and he announced that his parents were coming for dinner that night. I still had never met them.

"My ma wants to meet the girl who captured my heart," he said as he planted a sloppy kiss on me. He still smelled of alcohol from the night before. I tried not to turn away as I suppressed the urge to gag.

"Oh, that's great. I would love to meet your parents," I said, having always wondered why I had never met them before. "I'll make dinner. I haven't had a chance to really pull out the stops in a while!" I was excited. I began to plan a menu in my head.

"Now, Roxie, nothing fancy. My parents are humble folk like me. Make something simple," he reminded me as he put a ball cap over his blond hair.

I stopped. Simple. I could do that. "Of course, Ray. I'll make some good Southern comfort foods, how's that?"

When he nodded and went to the bathroom. I quickly got up and jotted down a grocery list, thinking of all the rich, buttery foods Tarek would have made for a family gathering. Maybe I should call him for a recipe. I was glad I was off work that day so I could clean the house and prepare a meal for my new family.

I spent the day cooking and cleaning. I would pop one thing in the oven, and then clean up all the mess that went with it. And in between, I scrubbed the bathroom and anything else that I could manage to spray down. I was exhausted, but enthusiastic.

Finally, everything was done and I had the meal on the table. Fried chicken, okra, scalloped potatoes, fresh macaroni salad—a Southern table if there ever was one. I had worked hard on this meal, and it felt great. I forgot how much I loved to cook for fun and not for work. Everything was in place, myself included. I was wearing a simple black dress, low heels, and my hair was styled. I felt like a million bucks. Until Ray came in the door, that is.

"What is all this?" he asked, not looking amused. He took off the ball cap, and I could see the vein on his temple bulge. His face turned red despite the smears of grease and oil. I wasn't sure why, perhaps he had a bad day at work.

"I'm meeting your parents for the first time. I made a special dinner," I said with a smile, ignoring his bad attitude. "Surprise!" I stepped back so he could see the entire table. I hoped it would better his mood with company coming.

"What – what is this? What were you thinking? My parents are mountain folk, do you want to shame them?" Ray shouted at me. I wasn't sure why he was shouting.

It made me shake. It made me furious. What right did he have to talk to me like that? I thought about my mother and all the times she never spoke against my father. About how he walked all over her for the twenty-five years they were married. I wasn't going to let my husband treat me the way my mom was treated.

"I was thinking I wasn't going to have crap for dinner yet again, Ray," I shouted back. It felt freeing to speak up after weeks of him talking down to me.

And that's when it happened. He smacked me across the face and sent me stumbling across the room. I hit the wall and slumped down. I stayed where I landed, too terrified and shocked to move.

Ray came and stood over me. His faded blue jeans were close enough I could see the grease stains on them, his face sneering at me. I looked up at him, willing myself to be defiant, but it did not come. Wasn't I supposed to love him? Wasn't he supposed to love me?

"Look what you did, Roxie," he scolded me like he would a child. "You made me do that. I didn't want to. Go clean yourself up before my parents get here."

He did not offer me a hand to get up. He walked away with me still crumpled up like a used tissue. I righted myself and got on my feet. My jaw was throbbing, my ears ringing. I made my way to the mirror. My perfect hair was ruined. My makeup was all over, mascara running down my cheeks, lipstick smeared. No amount of makeup, however, could cover my cheek. The throbbing and aching I could deal with, but the huge red handprint, I could not. How could I hide this? Ray's parents would be ringing the doorbell in minutes. What would they think of their son hitting his wife?

I stumbled to the bathroom, wary of where Ray might have gone. I locked the door and washed my face, not caring about the pain that shot out. Almost raw, I finally dried and looked at my face. Yes, my cheek looked as though it had been tattooed with a red hand print. Ray's hand print. I carefully redid my makeup. I caked on the foundation and powder. Then I applied the blush. And more blush. And more still, trying to hide the mark as best as I could. Then I caked it onto the other cheek to make it match. I felt like a clown, and I hated clowns. I tried to do a more dramatic eye in hopes of drawing attention away from my cheeks.

Without hope of improving anything further, I sighed and gave up, throwing the makeup in the drawer and slamming it shut. I took a deep breath, realizing my husband had just hit me.

I repeated it in my head.

My husband hit me.

Remi would have never done this. Even Josh would not have done this. I hadn't missed him since he had left, but I was suddenly wishing he was around again.

I didn't have time to cry or dwell on what had happened, because the doorbell rang then. And Ray yelled for me to get it. I was still angry, and we would have to talk about it after his parents left. But for now, I knew how to be a wife and a good hostess, and I would do what I could to make a perfect first impression on my new in-laws. I was, after all, the daughter of a retired senator. And Momma would want me to make a good impression. First impressions were everything.

I opened the door and nearly gasped. My new mother-in-law, at least that's who I assumed was before me, wore nothing more than a skimpy tank top with her unbound breasts spilling forth. Her middle was not trim, but that had not stopped her from wearing the tank top tucked into skin-tight jean cutoffs. She looked like a cheap hooker. Suddenly, my makeup did not feel so overdone. Once again, I thought first impressions were everything.

"You must be Roxie," she said with a deep, husky voice. I imagined it might have been melodious once upon a time before the smoking had taken over her vocal chords. She flung a bag of potato chips at me and sashayed past.

"Hey, sugar," came a voice from behind her. Ray's father gave me a nearly toothless smile. His hair was matted under his baseball cap, and his clothes looked at least two sizes too big. "Nice to meet you," he said, extending his hand to me. At least he seemed polite.

My automatic reaction was to shake his hand in response, but I immediately regretted it. He pulled me into a bear hug and his odor – something akin to grease, fried food, and sweat – assaulted my nose and eyes. If I wasn't careful, my mascara would run again. And his breath felt none too good on my cheek either.

When he released me I choked out, "Mr. O'Toole, it's a pleasure to finally meet you and Mrs. O'Toole."

My momma always said my charm school education would come in handy. And it did for sure on this day. I hoped my momma wasn't looking down on my life at this point. But I couldn't think about that right then. I had my new in-laws to entertain.

"Call me Phil, or just Daddy," came the reply. "And you can call Ray's momma Eileen. Or you can call her Momma if you like."

I thought it would make me sick to call either of these people Momma or Daddy. "Thank you, Phil. Eileen, please come in," I said. Remembering the chips Phil had crushed between us, I added, "Thank you for bringing these. That was sweet of you. Dinner is ready, right through there." I directed them toward the dining room.

"Ray, honey, your parents are here," I said aloud, but I wasn't sure where he had gone after our episode earlier.

"Bring them on in, Roxie," he called back. He was in the dining room. We entered and my jaw went slack. He had changed into chinos and a buttondown shirt. His blond hair was slicked back, and he had shaved. How had he done all that so quickly?

"There's my baby," Eileen cooed as she hugged her son.

Everyone came into the dining room and looked at the table. "What is all this crap?" Eileen asked bluntly.

I had to squelch a gasp.

"Roxanne is a professional cook, Momma," Ray said as he sidled up to me and put his hand around my back. "She made all this. From scratch."

"Woo-wee. Like at a restaurant?" asked his father, this toothless grin showing through.

I knew these were not well-educated people, but I still took offense to the question. Of course like at a restaurant. I tried to answer without sounding snobbish. "Yes, sir. I'm not the head chef or anything at the moment. I work at Pixie's as the sous chef. But I hope to one day be the head chef of a nice restaurant. I hope you enjoy the meal."

"You know my favorite restaurant? Denny's. I love Denny's food. Could you cook at Denny's with your fancy cooking education, Rosie?" Phil smacked his lips and hands at the same time.

"It's Roxie, Mr. O'Toole. But that's okay," I said, trying not to be angry. He was older, maybe my name just slipped his mind. And I refrained from saying that anyone could cook at Denny's. All they needed was a fryer and ketchup. Ray was apparently not too happy I had corrected his father. He pinched my back until it hurt. But I shot him an angry glance and stepped away.

"I hope you enjoy everything. I went with a good ol' Southern supper," I began, clapping my hands together. "I also made two pies for dessert, pecan and peach. I wasn't sure what you would prefer, so I made both," I said, blushing at the amount of food I had made.

"This is like a five-star meal, Raymond," Eileen O'Toole said, her eyes darting all over the table like a ravenous wolf eyeing its prey. "You must have spent a fortune on this." She sat at the head of the table, where I should have sat. But she was my guest; I forgave it and sat to her left. Ray sat opposite his mother and Phil was across from me.

"That's my Roxie-baby," Ray beamed. "She's a good girl, this one. I had to talk her into keeping her job. Wants to be a little momma, this one."

I stared at him. He was absolutely unbelievable. We had not discussed children beyond thinking they were cute. And I certainly never even entertained the idea of quitting my job. That had been his idea. I kept my mouth shut, though. I figured it was the safest option.

I ate in silence as the three O'Tooles ate and drank their fill. Ray and his parents ate quick and loud. Now I knew why I should not have gone through the effort. I couldn't imagine that they had tasted anything as they inhaled. They went through twelve beers and two bottles of wine between them. I never finished my first glass of wine. Their conversation was just as loud and none too polite, either.

I sat hunched over in my chair, silent, my arms protectively in front of me, my face stinging from Ray's blow earlier. I wished I had some painkillers in front of me, for more reason than one.

The entire night was awkward for me. Though it shouldn't have been, because nobody paid an ounce of attention to me the rest of the night. They were all drunk by ten o'clock. I offered to call Phil and Eileen a cab, but they insisted they were fine to drive. I was uncomfortable with the idea, but my own head was throbbing from a mixture of the blow before dinner and the noise and smoke. I wanted them to leave.

With his parents gone, however, Ray turned his attention to me once again. "I told you not to do nothing fancy, Roxanne," he sputtered. His breath reeked. In fact, his whole body reeked.

I wanted to placate him. I needed to placate him. I just wanted to get through the night and on to tomorrow. "I'm sorry, Ray," I cooed, "I only wanted to make a great impression. I think everything went well. I loved meeting your parents. Your dad seemed especially sweet."

"I saw you eyeing him," Ray said as he stepped close to me, a sneer on his lips.

What did he mean eyeing his father? "No. I wasn't eyeing anyone. I was trying to be polite and kind to all of you."

He raised his hand to me as if he would slap me again. I tried not to flinch as my hands instinctively came up to block him. Where had this Ray come from? What had happened to the sympathetic man who had worked his magic on me?

"Oh, sweet cheeks, I don't want to hurt you," he said as he put his arms around me. He nuzzled into my neck and I welcomed him despite his odor.

I took in a breath, finally. I felt like I had not been breathing at all. Maybe I needed to keep Ray away from alcohol. I knew from my years at Greene's what it could do to some people, and I knew how dangerous it was. I helped Ray to bed where he began snoring before he even hit the sheets.

Chapter Ten

THE THROTTLE VALVE

I felt like I had to tiptoe around Ray now. The littlest thing would set him off, and I didn't want to be that thing. The slaps and punches had become more frequent. I knew it was wrong, I wasn't stupid. I had been raised better. But I thought maybe I could get Ray help. And I thought if I tried anything drastic, I would wind up hurt even more.

And I wanted the relationship to work. I was, after all, only twenty-five and on my third marriage. I missed Remi and even Josh. I wished I had taken Adam up on his offer to move back in with him. I wished my father was supportive, and I could reach out to him for help. He wouldn't want this for me, would he?

But there was no point in wasting time on wishes. My life had become about survival.

Days later, we were out with some of the guys Ray worked with and their spouses. We had gone to a local bar to play pool and drink beer. It wasn't a crowd I would have normally spent time with, but I wanted to fit in, and I wanted to keep Ray happy. A happy Ray was safer for me. One of the wives had been perfectly sweet and made an effort to get to know me better. Her name was Darla, and she was married to Ray's boss, Mike.

"Don't you want a beer, Roxie?" Darla had asked me.

"No, thank you," I said. "I used to work at a bar, and now I rarely have anything. But thanks for asking."

Darla leaned across me to get a pool cue and placed her hand on my upper arm. The same arm Ray had bruised the day before. I gave a little cry and winced. I didn't want to call attention to it, but it was too late.

"I'm sorry. Are you okay?" Darla took hold of my elbow and lifted my shirt sleeve. The purple hand mark was still clear as day. She gently made me stand and led me to the ladies' room without a word. Once the door closed, she exposed my entire shoulder.

She studied the marks. Some were fresh and deep purple, while others were older and had faded to a pale green. I held my breath as Darla looked me over.

"What happened? Did Ray do this to you?"

I stammered, unsure what to say. Do I admit the abuse or try to cover it up? How could I cover up an obvious handprint and other marks? I couldn't very well say I walked into something hand-shaped. So instead, I said nothing, wishing to disappear into the wall. Why wasn't I fading into oblivion? Tears began to stream down my face, but I didn't feel them at all.

"Roxie, I realize you don't know me, but this is not okay," she said as she tucked some hair behind my ear. "Don't let anyone do this to you." She was filled with concern and compassion.

I wanted to cry and fall into her arms and tell her everything. But I didn't. I steeled instead. "You're right, you don't know me." I pulled away from her and wiped my face.

She stepped back and thought before speaking again. "Sweetie, there is a big God out there who adores you for you. And He would not want anyone to suffer under the abuse of another. Please let me help you."

Looking into the mirror, I began to reapply my make-up. Ray could not know I had cried or said anything to anyone. I considered the words Darla had said. A God who loves me? Hardly.

"I'm sorry," I whispered as I brushed past her and went back into the smoke-filled main room.

I spent the next hour keeping to myself. I didn't speak unless spoken to, and even then, I kept responses as curt as possible. It wasn't until Ray finished a game and lost fifty dollars that his anger rose and he came to me for the first time all night.

A quick look at the table full of empty beer bottles told me at least six of them were his brand. That was the threshold I had learned. Six was where he went from sloppy to mean. I whispered to myself that he wouldn't hit me here in front of everybody. I could see Darla watching me cautiously. I wanted to throw up. I said a silent prayer to the God Darla had mentioned, pleading for Ray to not hit me right then.

"Fifty bucks ain't nothing, Joe," Ray said to the crowd. "See this pretty little thing here? My Roxie." His words slurred. I braced myself. "My Roxie is loaded. Got a ton of money, this one!" I paled. Was he really saying this to a room full of strangers? What made him think I had a bunch of money?

"Tell them, Rox. Tell them you got all this dough but

won't let me have any." He bent down and put his face in mine.

"This is not the place, Ray," I said in a low voice. "Let's not talk about this here." I kept my eyes down. I would not meet his gaze. He jerked my head up so I had to look at him, and he squeezed my chin in his large, calloused hand. My jaw felt like it was going to pop.

"You look at me, you witch," he fumed. He spewed spit as he spoke. "Tell them how your ugly foreign husband left you all that money, and you won't let me have it! Not even a penny!"

I was dumbfounded. I had no idea where he had gotten this idea.

Out of the corner of my eye, I could see Darla push Mike toward us. Mike jumped up and came at Ray. "Hey, man. Don't manhandle your wife. You need to cool down." He pulled Ray's arm, and I fell from my chair when Ray released me. Nobody came to my aid, not even Darla. I didn't blame them.

We left after that. And I quickly forgot the entire evening, because Ray erased it for me.

Ray was waiting for me two days later when I got home from Pixie's. He sat at the bar in the kitchen, taking a swig from a beer. His shirt was still crisp as if he hadn't worked at all that morning. His expression was relaxed, pleasant. That was the look that had first attracted me to him. But there was something in his eyes that screamed out a warning to me.

"You're home early," I said, trying to sound cheerful. "What a nice surprise." I leaned in and gave him a kiss on the cheek. He was my husband, I reminded myself. I was supposed to kiss him and not want to run away.

"Where's the money, Roxanne?" His eyes were like slits, and they followed me across the room.

"What money, sweetie?" I still just smiled. I didn't know what else to do. What money did he think I had tucked away?

"You were married to that rich French guy, weren't you? And you divorced him, so you got half of his loot. So, where is it?" He took another drink from his beer bottle.

I shook my head. I had no idea where he had gotten this idea. "Ray, there is no money. The only thing Remi gave me was the money he got from selling his car. That was it. Nothing else." Yes, he had given me a check for something marvelous, but Ray... Ray was not it. I never mentioned it to him, and it sat safe in a deposit box at the bank.

He stood and got close to me. Ray towered over me. I came only to his shoulder. What had before been comfort and strength was now terrifying and brutal. I folded my arms as a buffer between us. "You said he was some sort of French royalty. That means money you should have gotten with your divorce. You said he paid you."

"Yes, the amount for the car. It was only about three thousand dollars. I didn't want anything more," I explained. I racked my brain and realized when I had first met him I had mentioned Remi had returned to his estate. That he was aristocracy. And then in one of our long conversations, I had maybe mentioned that he had given me some additional money. "I – I don't understand, Ray. Why do we need more? Aren't the bills paid?"

"I lost my job today, Roxie," he said, breathing heavily over me. The stench of alcohol that came wafting off him was unbearable. "Mike fired me, because he thinks I beat you. What did you tell him?"

I tried to back up, but he held my arms so I was frozen.

"No, Ray. Nothing. I didn't say anything. But the other night ..." He shoved me, and I couldn't finish my sentence. The words were knocked from my mouth.

"The other night, you sat in the bar acting like you were better than everyone else. High and mighty little Miss Roxie. Perched like a queen on your little stool, your leg crossed, showing off your skin like a common harlot." His thick, beefy hands clutched my arms like a vice. I was slowly losing the feeling in my hands as the bloodflow was cut off. "And I lost my job because of you. And I have a shark after me. So I figure you owe me money, Roxanne."

Chest heaving, I tried to reason with him. "I don't have any money, Ray. Just what I make from work. Nothing more." I tried to sound confident. I failed miserably in that.

Grabbing my shoulders, Ray shoved me back again. I was thankful I did not stumble. "You were supposed to have money. Why else do you think I was following you at Christmas? Why else do you think I was interested in you? You're the daughter of a crooked politician, you were married to some fancy French man. That means you should be swimming in dough, Roxie." He pushed me again, and I was in the hallway.

He stepped closer, and I stepped back. We did this dance until we were at the end of the hall, my back against the bedroom door. The knob pushed into my back, and I wished I could pull off the cold hard brass and hit him over the head with it. I prayed with all my might that someone – anyone – would knock on the door, bust through the door, anything. I prayed for someone to save me.

No one did.

In a flash, he had reached behind me and turned the knob. The door swung open, spilling me onto the floor. I slid back several feet on the recently polished hardwood. I scrambled to back up even more so I could stand, but he was on me in an instant. I reached above my head, trying desperately to grab onto anything that could get me away from him. I clawed at the floor. Then I began searching for something I could hit him with, but there was nothing. I was helpless.

So I gave up. I simply gave up. I didn't move as he beat me and abused me. I wasn't sure if I had mentally left my body or what, but I had no knowledge of anything for a time. My entire body ached, and the floor was cold and hard, but I did not move until I heard the snores telling me Ray was sleeping. Then I slowly got up and tiptoed to the shower and cleaned myself as best as I could.

I called in sick to work the next few days. Chef Tallant asked if I was okay, and I coughed into the phone and claimed I had some mutant form of the flu. I hid in the house and waited for the bruises and the memories to fade. After that, I made sure I was more accommodating when Ray approached me. I figured if I acted like I wanted Ray around, he wouldn't be so forceful. It was about survival at that point. He called me names and hit me while he was on me, and I tried my best to tune him out. I tried to detach from my body and close my eyes.

When I went back to work, Chef looked me over but didn't say anything. I was glad he didn't try to ask me questions, but I could see the concern on his face. I knew he knew. Part of me wanted him to help, but the other part wanted him to keep his nose out of my business.

My body was stiff and the amount of bending I did was painful, but I worked through it as best as I could. I had to. But after a few hours, Chef could tell I wasn't well, and my eyes couldn't prevent the tears from falling. I was sent home early.

After leaving Pixie's, I knew I couldn't go right home. It would make Ray suspicious. I went to Greene's to see Gina and my old friends. My body was still aching, but I tried to be strong and power through. And I needed an excuse for why I was home so soon that didn't include saying I was sent home because of bodily bruises. I realized I looked rough, but I didn't care. Greene's was a dive anyway, so I walked in with my food-stained clothes and worn out expression.

"Roxie DePrivé, it's been a while. What are you doing here?" Gina asked with a genuine smile on her face. "We've missed seeing you here."

"I know, I'm sorry. Between work and Ray, I don't have much free time," I said with a feeble smile. "How are you?"

"Busy as ever," she said as she wiped down the bar. I watched as she called out a greeting to a trio of women who came in and sat down. Her smile was infectious, and I found myself smiling for the first time in weeks.

"How are things with Ray?" Gina looked me over. Her smile turned hard and a crease wrinkled her brow.

I took a moment to assess my friend. Her inky hair was styled in shoulder-length box braids and her makeup was fresh. Her whole face looked dewy and soft despite working behind a bar for hours on end. It was a stark contrast from my grungy, mousy-brown hair in a ponytail and oily complexion still prone to breakouts. Gina's arms were toned and her body was sleek, unlike my sickly and gaunt frame. I could barely lift a cast iron pan anymore, I had become so weak.

I sighed. "Honestly? Not good, Gina." I wiped an escaped tear from my cheek. I could no longer hold my emotions in check. Exhaustion and depression had set in, and the tears began to flow.

"Give me one minute, sweetie, then I can step outside

with you," Gina said with a sympathetic look. She quickly went to the trio of women and took their orders, her expression nothing but smiles and delight. As she approached me again, her expression turned from delightful to concerned. I nodded as she went in search of someone to relieve her for a few moments.

I heard the trio of women begin to giggle. I longed to be carefree like them. While I knew no life was perfect, I figured their husbands or boyfriends didn't beat them. Their fathers probably had not disowned them or their mothers died of a heart attack.

I could use something to make me smile. Life had gotten me too down lately. I tried to listen to what was so humorous without making myself obvious. While keeping my head towards the bar, I angled my knees in their direction as if that would help me hear better.

"Are you sure?" the first one asked, sounding surprised.

"It can't be," replied another. I wondered what they were talking about.

"That's her. Senator DePrivé's youngest. Haven't you heard about her? She sent her mother to an early grave," said the first. I felt my back stiffen. She knew me. She knew my father. They were judging me.

"That's Jenny Dolinghouse's sister? There's no way! Jenny is so with it. She looks homeless over there." This came from one of the others.

"The DePrivés are an upstanding family, but that one there looks like a drowned rat," came a chortled assessment.

The third piped in, "What happened to her?"

I could feel their eyes boring into me as I waited at the bar. They were talking loud enough for anybody nearby to hear. They weren't hiding their conversation. I felt my whole body grow hot, and I longed to melt into the floor. I couldn't move from my perch, so I sat stiff, as if I was full of led. What had happened to those days when I was invisible?

"She's on her third marriage, this time to pure white trash," said the first. How did she know so much about me? "Her first husband ran off on her, you know the Keene family, Grace told me all about it. I heard the second was a marriage of convenience, not love. At least for him, poor girl probably pined after him. He was European and went back to wherever he came from. But I heard this third husband is pure trash. He's a gambler, too. She got her hooks into him, kicked his then-wife out and moved herself in. Who knows what they see in each other."

"She'll be looking to move on to another unsuspecting fool sooner or later," said the third woman. I could visualize them shaking their perfectly done hair at my expense.

"Better lock your husband up," one of them announced rather loudly. They all laughed.

They all laughed at me. I had become the brunt of town jokes and gossip. The husbands of these women probably worked with my father and brothers-in-law. This meant my family knew the slum I was living in and did nothing about it. I was truly dead to them all. My life had been reduced to a woman others had to keep an eye on for fear I would steal their man. It wasn't me, but it did not matter. I knew how it worked. Once marked, you were marked for good. Maybe I was no better than a harlot.

Gina reappeared, followed by an older man who was going to sit in her place for a few minutes. Her dark eyes showed nothing but compassion and a half-hearted smile came reluctantly to her face. "Ready to go talk, Roxie?"

I shook my head and wiped my nose on my already stained sleeve. "No, I have to go, Gina. I'm sorry. Ray'll be mad if I'm late."

I stood to leave and Gina placed a hand on my arm, her dark eyes boring into mine. "You can always come here, Roxie. Any time. Don't ..." she paused. "Just be careful, sweetie." I could see the concern in her eyes. I nodded and left the bar as quickly as I could, fleeing from the mocking laughter of the snobby women.

Chapter Eleven

THE BLIND SPOT

ot long after that, I was at home one afternoon when a knock came at the door. I was wary of anyone these days, so I hesitated to even ask who was there. But the knocking became more insistent.

"Ray!" a throaty female voice called. "Open up. It's Misty!"

Misty. That was the name of Ray's ex-wife. I rushed to the door and yanked it open. I stared at her, the woman who had gotten away from Ray. I didn't think of her as the woman who broke his heart any longer. Now she was the one who had managed to escape.

She stood before me with giant sunglasses over her eyes, her blonde hair pulled back into a high ponytail. Her clothes were well worn and too snug on her body, and the yellow top she wore revealed more of her cleavage than it should have. But she was trim and pretty, probably only a few years older than me.

"Well, I guess he did move on after all," she said as she sized me up. "Thought he might have when he stopped calling and asking me for money. I'm Misty McGee. Maiden name. No more O'Toole for me."

She stepped into the house without me inviting her in. I simply stood back and let her waltz in like she owned the place. I wasn't sure what to say. I had never dealt with an ex-wife before. But Misty seemed to have plenty of words for the one-sided conversation.

"This isn't a bad little house Ray found out here. Or was it yours to begin with?" She moved her sunglasses to the top of her head and eyed me. When I shook my head, she continued, "Well, anyway, I only came out here because I'm tired of the collectors calling me up. Now that I know this is the right spot, I'll send 'em here and you can deal with them. Do you have collectors bugging you yet?"

I had no idea what a collector was. Did she mean a bill collector? As far as I knew, we were current on all our bills. I shook my head.

"Do you talk at all?" Misty asked as she sat at the meager little kitchen table. She crossed her legs and swung her pink-painted toes in quick cadence.

"Yes, of course I talk," I responded, shaking my head. I hadn't moved from the spot at the front door.

She smiled at me. "Oh, good. I was afraid Ray had gotten himself a mute or something. You got anything to drink around here?"

I moved quickly to the kitchen. "I have sweet tea if you'd like some." I got a cup down from the cabinet and opened the fridge.

"Tea? Sure, why not," she said with a snort. I poured a glass and handed it to her. I got down another glass and poured one for myself as well and sat across from her.

We sized each other up for a moment. We were roughly the same size, but that was where the similarities ended. She looked vibrant, healthy. I had seen myself in the mirror that morning. I had dark circles under my eyes and my cheeks were hallowed. My hair hung lifeless around my shoulders. I looked like a haunted, ghostly version of my old self. She looked like someone who had survived. Misty seemed outgoing, commanding, the type who didn't put up with anything. How had she gotten away from Ray?

"You're Misty?" I finally asked.

"Yes," she confirmed. She twirled a lock of her hair.

"You got away ..." I said quietly as I stared at her.

Her eyes became as round as saucers, and she immediately understood what I was saying. "Oh, no. No. Tell me he's not doing this to you, too. I had hoped it was just me he found to be a good punching bag."

She stood and began pushing on my clothes, exposing my neck and shoulders. Bruises were easy to find on me. She clucked over me like a mother hen, whispering that she knew she should have done something when she had the chance.

"Is he still gambling, too?"

"He said a shark was after him," I said in a timid voice.

"Yeah, well, they'll come here soon enough," she said with a snort.

"He thinks I have money," I told her. Why did I tell her that?

"Do you?" She stood to her full height and glanced out the window as if someone might overhear us, then sat again.

I took a long drink from my glass. I didn't know if I could trust her. "Not like he thinks."

"Oh, honey," she said, laying her long, manicured fingers on mine. "I'm sorry. You need to get away from him. I wish I had reported him when he did this to me. But I thought I could change him. But you can't change Ray O'Toole. What's your name, baby?"

I blinked. What was my name? It took a second for it to come to me. "Roxie. Roxie DePrivé."

Misty looked confused. "Are you married to Ray?"

I nodded, "Yeah, but I never changed my name. Haven't gotten around to it. He understood at first, but then it was just something to hit me about. But this is my third marriage, and I haven't changed my name yet."

Glancing at her watch, Misty stood suddenly, but she left a business card on the table. "Listen, Roxie, I gotta go. But hear me. Get away from Ray. Get as far away as you can and get a divorce. And get away before the collectors start banging on your door." She crossed to the front door. "And don't tell Ray I was here. It will only make things worse for you. Good luck, hon."

And with that, Misty was gone. I washed her glass out and put it back in the cabinet in case Ray noticed a second used cup. I tucked Misty's card for her hair salon in the bottom of my purse. And then I wondered how to get out.

Except Ray somehow knew Misty had come. I'm not sure how he found out. "You let Misty into this house? She'll lead the sharks right to me! What good are you? You dress like a hooker and flaunt yourself around. You were supposed to be rolling in European dough," he said. My stomach dropped. "You're wasting my time, you good for nothing bag."

He climbed on top of me, straddling my legs so I couldn't move. I began to cry. How many people were whispering behind my back, spreading rumors that weren't true? And how did I combat the viciousness that was the rumor mill? I didn't have much time to think though.

The blow to the face came first and thankfully knocked

me out. I didn't feel the rest of the punches that came after. And I didn't feel him drag me to the car where he drove me to Greene's, leaving me unconscious outside until morning when I was found, bloody and bruised by Gina.

❦

*G*ina took me inside and washed me up. She kept extra clothes in her car and while they didn't fit me, they weren't soiled and caked with blood. She called Chef Tallant and told him what had happened. Then she said she would call Adam.

"You can't call Adam," I protested. "Please."

"Who else might I call then? Your father? I heard what those women said after you left here a few weeks ago. And I put them in their place, too. But I don't think your family would be welcoming you back." She was right, I knew. I had nowhere else to turn. She and Adam were the closest thing I had to family now.

"Call Adam," I said weakly. "He may not come, but call him anyway."

I should have known he would drop everything for me. He was at Greene's within the hour. Gina had fed me and kept steaming coffee in a cup for me so I felt marginally better when he showed up. I cried the world's ugliest cry when he rushed into the bar with such a look of desperation on his face.

"What happened? Oh, Roxie, I knew that guy was bad news," he said as he took me by the shoulders. I yelped in pain and he released me quickly. "I'm so sorry. You need to go to the hospital."

"She won't go, I tried," Gina said as she prepared the bar for their opening in a few minutes.

Adam looked at me with a stern expression. "You're going. You are cut and bruised. You could have broken bones, Roxanne." He looked over me and spoke to Gina. "What else did he do to her?" I hated that they were talking around me and treating me like a child, but I was too tired to argue.

"This isn't the first time this has happened, I'm afraid. I've suspected it for a while and when I called her boss at the restaurant, he said it's been going on pretty much since they got married," Gina confessed.

I thought I had done a decent job of hiding it. I had no idea that everyone knew and hadn't said anything about it.

Continuing, Gina whispered to Adam, "He's hit her, probably kicked her, and more, I'd say."

I watched as Adam's eyebrows went up with question. "More?" Tears slipped down my cheeks. Inside, I was screaming for Gina not to tell him.

I didn't hear Gina's reply, but Adam's response told me exactly what she has said. He fumed and slammed his fist onto the bar. I was mortified. My eyes closed in a vain attempt to hide.

"Can you stand?" Adam was in my face and when I opened my eyes, his were boring into mine.

"Yes," I said, unsure why he wanted me to stand.

"Good, let's go. I'm taking you to the hospital." He gingerly took my arm, and I winced.

I didn't argue. I was too exhausted to argue and too used to being punished for talking back. I stood and allowed Adam to take me to the hospital.

I had two broken ribs, some severe bruises, and a sprained wrist. The doctors said I was lucky. They also sent in a social worker to talk with me about pressing charges. I refused. I told them I just wanted to be safe. Then I thought about Misty. And I thought if Ray had done this to her and to me, who else had there been? Or who else might there be?

With Adam holding my hand, I agreed to press charges with the understanding that I would never have to see Ray again. I was assured with my help, he could be put away for a long time and not be allowed to hurt women again. I also gave them Misty's information in hopes she could also help put an end to Ray O'Toole's abuse.

"Why didn't you come to me for help?" Adam pressed me, his blue eyes boring into my brown ones.

"I was too scared," I admitted.

He paced in front of me. "I don't understand why you went out with him in the first place, Roxanne." His concern was endearing, but I had no fight left in me.

"I went out with him because I had just talked to you and you were with a woman. It was Christmas, I was alone. No family, no friends. I needed someone, and he was suddenly there," I choked out.

"When was this?" Adam looked alarmed.

"I think a week before Christmas."

"Cripes, Roxie, that was probably Maria, my secretary. It was our Christmas party," Adam told me. "I should have invited you to it. I'm so sorry."

I had put up with months of abuse because I had been jealous of Adam's secretary. Why hadn't I asked? Why had I made assumptions? I could have avoided so much if I only thought before I acted. I cried even more. Adam stayed with me the entire time.

Outside of the police line-up, I never saw Ray again. My divorce was granted immediately, and for that, I was thankful. Marriage number three had lasted all of four months, even shorter than my time with Josh. Eventually, Ray was sentenced to twelve years in jail without the option of parole, and he would be a registered sex offender once he did emerge from his dungeon. I kept in touch with Misty, who was a godsend when the nightmares came.

Adam and his beautiful lake house welcomed me home, this time to the room right next to the one I had shared with Josh. While the house held its own bittersweet memories, they were a far cry better than the pain of what I had endured with Ray O'Toole.

Chapter Twelve

FLESH OF MY FLESH

We fell into an easy rhythm, Adam and I. It was like the past five years hadn't separated us. He went to work during the day, and Chef Tallant let me pare down to part time for a while, and on the days we would both be home, I made dinner. I loved to cook and he loved to eat. He joked that he would have to start working out harder to keep the spare tire from around his middle.

Adam enjoyed playing little pranks on me, like the time he made the front door handle fall off when I pulled on it. He feigned panic until he began to laugh hysterically and produced a screwdriver to reattach it. Soon I was in on the act leaving little surprise jokes for him. One time, he had peppered our popcorn bowl with cayenne, hoping I would choke on the heat. Little did he know I liked heat in my food – even my popcorn – and he was the one who wound up with tears in his eyes from both the laughter and from the spice. To pay him back, I made him a fake cake. What he thought was a vanilla-frosted cake was really a meatloaf with creamy mashed potatoes for the icing. He wound up eating it for supper.

I began running with him in the mornings before going to work. We would start off near the house with a little conversation, but our discussion decreased as our pace increased. We would talk about our childhoods – his in Charleston with social climber parents and mine as the lackluster daughter of a senator. We talked about our dreams of the future. Adam knew exactly what he wanted from life. He wanted to retire early, find the woman of his dreams, and enjoy life. I was living my dream of being a full-time chef-in-training, but I couldn't help but feel there was something more. Even with three marriages behind me, I wanted to find love and have children. I wanted the American dream. I was only twenty-six, after all.

Reluctantly, I shared these dreams with Adam. At this point, he knew me better than anyone else did, and I felt that I could trust him.

"I still want to find love," I told him with a sheepish grin.

Adam wiped his brow as we turned a corner. "You don't think you've found it at all?" He didn't ask to mock me, but to really ask.

"I was foolishly and deep in puppy love with Josh. It wasn't love at all, just attraction and infatuation. Ray was merely me trying to cure my loneliness. I did love Remi, but not romantically. He was like a brother. I want real, passionate, romantic love. Something that will last forever," I said wistfully.

Adam replied, "I think we all want that, Roxie."

I struggled to keep up with him and I said, "I never realized before that love was such hard work."

"Rox, love is a verb, not an adjective. It's an action, not a feeling," he said half-heartedly before taking off ahead of me.

Back at the house, I turned on a pot of coffee as I always

did. We would both shower, separately, of course, then sit down for a cup. I tried to shed the jacket I had been wearing but my zipper was stuck and Adam had already gone back to his room. I tried pulling it over my head, but it wouldn't budge.

I went to the door of Adam's room and knocked. No answer. I bit my lip before deciding to call out. "Adam? Adam, I need some help." A few seconds later, I heard some fumbling, and the doorknob turned. I stepped back.

When he opened the door, I nearly gasped. He stood before me shirtless, with nothing but a towel around his waist. At least, I assumed there was nothing under it. I knew Adam had freckles on his face and arms. I had no idea there were freckles on his shoulders and chest. I didn't know one could get freckles on one's chest. I tried not to stare at the impressive, muscular body before me. I knew I turned bright red.

"What's wrong, Roxie?"

I stammered. Was something wrong? I couldn't remember. "Um. Um. My jacket. My zipper is stuck." I motioned to the zipper stuck at my neck. "I'm sorry. Can you please see if you ..."

He smiled and took his hand from his towel. I looked to the ceiling in case the towel dropped. Adam fumbled a second with the zipper, his hands at my collarbone. I held my breath. With a yank, the zipper loosed and Adam put his hands back on the towel.

"There you go," he said. I tried not to look directly at him.

"Thank you, Adam. I'm sorry to distract you." I smiled and turned to go.

"No problem. You're never a distraction," he said suddenly.

I stopped.

I debated turning and falling into his arms. I debated kissing him. I debated many things in the next split second. My lips turned up into a slow smile while my back was to him. Then I turned casually and glanced back, the smile still on my face. I saw him. I saw his face split into a huge grin, one hand on the towel around him and the other resting on the frame of his door. His expression carried from his lips up to his deep aqua eyes. I knew I would never forget that look for the rest of my life. My own smirk grew and I made myself turn and walk away from him, knowing he would watch me until I turned the corner.

After my shower, I came out for coffee to find Adam with two cups already poured. He was dressed for work in a sage green button-down and chinos. He looked wonderful in that shade of green. I was dressed for a casual day in blue jeans and a purple T-shirt. I was off work and was ready for a day of relaxing. My feet were bare and my hair was still wet, making spots on the shirt as it hung over my shoulders.

"Dinner tonight?" I asked, trying to be as nonchalant as possible after our exchange pre-shower. I chose a cup and took a sip as I leaned on the counter.

"I can't tonight, Rox, I have a ... thing," he said, looking away from me. The smile from before was erased, and Adam looked uncomfortable.

I chuckled. "A thing? What thing?"

"Um, nothing. Just a thing. I won't be home until later tonight. Sorry." He was lying. I could tell. My amusement from earlier was gone.

"You can't tell me?" I said with a nervous smile. I took another sip of coffee. "What, do you have a date or something?"

Adam turned from me and cleared his throat.

"You do have a date!" I exclaimed. "You have a date?" I felt hurt but knew I had no reason to. We weren't an item. We weren't dating. Adam had every right to go on a date if he wanted.

"I'm sorry, Rox."

I shook my head, my hair sending drops of water flying. "No, no. I'm happy for you. You've said before you hoped to find the right girl. I hope you have fun tonight."

"It was a setup," he explained. "A guy I work with, Rob, insisted on setting me up with his girlfriend's sister for some Christmas party thing. I couldn't say no. I owed him a favor."

"You don't have to explain to me, Adam. You are entitled to date anyone you want." I needed to get out of the room. I looked around and quickly spoke again, "I need to dry my hair. I have errands to run. I guess I'll see you later."

"Roxanne." I could hear the desperation in his voice.

"We'll talk later, Adam. Have a good day," I called out before my voice could falter. I stayed in my room until he left. I never dried my hair. I spent the morning cleaning the house, my go-to when I felt the need to do some deep thinking. And Momma had always told me to think before I acted. Why had I never listened to that advice before?

By the time Adam got home, it was late. Later than I would have thought for a blind date. Of course, he could stay out as late as he wanted. He never had to explain anything to me. I was lying in bed facing away from the door, waiting to hear his footsteps go down the hall. I heard them approach my door then stop. They went a few steps past, but then turned back.

He knocked lightly on my door. "Roxie?" I didn't move. I shut my eyes, hoping he would walk away. He knocked again. "Rox? Are you awake? I wanted to talk, um, to you."

I sighed. "About what?"

"Stuff," he said through the door.

"Come on in," I said.

He cracked the door open, and a thin stream of light came through.

I sat up, letting the blanket around me fall to my waist. Adam came in and sat when I patted the bed, though he sat several feet down. The soft glow from the bedside lamp illuminated us.

"I'm sorry," he began. His eyes were focused on the floor and the color in his cheeks was high.

"For what, Adam? You've done nothing wrong." I drew my knees to my chest and hugged them.

"I've been lying," he admitted.

My own cheeks flushed at his admission. Had he been dating someone for a while now and not told me? I wasn't sure what to think.

He answered before I could ask. "I've been lying to myself and to you. About how I feel." He inched closer to me.

I cleared my throat. "What do you mean?" I could feel my heart beat faster and faster until I thought it might give out. What would he say?

"I don't know how you feel, Roxie, but tonight really brought my true feelings to the surface." He looked anxious, I wasn't sure why. "This date tonight. The girl invited me back to her place ... well, I'm sure you know why."

"I don't need to hear this," I said, edging away from him. I wanted to put my hands on my ears. Even at my age, I didn't need to hear others' escapades.

"No, you do," he said hurriedly. "I went to her apartment, but the minute she closed the door, I only had one thing on my mind."

Shaking my head, I repeated, "I really don't need to hear this, Adam. It's none of my business."

"You."

"What?"

"You were the one thing on my mind, Roxie. You. I looked at this woman, who was beautiful in many ways. But she wasn't you. I don't want to be with anyone but you." He smiled and inched even closer. His hand closed over mine. "If you want me in return, that is."

"I ... I don't know what to say," I said. I blushed and moved to stand on the other side of the bed, putting space between us. This was what I wanted him to say, but now that he was saying it, I felt panicked. I was a grown woman, but still a woman thrice divorced. I didn't want another man to come into my life just yet. Did I?

"Roxie," Adam said. He came close until he was standing only inches in front of me. His blue eyes searched my brown ones. "Roxie, you are the most exquisite woman I have ever met. Would you move in with me?"

"Don't I already live with you?" I furrowed my brow, confused, but my eyes never left his.

Adam cupped my cheek with his hand. He leaned down and kissed me lightly. Despite how his lips barely brushed mine, I felt sparks of electricity speed throughout my body. "You live in my house. I want you to live with me, doll face."

Suddenly, I understood. He wanted me in his room with him. I wasn't sure I was ready for that move. We had been spending a lot of time together, but never had either of us mentioned being in a relationship. However, I could no longer deny my feelings for Adam.

He could sense my apprehension and immediately began to backtrack. "You don't have to," he said, stepping back. "I know it's quick. I know you've been hurt. But I've wanted to ask you this since you came back two months ago. Honestly, I've felt this way for years. I've actually wanted you from the moment you walked through my door with Josh, but I couldn't have you. I've dated other women who could never compare. You're all I think about, Roxie."

I smiled. I stepped closer to him and linked my hands around his neck. I nuzzled my head against his chest and felt the roughness of his beard on my cheek. Finally, a man who wanted me for me. He knew it all, he knew my past, knew the secrets. And he still wanted me. "Yes," I said. "Of course I'll move in with you."

He picked me up and swung me around. "Oh, Roxie, this is the happiest I've been in a long time."

And he kissed me again, this time deeper and more passionate. I could feel the longing behind it. I could feel the need behind it. And even though I could tell he was hungry for me, I knew he would be patient if I needed. But that just made me want him all the more. He led me back to his bedroom where I promptly moved in and made myself at home.

We didn't keep our relationship a secret, nor did we shout it from the rooftops. It was an easy transition, and Adam and I spent our free time together as we had been doing. Not much had changed between us, to be honest, except we were open in our admiration for each other and where we laid our heads at night.

The master suite in his house was amazing. I had not taken the time to examine it before. This room was different from the others. No soft, natural tones occupied this room. It was decidedly male. The walls were a steely gray color with no artwork adorning them. A lone mirror rimmed in black stood above his black dresser. A small bookshelf that was overflowing with books sat across the corner, and a strange piece of abstract art sat on top. His king-sized bed was massive and covered in a gray duvet. It looked and smelled masculine, but it was still friendly. I loved every part of it.

He had moved my dresser from the guest room into his and aligned it on an empty wall. He also made room in his closet for my belongings as well. At first, I was uncomfortable with him doing that – what if he changed his mind, and I had to move it back? But after a week, I knew there was no turning back.

Adam was amazing to me. He was attentive, he was interested, and I was completely in love. I woke every morning with his arm around me and went to bed each night with his kiss on my lips. Life was wonderful from the romantic walks along the lake to midnight movies.

It was during one of those midnight movies Adam first told me he loved me. Or, rather, tried to coax it out of me first.

"How do you feel about me, Roxie?" We were cuddled up on the couch, my head on his shoulder, his fingers running the length of my arm.

"You know how I feel," I said with a smile.

He craned his neck to look at me. "No I don't," he teased.

I wrinkled my nose at him. "I think you do. Can't you tell?"

"Tell me you love me," he said. It was more of a question than a demand. His voice was low and soft. I felt like an electrical current ran through my body.

I smiled in return and laughed. "And say it first? No way! You say it first." I sat up and faced him, our noses inches apart.

"I love you." His smile was huge, his eyes shining.

There are moments in life that you know you will remember forever. Memories of moments that will carry you though the rest of your life. This was one of those moments. A real declaration of love. For me. I could feel my heart beat faster and faster. My palms felt sweaty, and I knew I had the biggest smile of my life.

"You do?"

"I do." He kissed me, firm and deep. "I've always loved you."

"I love you, too, Adam," I said. "What do you mean you've always loved me?"

I took him in. His wavy hair was flattened from the ball cap he had worn earlier. His blue eyes nearly danced with joy. The auburn stubble along his jaw reminded me of Harrison Ford in the Indiana Jones movies. So handsome. His T-shirt clearly outlined his well-toned body. A muscular chest, taut abs, slim hips. I could just picture the freckles that made their way down his body. I bit my lip as I felt the heat rise.

"From the first time Josh brought you into my house, I was captivated by you," he admitted. "Why else do you think I asked you to that dinner with the Sweeneys?"

I shook my head and laughed. "I have no idea. I always wondered why. It was a little strange."

"I wanted you. I didn't need you there. I wanted you there," he said sheepishly. "You bolstered my confidence."

"I thought you were kinda creepy to be honest. Like you could see through me," I told him, remembering how I felt when we first met years before. "But I knew something was there. When you slipped me that envelope that night, your hand stayed on my knee. I could feel it. I could feel the heat deep in my stomach. Now I know what that was. It was this. Happiness. Josh told me I whored myself to you for the money."

Adam pulled back, and I could see anger flare on his face. "What? Are you serious?"

I nodded and shrugged. "When he called after he left. He said he took the five hundred. When I told him I had worked hard to earn my money, he said I had whored myself to you."

"What a piece of work he is," Adam said, shaking his head. "I'm so sorry you ever ..." his voice trailed. Then his face softened, "I'm just sorry, Roxie. You will never be like that, doll face. You do work hard. You are a strong woman. I'm really glad you're here now. None of the rest of it matters."

I beamed at his words. "I am much better off. Let's not talk about it anymore. He's gone. Remi's gone. Ray's gone. All gone. A thing of the past." I wrapped my arms around Adam again to feel the realness of him. "I am so glad you're in my life now. I do love you, Adam."

Chapter Thirteen

WITH THIS RING

A week later, Adam announced that his mother had invited herself to dinner that night. "I hope you don't mind, Roxie. This way you two can meet again, and I can introduce you as my girlfriend."

I tried not to think back to meeting Ray's parents and the heartache it caused. Adam's mother had been a perfectly nice woman when I met her before. She was someone I thought my own mother would have liked to be around. "It sounds delightful. And nerve-wracking. What do you want me to make?"

"Her favorite is shrimp scampi," he said with an unsure smile. I laughed and nodded. That was easy.

As we began to make dinner, we fell into an effortless conversation and a rhythm in and around the kitchen. We worked well together, Adam and me. It was so wonderful. We barely had enough time to change clothes before the doorbell rang. Adam zipped my dress, kissing the back of my neck before replacing my tawny hair over my shoulders. We rushed into the kitchen, Adam going ahead of me to get the door.

"Oh, Adam, darling, thank you," said Linda Joyce in her Southern drawl as she stepped into the foyer. Once again, she was immaculately dressed, this time in a casual navy blue blouse with an emerald green skirt.

She carried a bag into the kitchen and eyed me. "Oh, I didn't realize you had someone else coming for supper," she said with a tight smile toward me.

"Mrs. Joyce, it is nice to meet you again," I said, stepping forward.

"Mom, you remember Roxie," Adam said, stepping past her toward me.

"I'm not sure I do." She tried to place me and examined me closely.

"We met several years ago, Mrs. Joyce. Don't worry about not remembering," I assured her.

She handed me the bag she carried. "I brought some dessert."

"Oh, thank you," I said, pulling a pie from the bag. It was store-bought. I tried not to scrunch my nose at it. "I think we have some ice cream to go with this later."

Linda turned her attention to her son. "It's so nice to see you again, my dear. What has been going on with you since we spoke last week?"

"Well, Mom," Adam said as a smile came onto his face. "I thought this was a perfect opportunity to talk with you and reintroduce you to Roxie. We're together. She's my girl-friend. I wanted you to get to know her some."

For her part, Linda Joyce sure acted happy. I wasn't sure if she actually was or not. "Oh, what a wonder!" she exclaimed. She looked me up and down again. "Who did you say your people were, dear?"

I straightened my shoulders. "DePrivé, Mrs. Joyce. My

father is Dennis DePrivé, the former senator. And I believe you know my sister, Jenny Dolinghouse."

The real smile emerged then. "DePrivé? I had no idea! I know your father and your sister. Such good people, your family. I knew your mother, too," she said.

I nodded, still unable to speak of my mother without crying. Momma always said there was a time and a place for tears, and this was not it. I returned her smile.

"I didn't realize they had so many beautiful daughters. There are what, three of you?" She patted down her hair as Adam poured white wine for everybody.

"Four, actually. Jenny and Shelly are the eldest. Lori is a year older than me, I'm the baby," I said. I wondered if she had heard about me. Dennis DePrivé's vagrant daughter.

She stopped and squinted her eyes as she looked at me. "So, you're the youngest." She knew. She knew who I was. If Adam and Josh were cousins, of course she knew Josh's mother. She knew my past. I could feel it. Was she silently judging me?

"I am," I confirmed, knowing my cheeks were blossoming into a bright pink. I set my glass down and wrapped my arms around my waist.

"You're the one who shacked up here with..." she began, pointing a manicured finger at me. Thankfully Adam interjected before we finished her sentence.

"Mom, Roxie and I prepared a wonderful meal for you tonight. I hope you like it," Adam said, like a little boy who wanted to please his mother.

I was thankful for the distraction. Food brought people together. Maybe Mrs. Joyce would hold her judgment until she got to know me more. She smiled and nodded to her son. When she turned away from me and was out of earshot, I sighed heavily. The scrutiny was almost too much for me.

"Rox? Are you okay?" Adam placed his hand on the small of my back and brought me back from my panic.

I slowly nodded. "Yes, sorry. I'm fine. Are we going into the dining room?" When Adam nodded in response, I motioned for his mother to lead the way.

Suddenly, I had a vision of a little boy who looked exactly like Adam – red hair, quirky smile and all – running through the house. But not Adam as a child. A child of Adam's. I felt an amazingly strong urge deep within my belly. It was almost an ache. I felt anchored to the floor where I stood with this vision running through my head. And I smiled.

Past or not – Adam was my future.

❧

This time I had a proper spring wedding. Poofy white dress, church ceremony, reception, everything. My father and older sisters came to the wedding simply for appearances and because they knew the Joyce family, but my dad did not walk me down the aisle. Adam and I walked together.

The minister spoke of love and commitment. He read some verses from the Bible that were about love and how love was the greatest thing of all. I agreed wholeheartedly. I looked into Adam's eyes as we said our vows. His eyes were like pools, and I hoped to be lost in them forever. When we said, "till death do us part," we meant it. We had even discussed it beforehand. Adam said divorce was not an option in his mind. Marriage was forever. And he was my forever.

When the minister told Adam to kiss me, he smiled slyly and cupped his hand behind my head and drew me toward him. He laid his lips on mine as if it were the first time. He was gentle yet firm, and my entire body felt electrified. When he broke away, he whispered his declaration of love to me. I could have melted right there.

We honeymooned on a cruise ship bound for the Bahamas. It was amazing. I had rarely ever left South Carolina before, let alone needed a passport. The water was crystal blue, the food was abundant, and my groom was the most amazing man I had ever met.

Room service became well acquainted with us as we took several meals in our suite. Adam hand-fed me strawberries and we dined like kings. And when we did emerge from our room out into the daylight, we lounged by the pool. Adam had taken me shopping and told me to pick any bathing suit I wanted. I had chosen a fire-engine red two-piece. Not a bikini, but a two piece all the same.

Back at home, we fell into the same routine we had before. Except this time, I was Roxie Joyce. I could not wait to change my name officially and practiced writing it the way a twelve-year-old with a crush would. I loved signing my name.

It was an evening two months after our wedding when I was in my cleaning and singing session in the kitchen. I had taken up singing along with pop songs on the radio, scrubbing the countertops to the rhythm.

Without warning, a strong, masculine hand was wrapped around my neck. I jumped and screamed aloud. My heart raced and tears immediately sprang to my eyes.

"Don't touch me!"

Adam's hands lifted as if I was on fire, and it almost felt like I was. "Rox, doll, it's me."

I turned against the counter, wet rag forgotten as hot tears stung my eyelids. My throat felt constricted, and I couldn't get a deep breath. I slumped to the floor with my head between my knees, gasping for breath.

"Roxie, what happened?"

No words formed in my mouth, but my head was screaming, "*Ray! Ray happened.*"

Adam sat across from me but did not touch me. He waited for my breathing to slow, my head to lift. Silently, he raised an eyebrow as my eyes met his.

"I'm so sorry, Adam. I'm so sorry."

"No. You don't need to apologize. Can you tell me what that was?" He scooted a little closer to me, but still did not touch me directly.

Inhale, exhale. "That was a scar. Ray would often choke me. He apparently got a thrill from putting his hands around my neck. While I know you would never hurt me, my body doesn't. I don't know if I will ever be able to forget."

When I looked up at Adam, he had tears in his eyes. He stuffed his hands in his pockets and backed away from me.

He thought I thought he would hurt me. And it was agony to see that look in his eyes. I know he would never, but my body would not think rationally. I reached my hand out to him and he took it in his.

With a shuddered breath he whispered, "I'm so sorry, doll. I just didn't think. I'm so sorry."

We sat like that for a few minutes. I don't know what Adam was thinking, but I was thinking how I didn't deserve the man that Adam Joyce was. I questioned how he could love someone as broken as me.

As my breathing returned to normal, I moved to be next to him. "I'm sorry I reacted that way. I know you wouldn't hurt me."

His arm went around me and pulled me close. I closed

my eyes and wished the memories of abuse away. We stayed like that until I began to drift off and Adam led me to bed.

❧

a few weeks later, Adam and I were cleaning up after dinner when he stopped and stared at me.

"What?" I couldn't hide the shy smile that crept onto my face with his gaze.

"A few weeks ago, I wanted to talk to you about something, but that's when ..."

I stopped him there. "Yes." I nodded and gulped a little, forcing a pleasant expression. "What's up?"

The last dish was put away, and he leaned against the black marble counter. "Well, doll, I was thinking," he started. But he stopped himself and licked his lips.

I turned to him and matched his stance, right hip against the cold granite. "What were you thinking, my love?"

He sighed. "This house needs your touch. What about redecorating?"

I chuckled at him, "Why? I love this house. It's so calming with the yellows and greens. Everything is so peaceful."

"But it's not personal. I want you to put your touch throughout the house. Make changes. You have a great eye."

I studied his face. I felt like there was something more he wasn't telling me. Was he thinking of selling the house? Did he want to downsize? I asked him if he wanted to sell the house.

"No! Not at all. I thought it could use some updating, and your feminine touch. Maybe in some of the spare rooms. Paint, new furniture," he suggested.

"If that's what you want, Adam, sure. I can go pick out

paint and furniture. Why the spare rooms, though? Nobody ever goes in them," I mentioned.

He shifted so he was facing me completely. "What if we needed to go into them more?"

Fully perplexed, I took Adam's hands. "I don't know what's going on, but give it to me straight. Is your mom moving in or something? Are you taking on another homeless cousin and his child bride?"

"What if it wasn't a child bride but our own child?" he asked, his face beaming, his eyes twinkling at the idea.

"What?" I said as I nearly choked. "We just got married."

"Yes, but we've been together for months. We've known each other for years. Maybe the ring is still hot on your finger, but the desire is there for me. We have six bedrooms in this house. Don't you want to fill them up?"

Adam moved toward me, his hands reaching for mine. I could see the hungry look in his eyes. That look always got him what he wanted. I recalled the vision I had months before, the vision of a little boy that looked just like Adam running around. I could feel that urge hit me like a ton of bricks all over again.

"Of course I do, Adam, but is this the right time?" I protested, trying to be reasonable.

"It's not like you'd have a baby tomorrow. And it could take a few months of trying, you know? We could have a lot of fun trying," he teased. "And it will be the right time." His smile grew. It was infectious.

Smiling in return, I opened my nightstand drawer and pulled out my pack of birth control pills. "Are you sure about this? It's a lot of responsibility."

He reached over and grabbed the pills and flung the pack across the room. Then Adam nuzzled his face into my neck, making me squeal.

That was the night we decided to become a family of three.

$\mathcal{S}$t was also the night that began a roller coaster ride of emotions, of negative tests and us both wondering what was wrong with us. After a few months of having fun trying to get pregnant, nothing was happening. I tried to release that frustration in cooking and cleaning. The house was spotless and we were eating more than ever. Thankfully, our morning runs kept us from getting fat. Though I longed for the girth of a swelling tummy.

After another unsuccessful month, I felt like a ticking time bomb. "What's wrong with me, Adam?" I leaned on his shoulder and sniffed back tears.

"Hey," Adam said, pulling me back so he could look at me. "Nothing is wrong with you. If I'm putting too much pressure on you, we can stop. It's not a big deal to wait a while longer if you want, Rox."

"Adam, when we were dating, actually that night your mom came for dinner, I had a vision," I said with a deep breath. "A vision of a little boy with bright red hair running around this house. Not you as a child, but your child. And I felt an ache to make that happen for you. And ever since you said you wanted to try to have a baby, I have felt that ache intensify. I want this, Adam. I want to have children so much it hurts."

Apparently, I had not released all my frustration into cooking and cleaning like I had thought. A flood of tears came, and I did not care. I cried, certain that my past was costing me the one thing I wanted – children with my husband. I didn't know what to do.

Once my tears were mostly shed, Adam spoke firmly to me. "Roxanne, we will have children one day. I promise. What if we adopt?"

I had never considered it before. "I don't know. Perhaps? But I really want to experience pregnancy at least once. Not to mention it being insanely expensive."

"I tell you what. Why don't we talk to a doctor about this? Maybe they will have a suggestion? And maybe – maybe we should pray. And go to church."

I looked at him for a moment, unsure if I heard him correctly. "Church? What would that do?"

"Well, I know you were raised going to church. So was I. Don't you remember being taught that God answers our prayers? Maybe if we go to church and pray, it will happen. And you can call your lady doctor and talk with her, too. We'll get God and science behind us." Adam raised his fist in victory.

I laughed. And I sighed. Adam always had a plan, and it was a good thing, because I was not much of a planner. I would call my doctor. We could go to church a few times and see if that helped, too.

That Sunday, we went to the church closest to the house. It was a small church, probably not even a hundred people in all. We were stared at, obviously newcomers. An older woman approached us as we awkwardly came down the center aisle.

"Hello and welcome!" she said with a deep Southern drawl. "Y'all must be visiting us this fine morning. Please do have a seat." She pointed to the spot to our left. "Right here, front and center. I'm Alma, the pastor's wife. We are so happy you came today!" She hugged us both and retreated to the front pew as the music began.

"She was sure happy to see us," I whispered.

"I think we're the first new people they've seen in years," Adam said with a smile.

That church was not for us, we decided. After being forced to stand in front of everyone as newcomers, Adam and I both felt the urge to run the opposite direction.

The next week, we tried a more contemporary church. This one had a rock band, which reminded me a little too much of a previous life, and after running into Josh's mother – who shot me nasty looks the whole time – we decided not to return there again either.

I did learn in that time of searching that there are a variety of churches to fit the many different needs of the people in the world. Those two, however, were not the best choices for us.

I was only willing to try one more time, and Adam picked a church that wasn't too far from home. It was a decent size with a few older families and a few younger ones. The music was upbeat but nothing like Nirvana. Nobody made us stand against our will, and nobody gave us mean glances. It was pleasant, inviting. We liked it immediately. The preacher spoke of redemption, a message I thought seemed to be aimed right at me. Adam and I both decided it was worth going again.

With that in place, I finally had my appointment with my doctor.

"Roxanne, you're still young. Why the rush to have a baby?" Dr. Drummond looked at me sternly. She was a young doctor, but obviously did not understand what happens when someone feels such an urge to get pregnant.

"My husband and I have been trying for a few months with nothing happening. It's not a rush," I explained. "More just not understanding why it's not happening."

She asked about my daily routine and what chemicals I

was around. When I told her about my cleaning habits, she told me to cut back. "Some of those chemicals could be preventing pregnancy. And, you've only been off the pill for a few months, Roxanne. It can take anywhere from three to six months for them to completely wear off. Relax, give it time. If you're not pregnant within a year, we'll see about some tests to determine what's going on."

The doctor also suggested staying off my feet. But life as a chef meant I did nothing but stand on my feet.

Clean less, give it time. Didn't Dr. Drummond realize that cleaning was how I dealt with stress and how I passed the time? And that cooking was my passion outside of my family?

Despite that struggle, life with Adam was nearly perfect. We fit well together and knew each other's quirks. Adam Joyce made me laugh in a way I never had before. He was quick to show love without any conditions or expectations, which was something I was not used to in the least.

I never feared physical harm, nor did I fear coming home one day to find him gone. The baggage I carried from my previous relationships may have damaged me, but Adam was kind, patient, and compassionate.

Together we lived our best life. We continued to attend church, we traveled across the region to go to festivals and shows. Adam made sure I ended each day with a smile on my face.

That autumn, the whole world changed when four planes were hijacked and crashed. Terrorists had wanted to change the world, and they did. But instead of despair, our nation rose up and united. Adam and I volunteered through the church we were attending to send relief efforts to Washington DC and New York. This was the world we wanted to bring a child into. A world so full of love and goodness it needed to be shared with the next generation.

Professionally, Adam's real estate business was booming, and his face was plastered all over Columbia as the go-to guy for all your housing needs. He had several people working under him and we had saved quite the nest egg. As for me, I was still working at Pixie's as Chef Tallant's right-hand-lady. In fact, the local paper had done a write up about me. I hoped my father had seen it.

I had grown in so many ways since beginning anew with Adam. My life was almost picture perfect. Almost.

Chapter Fourteen

A GIFT FROM GOD

fter more than a year, Adam and I grew impatient. We loved being married. We loved being together. And we both longed to share our joy with a child. I saw new babies and pregnant women everywhere. I felt plagued almost, and the ache grew stronger.

I had found organic, non-toxic cleaners, so I was avoiding chemical exposure. I rested as much as possible. But the biggest change was that I left my job at Pixie's. It broke my heart to do so, but after months of praying over it, I felt it was the right decision for me. Adam's secretary had decided to move to Texas to be with her family, so I had taken over her position. The work allowed me to relax, have normal hours, and spend more time with Adam.

In the past year, we had joined the friendly little church that wasn't too stuffy or too loud. We started going to a Sunday school class, and went to pot-luck dinners. We fit right in, as if we had always been there. Over the summer, Adam and I were baptized into the faith, and we were never happier. We thought surely then, God would bless us with a child. But when another Christmas came without anything, we decided to seek more help.

We decided to pursue in vitro fertilization. It was invasive and terrifying, but Adam and I felt sure God was leading us, and this was what we were supposed to do. We sat anxiously in the doctor's office, waiting for our in vitro results. I took a deep breath, smelling that clinical, sterile smell all doctor's offices smelled like.

When I exhaled, Adam squeezed my hand. "You okay?"

"I don't know," was my honest reply.

Easter was just a few weeks away. We thought we could make an announcement on Easter Sunday at church and to our families if I was indeed pregnant.

A sonogram had been performed, but we opted to wait to hear the results from my doctor. In the event of bad news, I did not want to have a breakdown while the tech was working.

We sat nervously in the chairs as Dr. Drummond came in looking at a chart. Finally, she sat down and looked at us as if she wanted us to tell her the results ourselves.

"How are you feeling, Roxie?"

"Scared. Nervous," I answered. I did not want bad news, but I had to know. My palms were sweating, and Adam's left knee was bouncing out of control.

"Any nausea? Dizziness? Any cramping?" She looked at me closely. I felt scrutinized.

I stopped and held my breath. Did I feel ill? No. Did I feel crampy? No, not that either. "No, nothing. Is that bad?" I squeezed Adam's hand and took a deep breath. He squeezed right back. He was my rock.

"If you feel any cramping in the next few weeks, I want you to give me a call. Otherwise, I'd expect the nausea to hit in about two more weeks." The petite woman broke into a wide smile.

My mind went blank. What did that mean? Was she telling us something? I wasn't sure. I looked to Adam, and his face was just as blank as my own. He raised an eyebrow to me, as if to ask if I knew what was going on.

"I don't understand," Adam said for the both of us.

Dr. Drummond laughed. "Roxie is indeed pregnant. Here's the sonogram." She pulled a little picture out from the folder on her desk. Adam took it, and we both looked at it in awe. The doctor pointed out where the baby was, but we saw nothing but black and gray shapes. She assured us there was one tiny baby in there. "It looks like you should have this one right in time for Christmas. Congratulations!"

We shook her hand and left the office. Once outside, we sat on a bench and stared at the little picture. I was pregnant. I was finally pregnant.

"Adam," I whispered. I didn't have to say anything else.

"I know, doll, I know," he said back to me. And we clung to each other in that moment and cried with joy. We praised God for the miracle he had given us.

❧

*M*y pregnancy went as smoothly as it could have gone. I had minimal morning sickness, I began showing in my fifth month, and I craved tacos all the time. But not the delicious authentic ones. The greasy fast food tacos. I loved walking around town with my belly leading the way. I finally felt like an accepted part of the world.

Lori had welcomed me back into her life after I told her about my pregnancy. She herself was married with two little ones in tow. She lived about ten miles away, and she helped me shop for all those baby things I didn't know I needed. It was like old times, Lori and I together. A small portion of the rip in my heart was mended.

My sister, Shelly, called me on occasion, but Jenny was still chilly toward me. My father had sent a baby shower gift with Lori, which I took as a peace offering. The gift had made me cry—it was my mother's Christening gown, the one she wore when she was a baby. My sisters and I all wore it as well.

Linda, for her part, was more than excited to finally be promoted to the role of grandmother. She had known about my past relationships, but at Adam's urging she had looked past them, and she and I formed a close bond. She was amazingly helpful when it came to decorating a nursery and coming to doctor's appointments Adam couldn't make. She stepped into the spot my mother had vacated and was a balm to my soul.

❧

That fall, with me looking more and more pregnant by the hour, Adam told me that he had been given tickets to the Clemson versus Carolina football game right up the road in Columbia. Adam was not necessarily into sports, but his family had a history of loving Clemson, and my own father had attended the university for his undergraduate degree, so we happily accepted the gift.

We donned our orange shirts and found orange pom poms and headed out to the game. Despite the late November date, it was still a toasty eighty degrees outside and felt even hotter in the direct sun.

The game was fun to watch, but soon the heat got me. I

felt dehydrated and sick. With one look at my red and anguished face, Adam quickly ushered me to the first aid station.

"My wife needs help," He practically shouted as we entered the cool tent.

"What seems to be going on?" an older gentleman medic asked.

"She's pregnant," Adam said.

"I'm fine, just overheated and need something cool, and maybe with some sugar," I assured them.

The medic put me on a table similar to one found at a doctor's office. He checked my temperature and pulse and I closed my eyes, glad to be in a cooler spot. I immediately felt better being out of the glaring sun.

I could hear the crowd roar outside and the man commented, "Touchdown, Gamecocks."

Opening my eyes, I asked, "How can you tell?"

"Home team, it's louder. But I'm a Clemson fan myself," he said with a smile. Turning serious, he addressed my condition. "Missy, you got a bit of the heat exhaustion. What with the warm weather and you cooking a young'un and all. Cool down, have something cold to drink, and take it easy. Y'hear?"

"Yes, sir," I replied, returning the smile.

He handed me an ice-cold Sprite and I happily drank it. The fizzy bubbles felt wonderful, and the sugar helped me perk up a little.

"Does she need to see her doctor?" Adam rubbed my belly protectively. He kissed my temple, and I leaned into him.

The medic chuckled. "Not unless she's in labor, son. Now, y'all can hang out here for a spell, but I might recommend not spending two more hours in the sun."

"I'm fine, Adam," I assured him. "Really. How about we get out of here, and you find me some tacos?"

My husband brought his face in close to mine. He held my face in his hands and nuzzled in close. "I will get you anything you want, Roxie." He kissed my nose and I peered into his baby blues.

Thank you, Lord, for this man. Thank you for allowing him to wait for me. Lord, if it's not too much to ask, let our child fulfill that vision I had so long ago. I would love nothing more than a little Adam running around.

We thanked the kind medic and left the game behind in search of the greasiest tacos we could find in South Carolina.

Chapter Fifteen

O HOLY NIGHT

illiam Adam Joyce—Liam—entered the world on Christmas Eve. Adam was in the room with me while Linda and Lori waited outside. Labor took about ten hours, and I thought it would never end. My sweet baby boy weighed seven pounds, ten ounces and was twenty inches long.

Liam was born with a shock of red hair, though the nurses told me it would all fall out and likely come back blondish. With the vision I had had previously, though, I knew that would not be the case. My little boy would remain a redhead like his father.

We had chosen the name William for our little man because it meant "desired protector," and we wanted a strong name for him. And in the meantime, before he could be the protector, Adam placed a little brown bunny inside the hospital isolette with Liam as his protector. I watched as Adam smoothed Liam's hair and kissed his little forehead and my heart swelled beyond any measure I could have imagined.

As for me, I had decided to be a stay-at-home-mom to be

with Liam full time. We found a new secretary for Adam's office, and I planned to dote on Liam for years to come.

Chef Tallant, who had taken on something of a father role with me in the past several years, had inundated us with all kinds of wonderful meals, pastries, and even a baby chef set for Liam when he was born.

I still loved to cook and often catered little get-togethers for our church friends. It seemed my past had been mostly forgotten, thankfully, and I was just another mother in town. I wouldn't have wanted it any other way.

Being home with my little man was more than I ever hoped. I was completely in love with him. We explored and learned. I loved seeing the world through his eyes. I wished my mother could have met him, but Linda was a doting and loving grandmother. Adam would snuggle into the couch with Liam, and the two of them would nap on Sunday afternoons. It was like a dream life for me.

*L*iam was the most amazing child I had ever encountered, but I was biased. He indeed looked like his father with the shock of red hair I had envisioned so long ago. But instead of Adam's blue eyes, he had dark brown ones like mine. By the time he was eighteen months old, he had a smattering of freckles we called 'angel kisses' across his nose.

He knew all his colors, how to count to five, and we were working on his ABCs. Liam was the smartest baby in the history of babies, I was certain. He loved electronics and animals. As a baby, Liam lit up any room he entered with his infectious smile and bubbly giggles.

It was around this time, the vision came true. One night

after dinner, Adam was cleaning up, and I had told Liam it was time for his bath. He giggled wildly and went running down the hallway, his little feet smacking against the hardwood floors.

"Oh, no you don't, little man." I laughed as I chased after him, allowing him to be faster than me for a few brief seconds.

Every time he looked back to make sure I was behind him, he would shriek in laughter again and try to get a little faster.

My sweet Liam was wearing a little navy-blue cotton romper and laughing hysterically as I chased him. I had a sudden moment of inspiration. My vision of a miniature Adam came true. I stilled in my tracks and nearly wept with joy. I thanked God for my many blessings.

Adam was also completely taken by his son. He had introduced Liam to the world of video games and cheesy '80s movies way earlier than I would have liked, but Liam would have done anything in the world for his daddy. He wanted to follow Adam everywhere, and Adam was only too happy to oblige.

On a night I had miraculously gotten away from the house without my ginger shadow, I came home to the glow of the television still on, Adam snoring softly on the couch, and Liam watching his favorite cartoon puppies. Unlike his father, he was wide awake.

Upon seeing me, he quickly nudged Adam. "Tuh-oh, Daddy. Momma's home. Wakey up." He giggled as he jumped on Adam, brown bunny clutched in his fist.

Adam let out a loud groan at Liam's weight and caught him right before he could jump for me.

I bent down over the back of the couch so I was nose to

nose with Liam. "Busted, little mister." I rubbed my nose against his.

Brown bunny was thrust in my face as Liam mimicked, "Bussed, Momma. Bussed, Daddy."

"Yeah, Daddy is certainly busted." Adam sat up and turned Liam toward him. "I better get you to bed. Give Momma kisses. " He stood and passed Liam to me.

After a goodnight kiss, Liam hopped back to his father, and they went off to bed. I sat on the couch, still warm from where they had sat, and I sighed the most contented sigh I think had ever existed. My life was pretty grand.

I had just turned twenty-nine years old. It seems young still, yet I felt like I had lived an entire lifetime before Adam and Liam were a part of it. I attended our church's ladies' Bible study, sold cakes at all the fundraisers, and sang with the worship team. Yes, I sang. But singing for the Lord was vastly different than singing in a karaoke bar.

It was one night while I was at a church rehearsal that my world turned upside down.

Chapter Sixteen

STAND BY ME

I was at choir practice, Adam and Liam were running errands after supper. It was a typical Wednesday night, the warm South Carolina summer creeping up on us all. At about seven o'clock, shortly before we were scheduled to finish at the church, we heard sirens race by the building. It was an uncommon thing to hear, and many of us looked at one another in surprise.

A few moments later, one of the church's deacons came running into the sanctuary where we were singing. "Roxie! Come quick! It's Adam!"

My heart sank, and my knees went weak. It was one of those moments you never forget no matter how much time has passed. Without another word, I knew. The sirens had been for Adam and Liam. I didn't feel like I could move, yet before I had another thought, I was at the front of the church, getting in the car with Deacon Bob.

He raced about a mile up the road, where there were lots of police and ambulance lights flashing. I didn't wait for him to turn the car off. I tore from the vehicle and ran, spotting

Adam's silver sedan completely smashed. I tried to get to the car, but a police officer stopped me.

"You can't go through there, miss," he said, grabbing my shirt.

"Let me go! Let me go! That's my husband's car. He and my baby were in there." Sobs came out of me like I had never heard before.

The officer whisked me away to the ambulances. I saw Adam on a stretcher, an emergency medic getting ready to take him away. The officer explained who I was, and they let me go to him.

"Adam? Are you okay? Where's Liam?" I looked at my husband, the love of my life. He was covered in blood, and I was terror-stricken. He opened his eyes and raised a battered hand to my cheek. Relief flooded my veins.

"It's okay, doll, find Liam. I'm fine. Go to him," he said. Before I tore away, he grabbed me. "I love you, Roxie. With everything I have."

I kissed him and looked into his eyes. "I love you, too. I'll see you at the hospital."

The police officer helped me get to Liam before they took off in his ambulance. A pretty young medic was holding his hand while he was strapped to a tiny board to keep him still. Thankfully, he was not bloody like Adam had been. I was hopeful.

"Liam! Oh, my baby. Momma's here, baby. It's okay, Momma's here." I climbed into the back with him. He did not cry but whimpered instead. I kept telling him everything was fine, because Momma was here now.

Those moments in the ambulance with Liam were both silent and deafening. No words were spoken, but I would never forget the staccato beats of the machines, the hum of the engine, and the haphazard sounds of my tears falling onto Liam's pale skin.

At the hospital, Liam was rushed back to a room, and they let me stay with him as long as I was out of the way. I asked a nurse to check on my husband while I watched the doctors cut my son's clothes from his tiny body.

He looked so little, my Liam. Like a doll. I prayed and prayed for the Lord to save my family. I knew they would pull through. They had to. Machines started beeping and the medical staff began to move even more frenzied. I backed myself into a corner, wanting only to be by his side, but knowing that they could save him.

It was all a blur. A nurse took my hand and led me to his side. She spoke to me, but I heard no words. Suddenly I heard each staccato beep, every labored breath Liam took. It was all so slow. I looked at my child, his little body so still. His eyes looked up at me, and I put my hands on his chest. I stroked his hair, and I kissed his nose. I sang to him the way I did when I put him to bed.

And it hit me. This was it. This was what the nurse had said. This was my last chance to sing to him, to touch him, to smell him, to tell him I loved him. He looked so scared. I soothed him as best I could and prayed that God would do a miracle.

No miracle came. After a minute, the beeps began to slow. Each one spaced longer than the one before. It was both agonizingly slow and astonishingly brief. I let the tears slip down my cheeks, and I bent over my sweet son. I told him I loved him. I told him Daddy loved him. I told him his grandmother would be waiting for him in heaven. And in that moment, he was gone. I held Liam to me as he took his last breath.

I screamed out. My heart felt like it was torn from my

chest, leaving a gaping hole in its wake. Why? Why would God take this precious child from me? As a doctor took a step towards me, I snarled at him like a wild animal. I hovered over my child, my arms protectively covering his body. I had to keep him safe. It was my job to protect him, and I had already failed. I could not fail again.

A grandmotherly nurse with a sympathetic smile had to pry me off him. She said I had to go to my husband. She said they would bring me back after I saw Adam.

Adam. I had to tell him Liam was gone. It would devastate him.

I was rushed into another room where another medical team was working frantically. The nurse who had me by the arm said I was the wife, and they left me by his side while they continued. Everyone seemed to be covered in blood, Adam's blood. I shook my head in disbelief.

"Roxie," Adam moaned. "Liam?"

I shushed him and ran my hands through his gorgeous red hair. Someone whispered in my ear that he didn't have much time left. I don't know if it was a doctor or if an angel had sent me a message from heaven, but I knew I had to say my goodbyes.

"Oh, Adam, I love you so much," I said. I cupped his face in my hands, and I smiled at him through the tears. "No matter what, I love you more than anything. Please stay with me," I begged.

Adam's smile lit up. "Oh, Roxie, doll, there's Liam!" He looked past me.

I nodded as tears clouded my vision, "Yes, honey, do you see Liam?"

He nodded.

How could I do this? How could I say goodbye to the two men I loved most in the world? I looked around and saw that the doctors and nurses were now standing back, watching. I was sure Liam had come to get his Daddy. But that did not make it any easier.

"Adam, sweetie, please, don't leave me," I pleaded.

He looked at me, and I could see how full of love he was for me. "Roxie, Liam needs me now. I have to be with him. You will be okay, doll face, I promise."

I shook my head. I didn't want to be okay. I wanted to be with them.

Adam's eyes searched mine one last time. "I will always be with you. You are the love of my life."

"And you are mine," I told him. I leaned in and kissed him, longing to feel him hold me, but he couldn't move his arms. "Please, Adam, please tell Liam I love him, and he's my special little prince. I love you, Adam."

I kissed him one more time and laid my head on his chest. I felt his chest rise and fall, rise and fall, and then it stopped. I heard the moment his heart stopped.

❦

While Liam had been in his car seat, the impact gave him massive internal injuries and ruptured several organs, including collapsing his lungs. Adam lost too much blood and had more broken bones than I could name. They had been hit by a drunk driver who was going over eighty miles an hour in a thirty-five mile an hour zone. They were t-boned on the driver's side. The drunk driver died at the scene. He had been nineteen years old.

My mother-in-law took care of all the funeral arrangements. I was a basket case. I was thankful she was not. Even though her own son and grandson were gone, she was able to hold it together enough for the both of us. She had asked if I wanted them cremated, and I said yes, to put them together.

Father and son were buried a week later. Linda had ordered the headstone to read:

ADAM CALHOUN JOYCE 8/10/1973 – 7/18/2006

WILLIAM ADAM "LIAM" JOYCE 12/24/2004 – 7/18/2006

FATHER AND SON, UNITED ETERNALLY IN HEAVEN

FOREVER LOVED AND MISSED

After the funeral, Linda handed me some paperwork to sign. "What's this?" I asked, not caring much, but it had Adam's name on it.

"It's a trust Adam set up for you in the event that anything happened to him," she said with a sigh. She pushed her blonde hair from her face and wiped away a stray tear.

"A trust? I don't understand?"

She patted me on the back as I sat at the bar of my kitchen. Adam's and my kitchen. My hair hung in my face limply, and I knew my eyes were puffy. My mother-in-law still looked impeccable, even though I had seen her crying plenty in the last week.

"After you were married, I guess when you were pregnant, Adam asked me to help him with this. We went to our family attorney and set up a trust for you. If anything were to happen to Adam, you would get a monthly stipend to help make ends meet and cover any costs you and ..." she trailed off for a moment. "It would cover costs you may have."

"You mean me and Liam?" I asked, choking up again.

She nodded, tears spilling down her own cheeks. "Yes, it

was set up for you two and any other children you may have down the road. It's set to a specific sum, but you can adjust that with a call to the attorney any time."

"How – how much is it?" I knew Adam had made a fair amount of money, and he had been able to afford a six bedroom home, but I didn't know he had enough for a trust fund.

"I'm not sure exactly, but it's plenty. Adam's father left him a trust that he hardly touched. All that will roll into yours. I'd say your basic living expenses could be covered for many, many years if you live conservatively." She handed me a pen. "All you have to do is sign here, and the first installment will appear in your bank account on the first of each month."

I scanned the document for a number. I would start off receiving three thousand dollars a month. It seemed like way too much. But for now, I just signed the paper and handed it back to Linda.

Telling her I needed to rest, I retreated to the bedroom I had shared with my husband and wept.

I didn't want money. I didn't want any of it. Who wanted stuff when you were missing your very heart? That pain was one I would never forget.

Chapter Seventeen

LABYRINTH

I was a shell of myself after that, as I'm sure anybody would be. I quit talking to people, I quit doing anything except breathing, and I longed for that to stop as well. Members of the church came by and brought me food, but I didn't eat. A few people were kind enough to wash laundry and clean up some around the house. But I was unresponsive to them, and after about two weeks, they stopped coming. I became angry with church folks because they always seem to think after a major life upheaval, everything goes back to normal after two weeks. It doesn't. The grieving is just starting two weeks in.

Lori came by once a week for months. It was nice to see her again, or it would have been had I been in the mood for seeing her. She would bring premade meals for me and made me eat. They tasted like cardboard. She talked even though I didn't respond much. She wrote out thank you cards to those who had sent something to me. I hadn't asked, but I appreciated it. But even still, I only wanted to be left alone.

My father and older sisters came to the funeral. The

crash made headlines across South Carolina, and the media somehow knew that this was the son-in-law and grandson of Senator Dennis DePrivé. Even though my father had only seen Liam once, he came. And my sisters tore themselves away from their socially busy lives to pay their respects. I didn't really care whether they were there or not. Adam would have told me to take advantage of the opportunity, but I didn't. Just thinking of Adam made my heart feel like it was in tatters.

Eventually, it all stopped, though. My father's attention and that of Shelly and Jenny were short lived. The church pastor said he would give me time to grieve, and that I was welcome back to church any time I felt ready. I didn't hear from him again. And after four months of coming to the house frequently to help me, Lori said I needed to start doing things for myself again, and she stopped coming. When she would call, I would ignore the rings. I didn't want anything from anybody.

I was alone, and I didn't want it any other way.

Adam's mother called me once a week to check on me, but at that point, it felt like it was a formality. She reminded me that I could leave town and start fresh and that Adam wouldn't mind at all. I'm sure she wouldn't have minded either. The idea of escaping was tempting, but I wasn't willing to leave my memories behind. Besides, I had never lived anywhere else and the great big world scared me.

*A*bout a year after the accident, I began to rally once more. I was thirty years old and living the life of an eighty-year-old hermit. I called Gina, always my good friend, out of the blue. I just wanted someone familiar in my life again. She asked if I wanted to come work with her. She had bought Greene's and was turning it from a dive bar to a ritzy restaurant and bar. She said she had been waiting for me to call so she could offer me a job.

"I'm not sure I'm ready, Gina," I said. I had gone into survival mode for the past year, and while I had never been a social butterfly before, now I was completely inept.

"Sweetheart, you listen to me. Life is rough. I know you know that. You've been through more than your fair share of horse manure," she said with her sassy Southern accent. She always reined in her language around me. "But you need to rejoin the living. You will never get over losing them, but you have got to stop losing them daily."

It was a slap in the face. She was right. Every day, I relived the death of my family, replaying the blood, the last breaths, and every day, my world shattered again. It was a horrible cycle, and I had been punishing myself for not being with them that day. I reimagined that day over and over again in different scenarios and each time, they still ended up leaving me. I needed to find something else to occupy my time. I agreed to come to work for her.

It was the best decision I had made in a year. It took some time, but I finally came back out of my shell. I laughed, as foreign as the sound was to me. I smiled, and it made my facial muscles sore. I was exhausted from physical exertion, not from sorrow. I began to sleep better, and I stopped crying every single day. I designed the menu for Greene's and oversaw the kitchen, cooking often but delegating much of it to the kitchen staff.

I also began to see a counselor. I know the old cliches, but my therapist was incredibly helpful and helped me over a lot of my survivor's guilt and my feelings of, well, everything.

❧

*I*t was about six months after I went back that I met one of the first responders who had come to the scene of Adam and Liam's accident. I didn't know it at first, but when someone asked to see me, I was met face to face with a ruggedly handsome man with dark cropped hair and warm brown eyes. He was wearing the T-shirt of a local fire department, and it showed off his biceps nicely. I almost blushed when I saw him. I was immediately angry at myself for feeling attracted to the man.

"Are you Roxanne Joyce?" he asked. I could see him swallow a lump in his throat.

"I am," I said, still unsure of who he was or why he would want anything to do with me. While the rumors about me had quieted, I was too accustomed to them, so I was automatically suspicious.

"My name is Will Worthy. I was a fireman called to the scene the day your husband and son were in the accident," he said with a hoarse voice, not meeting my eyes.

All the air in my lungs rushed out, and I felt like the world would go black. I grabbed hold of the chair next to his for support. He rushed to my side immediately and called out, "Can I get a glass of water for her?" He took my elbow and led me to sit.

Gina quickly arrived with water, "Roxie, what's wrong?" She glared at the man who was fanning me with a menu. "Who are you?"

I couldn't see him, but I heard him respond, "I'm sorry. I was there when her family was in the accident. I just, I just wanted to check on her and give her something. I don't mean any disrespect."

I took a long drink of the ice-cold water Gina handed

me. "I'm fine, Gina. Really. He just surprised me is all." I looked to the concerned man before me. "Please, sit down. Tell me everything."

He sat at the table directly behind him and motioned for me to join him. Gina backed away, but still hovered close by the table. Always my protector, I did love her so.

"I'm sorry to distress you, Mrs. Joyce," he said. His eyes were kind, and he offered me a half-smile before scooting his chair in.

"Call me Roxie. Mrs. Joyce is my mother-in-law," I said with a feeble smile. "What did you say your name was?"

"William Worthy," he said, clearing his throat. "But please, call me Will."

"Alright, Will. My son's name is William. Was William. We called him Liam. Please tell me everything," I repeated. "It's all such a blur for me, and I really never bothered to find out what had happened before I got there. I never wanted to know."

He gave his account of what had happened. What the cars looked like when he arrived, how they had to cut the car open to get Adam out. He told me how he had personally pulled Liam from the car and sang to him. He had smoothed his brow and told him everything would be okay soon. He said he had a daughter himself, and he treated Liam the way he would want his own child treated.

I cried. More than cried, I sobbed. But I heard every word he said. I think people around me were crying, too, I really wasn't sure. At some point, Will took my hand and held it as he told me everything. As he finished, he reached below the table and pulled a little stuffed rabbit from somewhere.

"This was at the scene. You had gone in the ambulance, and we were helping to clean up the road debris. This little guy was sitting outside your husband's car," he said. I could hear the lump in his throat. "I'm sorry it's taken so long to bring him home."

It was Liam's favorite bunny. He carried it everywhere with him. It was like touching Liam to feel the soft fuzz under my fingertips. I hadn't been able to find it after the accident and thought it had been destroyed. I took it from the man before me with trembling hands. I looked at the worn brown fuzz and floppy ears. I brought it close and inhaled it. Tears trickled down my cheek. It still smelled like him. After a year and a half, it still smelled like Liam.

That bunny still sits on my dresser, and I greet him every morning. It's a ritual and my way of saying good morning to my little boy every day.

I looked from the toy to its rescuer. "Thank you," I whispered. I closed my eyes and remembered my son. I remembered tucking that rabbit in with him in his bed the day he was born. I remembered him dancing with it in the kitchen as I made dinner. I remembered Adam and I kissing the toy goodnight before kissing Liam. My heart broke, but then something new happened.

I smiled. I opened my eyes and brought my hand to my lips to be sure I wasn't mistaken. No, sure enough, a smile graced my lips. I felt great joy in remembering my sweet family. Yes, the sadness and heartache was still there, but my memories were sweet, and that was what mattered.

"Thank you, Mr. Worthy, for bringing me this. It means more than I could ever express," I again rubbed my cheek on the soft fabric. "Please let me buy you dinner as thanks for helping my husband and son."

"No, ma'am, that's okay," he said, standing.

"I insist, please. It's the least I can do." I stood and wiped the stray tears from my cheeks. "Give me one minute to put this away, and I'll make you my special."

"Sure, Mrs. Joyce, that'll be fine." He took his seat again slowly and nodded.

"Roxie, please," I said, excited to do something in return for someone who had done so much to ease my own family.

I went into the kitchen and set to work. I decided to make him the best comfort food I knew of – tomato soup and a bacon grilled cheese on artisan bread with applewood smoked bacon and three kinds of cheese. Simple, yes, but I'd never met a Southern man who didn't love comfort food.

After he savored each bite of the food I had made him, Will approached me shyly. "Roxie, that was truly the best food I've ever had. My daughter loves to cook. She would love to learn how to make something simple."

"How old is she?"

"Just six. I know she's still little, but she's smarter than any other kid." He quickly whipped out a picture of a lovely little girl with dark hair, a smattering of freckles, and a missing tooth.

"Her mother doesn't cook?" I found myself asking. Was I really contemplating teaching this man's daughter how to cook?

"We're divorced. But her mom isn't much of a cook. More of a microwaver." He chuckled and shook his head.

I looked him in the eye. Something about this man made me trust him and want to help him. After all, he had been one of the last people to comfort my son. "I'd be happy to show her around a kitchen," I offered.

We exchanged phone numbers, and he said he would call me next time he had his daughter at his house.

❧

*W*e talked after that on the phone several times without actually meeting. Everything went considerably slow, which I liked. We spoke every few days, and I learned that Will wasn't just a volunteer firefighter, he was a professional one. He was close to his family, which included an older sister and a younger brother. His parents were still alive, and they all lived locally. They even had Sunday dinners together each week.

It was a clear June day when I got word that my father had passed away. I saw it on the news. Not even Lori had called to tell me. Of course, my father hadn't really been a part of my life for many years, but the sting of losing a parent doesn't disappear.

I watched the newscast from my couch. The anchor's words were cold and indifferent. He mentioned the passing of my mother more than fifteen years before, and that the former senator had daughters and grandchildren, but we were not named. There was no mention of the senator's grandson being killed in a crash, and for that I heaved a sigh of relief.

I had to call the funeral home to find out when the service was. Will offered to come to the funeral with me, but I declined and attended alone. I remembered my mother's funeral and didn't want a scene this time around. I kept to the back of the sanctuary and listened to the pastor's passive words. I could tell his heart was not in it, for he did not speak with passion. My father had simply been a warm body in the pew, not somebody who was actively involved in his church. When he dismissed everyone to go to the gravesite, I left without speaking to anybody. Even Lori. She had spotted me coming in and had motioned that she wanted to talk, but I slipped out before giving her the chance. I didn't want to hear how great her life was or how I had let grief be all-consuming. As if there was a time limit on grief.

If there is one thing I have learned in all of this, it's that there is no limit on grief. It doesn't matter if you are grieving a death or a divorce. Grief is still a cloak that will tempt you to the depths as long as you let it.

My steps down the church stairs sounded hollow on the warm brick. A few men with loose ties smoked right off the church premises. Two had cameras. They immediately perked up to see someone coming toward them.

"Hey, you're Roxanne, right?"

I resisted the urge to roll my eyes. I was having déjà vu from my run in with the paparazzi in high school. I did not respond to the question, even though I recognized the reporter as Franklin Mitchum from Channel Five Action News.

But Franklin Mitchum knew who I was. He motioned to his cameraman, who immediately began rolling. "Mrs. Joyce. Everyone wondered if you would come to your father's funeral after he cut you out of the family so long ago. Why are you here?"

The other camera man from a rival station also began filming me. I was flanked on both sides, so I stopped in my tracks.

I looked to the man with the microphone, his lit cigarette burning away on the concrete below us. "I'm here because Dennis DePrivé was my father. A man I may not have gotten along with very well, but still my father and I loved him. By the way, your cigarette is still burning right next to your pant leg, Mr. Mitchum. You might go up in flames."

The man jumped as I slipped between the two cameras,

walking as steadily as I could to my car. While the cameras turned toward me, others began to file out from the church, and the two cameras swung back to the church. I pulled my sunglasses over my eyes and watched as the newsmen called out to my sisters, who walked out together. A united front.

I had lived without them for a long time at that point.

As it happened, the day after the funeral was my birthday. I really tried to sweep it under the rug, but my regulars, Tom and Paul, along with Gina and the kitchen staff, pulled off a little surprise for me. The guys had gotten me a little cake from a local bakery, and Gina put up streamers. It was all awfully sweet.

"How old are you now, Roxie? You look the same as you did when you first walked through the doors here," my favorite customer, Tom, asked.

I thought back. I had just turned eighteen when Josh and I had gotten married and I had taken a job at the bar. Now it was a high-end place, but the regulars at the bar were the same. I had changed myself. From a bright eyed, fresh-faced youth to a woman more than a dozen years older and not much to show for it.

My mousy brown hair had been replaced with L'Oreal's Sun Kissed Caramel to cover the grays that were emerging, much to my dismay. My size four Spice Girls dresses had been ditched in favor of size ten low-rise jeans. I had filled out all over, but I still thought I was pear-shaped. Adam and Remi had disagreed, and Remi had pointed out that booties were a hot commodity these days. It was a good thing, because I had plenty.

I sighed and leaned on the bar. "I'm thirty-one today, Tom. How did that happen?"'

He kissed me on the cheek and patted my head the way a doting uncle would. "If I were twenty, heck, thirty years younger, I would snatch you up, Roxie," he said with a hearty grin.

I laughed. "And I would happily go with you, Tommy."

His smile faded for a moment, and his old eyes looked into mine. "One day, a new prince will come to you, sweetie. I believe it. And he will sweep you off your feet."

"That's sweet, Tom, but I don't think I'll ever be swept away again." I took a deep breath. Thirty-one years old and already an old woman.

A baritone voice behind me said, "Can I at least try?" I turned to find Will standing a few feet away with a small bunch of flowers clutched in his hand. They were daylilies, some of my favorites.

Tom nodded in approval. "Now, there's a feller who looks like he knows how to woo a lady."

Will gave me the flowers, and I thanked him. I put them into a small pitcher of water and set them on the bar.

I showed him to a table and sat with him for a moment. "What are you doing here?" He smelled of smoke and his fingernails were edged with soot and ash from a day of fighting fires, but I still felt my belly flip-flopping. It hadn't done that in years. I wasn't sure I recognized the sensation.

"Well, I was thinking I could sweep you off your feet, but it seems you're not receptive to that," he said with a wink. "I wanted to see you again."

"Did you just get off work?"

He nodded. He looked tired and I could only imagine how hard it must be to work a twenty-four hour shift.

"How about some supper? I have the perfect thing for you."

I went back to the kitchen to whip up a plate of my modified fish and chips. The fish was bite-sized nuggets, and I hand-cut sweet potato fries. It had been a tremendous hit with the diners. I sent it out to him via Gina who was dying to get a second look at him.

When she came back, she winked and cackled at me. "He's handsome, Roxie. I can't believe you've been talking all this time but haven't seen him in months."

"I know," I told her in a hushed tone, even though Will could not hear me.

Crinkling her nose, Gina pushed, "Tell me all about him!" She leaned into the counter and batted her eyelashes playfully at me.

I thought for a moment. "Well, his name is William, just like my Liam. He's thirty-three. Divorced with one daughter." I looked through the window in the kitchen door toward him. He was happily eating. I gave a little sigh.

"You've got it bad, Roxie," she teased. "And I'm so glad to see that. You deserve it. You really do. Everyone needs a second chance."

I looked at her and smiled through pain. "How many second chances can one person get? I've been married four times, Gina. I can't be heartbroken again." With that, I wiped away a stray tear and walked away.

I liked Will. He was easy-going, fun to talk to, and didn't treat me like tainted meat the way so many others did. But I meant what I said about not wanting to be heartbroken again. Four marriages behind me, and I was barely into my thirties. Surely, that was some sort of record. I laughed at myself – maybe I should call the people at Guinness World Records. I tried to clear my head and think positively. Even if I wasn't looking for romance, I was always looking for a friendly face. And I was happy to have found one in Will Worthy.

I smiled at Will as I picked up his empty plate. "Was everything okay?"

He patted his flat, firm stomach and said, "I'm stuffed. That was delicious. Was that catfish?" He ran a hand over his dark buzzed hair, and I watched his muscles flex. I suddenly felt like a woman again, noticing a man's muscular arms.

I blushed a little. I couldn't believe I was blushing. "It was catfish. I'm glad you liked it. Cooking is the only thing I find solace in these days."

"Shame you have to work on your birthday," he said, drinking from his glass of sweet tea.

"I don't even think about it," I said. Then I eyed him. "How did you know today is my birthday anyhow?" I had not told him.

"I didn't, actually," he laughed. "Call it dumb luck. I thought I would come and ask you on a proper date and low and behold there's a crew of men around you with a cake."

I tucked my hair behind my ear and smiled. "Oh."

I wasn't sure I was ready for a proper date. Hadn't I just thought I didn't want anything romantic? Then why did my stomach flip when I talked to him? Why were my palms sweaty the moment I saw him with the flowers? And why did I desperately want him to actually ask me out? I wrapped my arms around my mid-section.

So I waited. He had said he wanted to ask me out, but so far no asking had happened. When he didn't say anything, I cleared my throat and asked, "Was there anything else you needed, Will?"

I guessed Will was a little absent-minded. He still did not ask for a date. "I guess, just the check."

Shaking my head, I told him it was my treat. When he insisted, I gently said, "You can get the tab the next time."

His eyes widened, and he finally caught on. "Oh, yes! How about Sunday? Can I pick you up early, around five? I have Sadie this weekend, and I drop her off with her mom at four."

I nodded, "Sure. That sounds lovely. Can I see another picture of Sadie, by chance?" He loved to talk about his little girl, and I felt like I knew her already.

Ever the proud father, he pulled several pictures from his wallet. "This is Sadie when she was a baby. And here's Sadie at about three. This is her first school picture from last year. She was so proud. And now here, this is the most recent from her dance recital." He pointed out each one.

Sadie was an adorable little girl with long hair the same color as her father's. She had a smattering of freckles that reminded me of Liam. He would be a few years younger than Sadie, his fourth birthday still a few months away. I felt the flood of emotions hit me. I would miss all this. I would miss school pictures and sports teams and baseball games.

I suddenly felt my heart pounding and like I couldn't breathe. I struggled to get air into my lungs and spots flashed in front of my eyes. The room began to close in on me, and I searched wildly for Will's face. Then I looked for Gina, my constant friend. I couldn't find anything.

I heard someone call out from next to me, "Are you okay, Roxie?" I felt hands on me, guiding me down into a booth seat. Someone fanned me and spoke in a soothing voice. Will's fingers pressed against my neck, checking my pulse. He was talking to me, but I didn't know what he said.

I hadn't realized my ears were ringing until they stopped, and I could hear again. Gina was hovering across the table with a glass of water. "Here, Roxie, drink this, sweetie." She held the glass up to my lips, and I took several swallows. She patted my forehead with a damp cloth. "There now, it's okay. I think you'll be all right."

I sat up slowly. I could feel my heart slow from racing to

just jogging. I took a few deep breaths. "Am I okay? That was a terrible feeling," I said, still feeling flushed. It reminded me of the time I had panicked when Adam had come up behind me.

Will spoke from outside the booth. "I'd say it was a panic attack. I've seen them before." He looked at Gina and said, "Keep her put. I have a medic kit in my truck."

"I'm so embarrassed," I said, sitting up further. My hands were shaking, and I couldn't hold still.

"Take it easy," Gina demanded. I could hear the concern in her voice. "What happened?"

Shaking my head, I considered what had led to my feeling so overwhelmed. What had happened? Will had asked me out. I had felt like a schoolgirl accepting. That wasn't it. He showed me pictures of his daughter. I had realized what I was missing with Liam gone. That had been it.

With tears in my eyes, I told Gina. I panicked because I missed my baby. I not only missed him, but I missed out on him. On raising him. "Please," I sobbed. "Please tell Will that I'm fine and to just go." I made my way to the ladies room where I splashed my face with water.

I listened at the door to hear what Gina would say, but I could only hear every few words. "I'm sorry ... misses her baby ... take care of her...don't worry." Will spoke, but I couldn't distinguish what he said.

Gina spoke again. This time I heard every word she said. "Next month marks two years since her husband and son died in that horrible crash. It was terrible. She's still heartbroken." She was quiet a moment, then said in response to someone, "She deserves happiness and a chance at life. She's still young enough to start again."

Start again? I had been feeling like a youthful girl just a few minutes before. Now I felt like an old woman. My entire body ached. I mentally went through the foods I had already prepared for the restaurant. There was plenty. When I was sure Will had left, I came out and told Gina I was going home. Tom offered to drive me, but I declined. I told him I was fine, just tired.

A note from Will sat under my windshield wiper.

I'm sorry if I distressed you in any way. I'll understand if you don't want to see me again, but I hope you do. I can't help but feel that maybe you are my second chance. And maybe I can help you heal. Please call me.

— *WILL*

I stayed stoic until I got home, where I curled up on Adam's side of the bed with Liam's favorite toy bunny and wept until I fell asleep.

I returned to work the next day, apologetic and appreciative to my friends. Everybody was concerned for me, but I told them working would keep me sane. I felt better after a night of self-pity and crying. I had sent Will a long text that morning, explaining that I did want to see him, and that I was so embarrassingly sorry for the commotion I had caused the night before.

He had texted back right away.

Will: Don't worry about it. I'm sorry if I made you upset. I hope I can right my wrong.

Roxie: You were not in the wrong, Will. I just realized all I have missed out on with my son. Please enjoy your weekend with your daughter. Hug her extra tight.

Will: I always do. I will pick you up Sunday. Send me your address, please. I plan to take you out for a night of fun.

I thought of him while I readied the kitchen for the day's work. With a deep breath I nodded to myself. Yes, I was ready for a night of fun.

The weekend went quickly for me, and I had thrown myself into work. And when I wasn't at work, I was busy scrubbing parts of my house that were already clean. It was what I did to relieve stress, and the idea of a real date with someone who wasn't an immoral gambler or a man in love with someone else had me tense.

When Sunday came around, I lounged in bed longer than usual. I wanted to take the day to pamper myself. I finally got out of bed after watching a morning movie on cable. I took a long shower, then plucked my eyebrows and painted my nails. I curled my hair and experimented with a few styles before deciding on just wearing it down. I searched through my closet and then searched again. Finally, I pulled out a purple paisley maxi dress and a black cardigan. I felt it was casual, but not too casual. I glanced at the clock. It was three o'clock in the afternoon. I still had two hours before Will came.

I wished I had girlfriends or a mother to call to talk about all this with. Gina and I had already dished, and she was enjoying a day with her own family. She had given me the lowdown on dating, as she was a serial dater – never a committer. I sort of thought that might have been my fault. I married every man I ever dated.

My sisters came to mind. I would have loved to talk to them. Lori and I hadn't spoken in a long time, and she was busy with her own life. There was nobody else for me to confide in. I brewed another pot of coffee and ate a BLT sandwich to tide myself over until dinner.

I wandered over to my picture wall and gingerly touched the large portrait of Liam. A deep sigh escaped my lips. He would be my baby forever. Did he remember that Will was the one who pulled him free of the car and saved his bunny? I hesitantly went over to my favorite photo of Adam and myself. We were laughing at a party, arms tangled up around one another, not a care in the world. We looked so happy. I took a steadying breath, telling myself not to cry, but a rogue tear escaped and trickled down my cheek.

"I hope you don't mind this, Adam," I said out loud. I put my finger to his face. "It's been almost two years. I'm still young. I don't want to be alone for the next fifty years if I live that long. I want to be with you, but you and Liam ...

"Will is an incredible, sweet guy. He pulled Liam out of the car that day. So he has seen my grief first hand. He has a daughter. Even if this is a one time thing, or something more, I adore you, sweetie. You are my true love."

A moment later the phone rang. I took a steadying breath as I picked my phone up from the kitchen counter. It was Linda. How had she known I needed a mother right then?

"Hello, Linda." I tried to suppress a sniffle, but failed. "How are you?"

She sighed. "I'm well. How are you, Roxie?"

A small smile came to my lips. "I'm not too bad. I was just looking at pictures and taking a trip down memory lane."

"I hope they're good memories, Roxie," she commented.

"Always. There's not a bad memory to be had." I sat at a barstool and tried not to pick at my newly polished fingers.

"How are things going at work?"

"Very well. It's been wonderful working again and being around people who care about me," I told her. "Is anything new with you?"

"I heard something funny I thought you might like to know." She giggled a little. "Word on the street is that Josh Keene will be playing with Jay Leno's band for a week starting tonight while someone else is on vacation. I thought you might like to sneak a peek at him."

I gasped. "Really? I'll have to set my DVR to record it! I haven't seen or heard anything about him in a long time." I wondered what he looked like now. Had he aged?

"I won't keep you, darling, but I wanted to let you know." Linda's voice was sincere and full of love.

"Linda? Can I tell you something?" I licked my lips. Would she be upset that I had a date? I wasn't sure, but I really wanted my mother in that moment.

"Of course, sweethea—"

"I—I have a date tonight. I was telling Adam and Liam all about it when you called. His name is Will Worthy, and he's one of the firefighters who responded to the wreck." Tears fell silently down my cheek. I didn't know what Linda would say, but I felt like I needed to tell her.

She was silent for a few moments, but I could hear her breathing. "I think that's lovely, Roxie. You deserve to find someone to make you happy."

I could only whisper. "Really?"

"Really." Then she added, "Tell me all about it tomorrow, okay?"

I smiled. "Thank you, Linda."

We hung up, and I took a few minutes to slow my breathing.

Chapter Eighteen

FLASHOVER

inally, five o'clock came, and Will Worthy was prompt. He rang the doorbell, and I made myself count to five and take one last look in the mirror before opening the door. He handed me flowers and took off his cowboy hat as he came through the door. I invited him in so I could put the flowers in water.

"It's been a long time since anyone has been in the habit of bringing me flowers," I said as I led him to the kitchen.

"That's a shame," was the only reply. I glanced back and saw Will taking the house in. I always forgot how impressive it was, and I recalled the first time I had walked through the doors in amazement. "How big is this house?"

I smiled. "It has six bedrooms, a gourmet kitchen, and we have a playroom downstairs that was a media room, then an actual playroom. Living room, dining room ... It's just a house." I filled a vase with water.

"You have six bedrooms?" Will put his hands on the kitchen counter and continued to look around. "Can I ask why?"

I didn't feel like my house was that opulent. I spent a

majority of my adult life in that house, so the size didn't occur to me too often. "It came that way. It was Adam's house, and then it was our house. And now it's my house. I know it's too much for me, but I've never been able to part with it." I looked up at him and smiled. "Shall we?"

We got into his pickup truck, and he pulled out of the driveway. I was a little nervous, to be honest. I had no idea where we were going, but I wasn't going to worry about it.

"I'm a little scared to take a professional chef out to a restaurant," Will said after a minute. "What if their food isn't up to snuff?"

"Don't worry. I like everything. I still love to go to IHOP every now and again just as much as I like fancier restaurants. And little hole-in-the-wall dives have some of the best, freshest food you can find," I tried to reassure him. Secretly, though, I hoped we were not heading to IHOP.

With a chuckle, I added, "Um, just don't take me to Denny's."

Thankfully, Will took me to a nice little place downtown called The Tiger's Den. It was cozy and dark and offered a wide variety of some of the best made from scratch comfort food you could ever want. As it turned out, the place was owned by my old culinary school friend and roommate, Tarek. It was a treat to see him again and introduce Will to someone from my past. And, of course, we got the choicest of fare.

After dinner, Will took me back to the firehouse where he worked. He showed me around and offered to let me slide down the pole. I politely declined, given that I was wearing a dress. A few of the men were sitting in the living area playing games, and Will happily introduced me. Then Will took me by the hand and led me to the kitchen.

"I thought we could just have some coffee, or a root beer,

and chat," he said. "Actually, not only do I have root beer, but I have ice cream if you would like a root beer float."

I giggled, pleased that he remembered my favorite drink. "I would love one." He made them up and took me into another small room with a television and some worn chairs.

"Please have a seat. Nobody will bother us here," he said with a genuine smile.

The television was on, but as Will went to turn it off, I stopped him. "Turn on Leno!"

"Leno? Why?" His eyebrows knit together.

Sure enough, the Tonight Show was starting, and there was the band. I got close to the TV and watched it for a second. It was then that I spotted the tell-tale blond locks falling over blue eyes. Josh.

It was only a split second, but he was playing the guitar on the Tonight Show. I couldn't help myself, I burst into laughter.

"What's so funny?" Will was truly perplexed now. He kept looking from me to the screen and back again.

"Oh, um, I'm sorry. That was someone I went to high school with. I heard he would be on the show tonight, and I wanted to see. It's been several years, but that was definitely him," I said with a shake of my head.

Well, I'll be – Josh Keene finally made it on television. I hoped he was happy and enjoying life. I didn't hold a grudge against him. After all, he had introduced me to Adam.

I looked to Will and felt slightly embarrassed. "I'm so sorry. I'm all yours now."

"Would you like a seat?" Will flipped the television off.

I chose a chair and sat, sipping my float through a straw. "What made you bring me here?"

"I may not live here, but it feels like home to me. And I didn't want to take you back to my house and make you feel unduly pressured about anything," he said with a shrug. "I thought we could just hang out tonight. I thought about taking you to a movie, but you can't talk in a movie. And I can't see your beautiful smile in the dark theater."

I blushed a little, uneasy with the compliment. Will brought another chair next to mine. I wanted to take the attention away from me, so I asked about his work. And the conversation journeyed from there. At times, we were in serious discussion, other times we were rolling with laughter. It was comfortable and natural. Will talked about work, about his divorce, and Sadie. I had already told him my history but told him more about Liam, and I apologized for the panic attack a few nights before.

"Hey, don't worry about that, Roxie." Concern shone in his eyes, and he laid his hands over mine. "If I lost Sadie, I would be a basket case. I can't imagine how you have felt these past few years. You've certainly gotten a few rotten tomatoes your way, but maybe ..." He licked his lips. "Maybe I could be a not rotten one?"

I chuckled at his analogy and nodded. "I would like that, Will."

He cautiously leaned in and brushed his lips to mine. A hunger I had not felt in a long time seemed to have awakened with that kiss. I leaned closer to him, urging him on. We broke away only because the fire alarm suddenly went off.

Will laughed. I was filled with worry about someone's house being on fire. "It's okay," Will assured me. "We're professionals. This is what we're here to do. It's late. I better get you home anyway."

He took me home and walked me to the door. "Thank you for a nice evening, Will. I really enjoyed it." I could feel myself grinning like an idiot, but I didn't care. I hoped he would kiss me again.

He did.

✿

*F*our months later, and I was completely smitten. Will and I spent every moment we could together. And finally, he introduced me to Sadie. I felt like I already knew her. We went to lunch, the three of us, and we all had root beer floats. Sadie asked if I was dating her daddy, and we said yes. She accepted it pretty easily, but I think Will had given her a heads up. After lunch, I let them go about their weekend fun. I didn't want to impede on her time with her father.

I felt like I fell in love with Will Worthy – and his daughter – at lunch that day.

It took six more months, which I was fine with, before Will proposed to me. It was a chilly April Sunday. I had gone to church with his family and Sadie, as I had been doing for a few months. At lunch, he got down on one knee and cried as he asked me to be his bride. I happily accepted. He gave me a small diamond ring, and I wore it proudly. Sadie leaped into both of our arms, thrilled to add me as a parent.

What a balm to my soul Sadie was at that time. While I will always bear a hole from Liam's passing, Sadie filled a new part of my heart.

Finally, I bit the bullet and called Lori. I hoped she would be happy for me. When I got her voicemail, I left a cheerful message for her.

"Lori, it's me, Roxie. I miss you a lot. And the kids," I said, willing my smile to reach through the phone. "I just wanted to let you know I've met someone. He's amazing.

He's a firefighter, and he has an adorable little girl. His name is Will, and he's proposed. I just – I really hope this is another chance for me at the real thing. We're planning a beach-side wedding in August. I hope you can come. Call me any time. I love you. Bye."

Lori never called me back. I tried emailing her, but it bounced back. I had joined Facebook finally and looked her up. She was happy and active. But my sister had shut me out. I couldn't blame her, though. I had shut her out first. I tried to shake it off. I had a new family now.

When the heat of summer arrived, I was ready for our big day. We planned an intimate and cheerful wedding for Hilton Head, where Will's family had a cottage. We would be married in the yard with just close friends and family. I invited Adam's mother, but she had declined. She did, however, give me her blessing and wished me all the best. Gina managed to leave Greene's for a day to come and serve as my bridesmaid. Will's brother, Tony, was his best man. Sadie, of course, was the flower girl.

Before the ceremony, I looked at the picture of Adam and Liam I carried in my wallet. "I haven't forgotten you, I promise," I said in a whisper. "But I think I can finally be happy again. I don't know how many chances I get, but I think this one is a keeper. Adam, you and Will would be great friends, I know." I choked back tears and tucked the picture away before heading down the aisle to my groom.

When I emerged from the house, I saw our guests smiling, and Will was front and center, grinning from ear to ear. He wore a light gray suit with a blue shirt underneath. It went well with my beachy look of a calf-length flowy a-line dress in a lush champagne color. I looked to Sadie, who was the picture of perfection in a beautiful sky-blue dress that matched Will's shirt. She waved to me. I gave her a little wave back.

The ceremony was brief, but meaningful. Once again, I promised 'till death do us part,' and the severity of that promise brought tears to my eyes. We included a small part of the ceremony for Sadie where we promised to love her and always be a family. I gave her a locket necklace as a wedding gift and told her she would always be special to me.

After the 'I Dos' and a passionate kiss, we celebrated with a seafood feast. I watched as Will danced with Sadie and Will's father, Bill, asked me to dance with him. He was a sweet older man who was still spry and light on his feet.

As he twirled me around the yard, he told me he was glad to have me join the family. "It's been a long time since Will was happy. He needs to be happy. And my Sadie-Bug, well, her mother's not the best person, so I hope you can be a good influence on her. I'm glad to have you join our family, Roxie."

Bill must not have known my history, because I could not believe anyone would think of me as a good influence. I was sure my father would have contradicted Bill if he had been alive and present.

It took me a moment to gain my composure before I could speak. "Thank you so much. I've certainly been nervous about becoming a stepmother. But I do adore Sadie. And Will." I looked over to him. "Will is just the most amazing man I've met in a long time."

When the song ended, Mr. Worthy wandered off for a drink, and Will's mother, Susan, approached me from across the yard. She bypassed a few well-wishers and beelined for me. Her frosted brown hair was cut short and spiked out around her head. It gave her a certain ... edge.

"This is a lovely wedding, Roxanne," she said, her voice a little dry. "I was hesitant when I first met you, because I had heard about you around town. I'm so glad to see that they were wrong about you. I don't know that I trust you, but Will and Sadie are happy, and that's the most important thing."

Reaching out, she took hold of my necklace – a cross Adam had given me – and straightened the chain so the clasp was in the back. Her move was bold, and I recognized it as her asserting herself as a superior to me. I understood, she needed to protect her family. While it saddened me that she did not trust me still, I could see where she was coming from.

I nodded in agreement with her. I had been a bad judge of character before. "You're right. I do have a not-so-pretty past. Mistakes have been made, but I haven't hidden anything. Will knows my entire story. I know how much you love Will and Sadie, and I can assure you, I love them as well. I didn't think I would ever love someone again after my family died, but my heart is overflowing with love for your son and granddaughter."

I watched as she sized me up. "I think you will be good for my Will and Sadie. I hate that I heard those rumors at all, but when it affects your family, you tend to perk your ears, you know?"

I nodded, unsure what rumors she had heard, but certain many were lies.

"I'm not well-liked in Columbia, and I know that. But gossip is just that – rumors that are not true. I have never taken anyone's husband away from them. I have never been involved with the sex industry. My first husband left me, eighteen-years-old and penniless. Then my dear friend was going to be deported – we were married in name only. My next husband was an abusive gambler I was lucky to get away from. It was Adam who was my true love, and if he were still alive ... Well, I'm just happy for another chance to get it right. And Will is the most amazing man I've met since Adam."

With a nod, Susan said, "Well, I hadn't heard everything quite like that. I'm glad you told me. I think I would like more details one day." She nodded again and walked off, looking confused.

As the night wore on, many guests made their way back to their hotels and quick weekend vacations. Sadie would be staying the night at the house with Will's family. He and I rode off in his pickup to a private honeymoon suite that was waiting at a nearby resort.

Chapter Nineteen

LIFE ABLAZE

I think Will and I were a typical married couple. He worked twenty-four hours then had forty-eight hours off, so it made for an interesting time of adjusting our schedules together. It felt odd moving out of the house I had shared with Adam, but I thought it was time. I debated putting my house on the market but figured I didn't need to make any impromptu decisions. Momma had always said to sleep on big decisions. So I decided to rent it out for the time being.

Sadie stayed with us almost every weekend, which made my heart sing with joy. It seemed Valerie was all too happy to have someone look after Sadie so she could go off with a boyfriend for the weekend. Will mumbled each time under his breath that Valerie could be doing better in the man department. I didn't think I detected any jealousy there, just a concerned father.

I taught Sadie how to cook, even though she had just turned eight. She was a quick study and was soon making us pancakes and scrambled eggs for breakfast under my supervision. She said she tried to show her mother that she could make a few things, but her mother had just handed her a doughnut and told her to scurry away. I tried not to judge the woman, but it was hard to think of Sadie not getting quality food and nutrition.

The hardest part of my new family was watching Will leave for work. It wasn't until we were married and living together that what he did for a living really hit me. He fought fires. And thankfully, he always won, but I worried that one day the fire would win. Most days he came home fairly clean, but on occasion, he came home covered in soot and reeking of smoke.

"Roxie, I've been doing this for a dozen years now," he told me in an effort to comfort me. "I know all the equipment. I know all the procedures. And we always know that life is more important than stuff. Say it with me, life is more important than stuff."

"Life is more important than stuff," I repeated. I repeated it like a mantra.

"If there's a serious risk to our safety, we let it burn," he said as he smoothed out my hair. "About a year before I met you, I went into a house looking for a young lady, just a kid, but she was pregnant. Her mother was outside already, and she was just screaming for her daughter. I ran in and found her. But as I brought her out, she kept asking for things. New things for her baby. I had to tell her no over and over. Why? Because all that stuff would have been useless if something had happened to her and her baby. Not to mention my arms were full of a pregnant girl. I didn't have room for clothes and toys. Life is more important than stuff."

In my head, I knew he was right. "I will do my best. It's hard to love someone who put themselves in harm's way day in and day out."

He ran his hand over his head. "Yeah, Val used to say

that, too. In the end, she couldn't handle the stress of me going to work. So she chose to leave. But I promise you, I will do everything in my power to come home to you and Sadie. Don't worry."

I hugged Will close. "I'll try not to. I just love you so much." I tried to ignore the faint smell of smoke and ash on his clothes. It was always on him, a constant reminder.

"I love you too, Roxie."

✿

One weekend when Valerie dropped Sadie off, she lingered on the doorstep after Sadie had disappeared inside. I could tell something was up.

"Did you need to come in and talk?" I didn't want to be rude to her. She was Sadie's mom after all. I needed to be peaceful.

A heavy sigh escaped her lips. "I guess Will is at work again?"

"Yes, but he gets off at seven. We'll have a late dinner. And he's off the next two days, so Sadie will see him all weekend." I tried to reassure her that Will would be with their daughter.

"Okay, that's good to know. I don't want to just, you know, dump her on you all weekend. I couldn't stand it when Will was at work. It would work my nerves." She picked at a loose thread and didn't meet my gaze.

"Will said you didn't like him being a firefighter."

She snorted. "Who would? The last thing you want is a call from Pete, saying something happened to the man you love more than your whole life. I couldn't take it, even got an ulcer."

Perhaps Valerie wasn't thinking about who she was

talking to, even though I knew she knew my history. I knew the feeling of having the man you loved more than life itself die in front of you. But all I could do was nod.

"Well, just please have Will call me tonight, okay? After Sadie is in bed is fine," Valerie requested.

"Yes, of course. I'll let him know." I moved inside the doorway.

"Fine, thanks." She turned, but then turned back and yelled inside, "Bye, sweetie!"

From inside, a content little voice called out, "Bye, Momma."

That night, Will called Valerie as he had been asked. I tried not to overhear as I read a book on our couch. Will paced back and forth on our back porch, and I could hear him argue with Valerie.

"You know I try to make sure I'm off when Sadie is here." He paused. "Roxie is a wonderful stepmother, she lives for that girl. Not like you and your parade of boyfriends."

This time the silence was longer before Will shouted, "Well, I didn't have to choose between you and my career. You made that choice for me. I will always put Sadie first. I'll see you Sunday when you pick her up."

He released a guttural yell of frustration and kicked our wooden privacy fence, making me jump inside the house. Never was I more glad I did not share children with Josh or Ray.

When you marry someone with exes, you don't realize the baggage that will come with that until much later in the relationship. While I had thought of Valerie as Will's ex-wife, I did not realize that she was essentially a third person in our marriage. I wondered if pieces of my former husbands followed us around as well.

❧

*W*ill's firehouse family became our family. His captain, Pete Henry, was a huge teddy bear of a man, and his wife, Beth, was the stuff grandmother dreams were made of. She was sassy and classy at the same time. I got to know Derek and George and their wives, Lisa and Kim. They were sweet, amazing people with patience and love to spread around.

Every year, the station held a barbecue contest. It seems a little cliche, but it was always highly anticipated. Will had an amazing barbecue recipe that was like nothing I had ever had before. But I was a chef, so I thought I could outdo him. Instead of there being one Worthy recipe, that year we had two.

Will's pork was always a little wetter than how I made it, and his sauce was mustard based. I made mine tomato based. I liked a wide smoke ring on mine, where Will's didn't have that thick layer of bark. We would see which of us would come out on top.

Captain Henry had called in a few judges for the contest. One was a professional barbecue chef with national titles under his belt, two were fellow station captains from other areas, and the final two were food science majors from Clemson University. I didn't even know you could major in food science.

Not only was the station championship on the line, but Will and I were playfully vying for the top spot in our household. We had developed a bit of a competitive streak between us. We would run together and see who could make it to a certain point the fastest, or on family game nights, we were constantly trying to beat the other's score.

"I've got this in the bag, Worthy," I teased.

"You only think you do, Rox," he shot back.

We stood face to face, staring each other down. It was almost comical, like one of those old western movies.

"Y'all are a little too into this," some said to us.

"No such thing with a barbecue title on the line," I said with a comical sneer on my lip.

Will stepped closer to me. I stepped closer as well. Soon we were nose to nose. In a flash, Will lunged at me and swooped me up in his strong arms. He kissed me as I laughed hysterically.

There were twelve entries in all, but I wasn't nervous. I knew I had my career behind me and my reputation on the line – well, my culinary reputation at least. My social one was still in shambles despite how much time had passed or how many people got to know me.

When it came time for judging, the barbecue master, who called himself Boss Hogg, oohed and aahed over each and every entry. He wafted the aromas up to his nose. He inspected the look and feel of each plate. I'm pretty sure he even attempted to listen to each entry as well. Then he tasted, eyes closed, nostrils flared. He savored the dripping, fragrant morsels before jotting his notes on his clipboard.

The other judges were not as fanciful in their taste testing. They gave each plate a sniff, then ate a few bites. All of them nodded with approval and wrote down their scoring.

Once the judges were done, the event became a barbecue feast, feeding all the families of the men and women who worked at the station. Cornbread, potato salad, and macaroni and cheese magically appeared, and everyone joined in on a grand picnic.

Will and I sat under a shady tree on a picnic blanket by ourselves. After inhaling his plate of food, Will laid down, his head resting in my lap. He looked a little forlorn as I ran my fingernails through his short hair. He always kept it cropped close to his head, and it almost felt like velvet when I ran my hands over it.

"You okay, sweetie?"

He looked up at me and smiled. "Yeah, I just wish Sadie was here with us," he admitted.

"I know. Me, too," I agreed with a sigh. Nothing was the same without Sadie. That child lit up our world in amazing ways.

The pangs of heartache crept up my body. I was missing Liam as well. He would be starting school, maybe playing t-ball or taking swim lessons. I imagined he would love to go fishing. As the panic rose in me, I fought to control my breathing. The years had not afforded me relief from the panic attacks, but they had granted me the wisdom to know how to handle them. I closed my eyes, recalling the words of my counselor. I thought of ten things I could see when I reopened them and took ten deep breaths. When my eyes opened, the attack was gone, but the hole in my heart would never disappear.

I leaned over and kissed Will, wrapping my arms around his torso. He put his muscular arms around me, and I felt safe and happy. I sighed with contentment. He was always the number one thing that got me through the panic attacks.

"Are you okay?" he asked me, concern in his voice.

I took a final steadying breath. "I am. I'm happy. I have you. I have Sadie." I smiled as I pulled back and looked at him. "And in a few minutes, I'll have a barbecue championship to celebrate as well."

A voice called out to us, "Hey, Worthy, results are in."

We rose and joined the rest of the crowd to see whose barbecue reigned supreme. All twelve plates were lined up. I was entry number three. Will was entry number ten. Seven

of the plates had honorable mention ribbons next to them –
but both of ours were still empty of a ribbon, meaning we
had placed in the top five.

Will was behind me, his arms on my shoulders. "I won,"
Will whispered to me as he hugged me from behind.

"You won second place, you mean," I retorted. He kissed
me on the cheek.

Boss Hogg cleared his throat. "This was some of the
finest 'cue I've ever had the pleasure of tastin'. I don't take
judging lightly, and I think my fellow judges feel the same.
Looking at the scoresheets, I can tell you this was a tight
race all around. But here are the top five entries. If I call
your name, please come up front. Will Worthy, Pete Henry,
Carla Jones, Eric Calvin, Roxie Worthy."

Will and I joined the others at the front of the crowd. I
held my husband's hand and squeezed it lightly. He
squeezed back. "I love you," he whispered. I whispered it
back to him.

"Now, in fifth place we have Carla Jones. Fourth is Pete
Henry," came the announcement. They both approached
one of the other judges and got their ribbons.

"In third place, we have Roxie Worthy," Boss Hogg said.
"That was some amazing 'cue, darlin'."

Defeated, I went up to accept my yellow ribbon. Will
whistled and hooted in support. Or maybe it was because he
was still in the running for first.

"Now, gents, we have our top two. Second place goes to
… Will Worthy. Which means that Eric Calvin is our winner.
Congrats, guys."

Will went up for his red ribbon and took a bow. Eric
followed, a sheepish grin on his face. A rousing round of
applause caused him to turn beet red as he accepted his
blue ribbon.

When Will returned to my side, I hugged him tight. "I am so proud of you. You should have won."

He smiled and his dimples made my heart melt. His dark eyes peered into mine. "Nah, you should have won."

I shrugged and winked at him. "Well, I did throw the competition so you would do better than me. We couldn't have your little woman upstage you, right?"

"You little siren. You know I beat you fair and square," he cried out, capturing me in his arms and rubbing his five o'clock shadow across my cheek.

That's how it was with Will. We had fun, and we were affectionate. And when Sadie was with us, she joined in on the playfulness, too. I was part of a family again and it was heavenly.

§➔

*A*s we rolled into fall and the holidays were approaching, Will and Valerie got into a heated argument about where Sadie would spend Thanksgiving. We were hoping to take her with us to Hilton Head for a relaxing holiday, but Valerie wanted Sadie to go with her to Atlanta. They had been invited by Valerie's new boyfriend to meet his family.

I listened to Will's side of the argument on the phone, nodding with everything he said. Valerie had brought a different boyfriend to each of Sadie's birthdays or school plays. The string of men really bothered Will. He got angry with each new one and muttered expletives over the choices Valerie made.

"Sadie will go to Atlanta over my dead body," Will mumbled as he threw a T-shirt into his suitcase. "I've met this guy, and I wouldn't be surprised if he was smacking Val around. I won't have Sadie around that."

I stilled. While Valerie certainly wasn't my favorite person, I would never wish abuse on anybody. I was forever thankful there were no children to witness what Ray had done to me. I fought to swallow, remembering the hands around my throat. I sat on the bed next to my half-full suitcase.

With tears in my eyes, I looked to Will. "Go over there and talk to her. You won't accomplish much like this. Have a face to face with Val. Sadie's at her friend's birthday party, so you can talk without her overhearing you."

Will stood in front of me and kissed my hair. "Maybe you're right. I just do not like the idea of Sadie being around that guy Val's with. Lloyd. Even his name is bad."

"Hey, be the bigger guy here. Go talk to her now. You know she's home." I wanted this mess over just as much as Will did. And I needed to know if I should pack a bag for Sadie.

"You don't mind?"

I shook my head.

He ran his hand over his hair before letting it come to rest on his hip. "Okay. It might be a while. I have a few things to get off my chest."

Nodding, I agreed. "You do. Go on. I have a new book I want to start reading anyway."

With a sigh, he ran his hand over the scruff on his chin. "Okay. I'll head over there. Be back as quickly as I can."

He kissed me again and left. I heard him grab his keys and the front door open and close. As I listened to his truck barrel away, I said a quick prayer that Valerie would be willing to listen to reason.

My suitcase was easy to pack, so I went to Will's and

folded his crumpled shirt. Then I moved to Sadie's room and went ahead and pulled a few outfits out for her, in hopes that she could join us for the holiday. I was glad Will was off work, since the year before he had worked and put out three turkey fires on his shift.

I settled onto the couch with a novel Gina had let me borrow. It was about a woman who falls back in time in Scotland. The book was huge and would probably take me a year to read, but Gina had promised I would love it.

After an hour of reading, I felt peckish and carried the book to the kitchen where I continued to read and make myself a BLT. It was a perfect and easy dinner. I wondered if Will was still at Valerie's. Would they stop their argument and eat?

I had never needed to see an ex after the marriage ended, let alone needed to sit down with them. How awkward that must be for them both. Having to sit with someone you used to love but now didn't. I was thankful none of my first three marriages had any children to have to consider. While I felt like Josh would have been pretty agreeable to deal with, I did not want to ever see or speak with Ray again. Of course, with Remi there would have been no need to worry.

I texted Will quickly to let him know I was in his corner. I sat back down and pulled a blanket over me and continued to read.

My eyes opened some time later, and I felt a little disoriented. I had drifted off while reading, the book sitting open in my lap. I yawned and let my eyes adjust to the clock. It was after midnight. I listened for a telltale sign that Will was home. Nothing.

"Will?" Again, nothing. I stood, wrapping the blanket around me. "Will? Are you home?" I shuffled into the kitchen and peered out the window. His truck was still gone.

I pulled out my Blackberry and dialed his number. Straight to his voicemail. "Will, it's after midnight. Where did you go after you left Val's?"

I wandered around the house a minute before deciding he had probably stopped at the station and lost track of time. Maybe he needed to play pool to blow off some steam. Nodding to myself, I thought that seemed the most likely. In our bedroom, I climbed into bed and curled up.

"Come home, Will Worthy," I whispered into the air before drifting back to sleep.

A crash woke me, and I bolted upright in bed. "Will?"

His head poked through the doorway. "Hey, babe, sorry I woke you. Go back to sleep."

I shifted and blinked to get a better look at him. "Where have you been?" The clock beside me read 3:27 a.m.

My husband's figure disappeared a moment, then he came fully through the door, but he stayed across the room from me. He ran his hand over his close-cropped hair. "Sorry, Rox."

My question was unanswered. "I figured you were probably upset and went by the station to blow off some steam. Is everything okay?"

A huge grin broke onto his face. "You know me too well, babe. I had some, um, pent up energy to burn off. We'll talk later." He took a few steps toward the bathroom. "I'm going to take a quick shower. Go back to sleep."

Relieved that he was home safe, I nodded and rolled over, my eyes closing on their own. I heard the shower water start, but I was fast asleep within moments, and I did not wake when Will slid between the sheets.

The next morning, I was gathering up laundry before

heading to work. I tossed our towels into my basket and picked up the clothes Will had been wearing the night before. They were still laying in a heap in the bathroom, and I shook my head with a little chuckle.

But as I lifted Will's favorite navy-blue shirt, a scent wafted up to me. Citrus and peach notes met my nose. Elizabeth Arden's Pretty. Valerie's perfume. I knew because Sadie had told me when we had gone shopping. Will's shirt smelled like his ex-wife.

I shook my head. Of course, it smelled like her. He had been at her house, probably sat on her couch. Perhaps after their fight, he had given her a little hug. They did share a child after all. They needed to be amiable to one another.

As I went back through our bedroom, I looked at Will, still asleep in bed after his late night. I almost went up to him to smell him, but then remembered he had taken a shower when he got home. I considered if that had been odd, but I wasn't sure. He worked nights before we left for Hilton Head, so I let him sleep.

But I chose to ignore the little red flag that popped up in my mind. Maybe I should have listened.

Later at work, I got a text from Valerie that Sadie would be able to join us and to pick her up Wednesday afternoon. I fired off a message, thanking her profusely and beamed the rest of the day. I knew we would have an amazing family holiday.

§♠.

*W*e were blessed enough to have Sadie the week after Christmas as well. I understood that she needed to spend Christmas with her mother. I wasn't heartless. I wished I could spend Christmas with my own mother. It had been more than fifteen years since I had seen her smile.

Will went to Valerie's to pick Sadie up while I prepared her favorite lunch and made sure the stockings were perfectly stuffed. Since we were doing Christmas a little differently, I thought it would be fun to do stockings right away and save opening gifts for morning. Everything under the tree was for Sadie since Will and I had exchanged gifts the day before.

My gift from Will had been a white gold pendant engraved with the words, "Will's Girl." It had been so sweet, almost like we were high school sweethearts. He told me he had gotten one for Sadie as well, which made me love it even more. He also gave me diamond earrings with the box hidden among a dozen red roses. It was probably one of the most romantic gifts I had ever gotten.

I gave Will a meat smoker with a matching apron, not nearly as personal and romantic. I also gave him a gift certificate for couples' massages. At least that was a little more personal. We had saved our stockings for when we would be with Sadie.

When Will and Sadie returned, he was carrying a big box of chocolates and wearing a new pair of sunglasses. He had a huge grin on his face. Sadie bounded over to the tree and shrieked at all the gifts with her name on them.

"This is so much more than I got with Mommy," she proclaimed. "Oh my gosh, look at this one." She grabbed the biggest box and hugged it tight.

I looked at Will behind me. "Oh, I do love to see her so happy."

With a gulp he replied, "Me, too."

I tilted my head to the side. He almost looked guilty, not meeting my gaze and swallowing hard. "Did you open your gifts from Sadie already? Is that where the shades came from?"

He pulled the sunglasses from the top of his head and placed them on the table next to the door where we kept our keys. "Oh, um ..."

"Those were from Mommy," Sadie explained. Her voice was sweet and melodic, and she batted her eyelashes as she spoke. "And Daddy gave her some really beautiful flowers."

They were exchanging gifts? My heart hammered in my chest. "Be right back, I'll grab the camera," I murmured, escaping to the bathroom. I took a deep breath.

He gave her flowers? She got him gifts, too? I reminded myself to breathe in and breathe out. Think rationally. Of course they would exchange gifts. They had been married. They shared a child. Being cordial to each other was necessary, wasn't it?

I had to get a grip. I wasn't sure where this paranoia was coming from, and I didn't like it. I trusted Will, didn't I? He wasn't running off. He wasn't hurting me. He loved me. He told me so with words and actions every single day. I shook my head, arms, and legs in an attempt to force myself to loosen up. I was being silly. Jealous, even. Wasn't I?

My apprehensions would not affect my holiday enjoyment with my family. I rejoined them as Will made hot chocolate, three mugs on the counter. He raised an eyebrow at me, but I just smiled. All was well, was it not?

Chapter Twenty

ASHES, ASHES, WE ALL FALL DOWN

*A*fter the holidays, I still had that nagging feeling that something wasn't quite right. Will was avoiding being close with me, he had taken on extra shifts at the firehouse, and he was often late in coming home from work. The easy conversations we'd always enjoyed had also disappeared.

Finally, I told Gina about everything as we were preparing to open Greene's. I told her all the different details that had been bugging me.

In all the years I had known Gina, she had been a serial monogamist like me, but had never walked down the aisle. She had been with her latest, Rob for two years. She was constantly saying she didn't see the need to have a piece of paper declaring her love to a man in a legally binding contract. She hadn't had any children, and now Gina was past the age of wanting to chase after little ones.

She eyed me, put her hand to her hip, and shook her head. "Rox, you know I love Will. He was just what you needed in a dark time, and I appreciate that so much. But I'm afraid maybe he doesn't need you."

"What do you mean? He does need me. He needs me to be there for him. And for Sadie, too."

Her long fingernails tapped on the pristine counter. "No, girl. Sadie has a momma and Will knows it all too well. I think he's messing around with her."

I gulped. The idea had been hanging out in the back of my mind for a while, despite my efforts to ignore it. But I had to disagree with her. "No, Gina, she's an alcoholic. She goes through a new boyfriend every few months. She does her best with Sadie, but I know Will isn't interested in rekindling their romance."

"You said you smelled her perfume on him?"

"After he had been at her house working out custody for the holidays," I argued.

"You said he gave her flowers? What kind?"

I squeezed my eyes shut and sucked in a sharp breath. "Apparently, roses. Same as he got me."

Gina took my hands in hers from across the bar. "Roxie, I love you. I hate to see you get hurt yet again. But I don't think your paranoia is paranoia. I think it's a real possibility."

My heart felt like it dropped to my feet. A mixture of anger and sorrow welled up inside of me. Gina wouldn't play games with me. She wouldn't hurt me on purpose. I knew she would do everything in her power to protect me.

"What do I do?"

She clucked her tongue before stating, "You have got to confront him. The sooner, the better. And you pray that we're wrong, and it's all a big misunderstanding."

I nodded as Gina patted my hands once more before walking to the front door, unlocking it, and flicking on the sign declaring us open. Nobody rushed right in, so I had a moment to collect my heart from the floor.

Two waitresses bustled about, wearing black slacks and emerald green tops. Gina returned to man the bar, and I went back behind the doors of the kitchen to oversee my staff. I had five cooks under me at Greene's, two of whom were currently working and prepping for what would probably be a slower lunch crowd. I told them we were open and reminded them to watch the temps of the meat they were putting on plates. They grunted their compliance.

All through the day, I worked absentmindedly and thought about how to confront Will about his relationship with Valerie. Then I would think there was no way he would be carrying on with her behind my back. He merely tolerated her for Sadie's sake. But then something else would come to mind, like how he was laughing over her text messages or he was lingering when he would take Sadie home. Then I would question him in my head all over again.

I was exhausted by the time I left at 2:30. I felt the need for a pick-me-up, so I thought I would treat myself to a cookie from my favorite bakery, Powder. I parked out front and smiled at the idea of eating one of their delicious black and white cookies. Perhaps I would get a few extra to take home to Will.

That's when I saw them. Will and Valerie, no Sadie in sight. Of course not, she was in school. But they were together, inside Powder at one of their little bistro tables. They were eating cookies and laughing. Will was laughing so hard he wiped his eyes with a napkin.

I could have used a napkin as well, but for an entirely different reason. My eyes lost their focus as tears welled up and spilled over my lashes. With a shaky hand, I threw the car into reverse and sped home. I didn't know what I would do, but I knew I had to get the truth from Will.

He came home an hour later, and I could smell that

perfume the minute he came through the door. I stood behind the kitchen counter, my head pounding, my legs shaking. I had my palms flat on the cool granite, holding me up. I was ready.

Will flew past me with a wave. "Big fire on Hemingway. They need backup before the whole neighborhood goes up in flames." He disappeared for only a moment before coming back out, ready to go. "I'm meeting them there. I'll be home as soon as I can."

With a kiss on my forehead, he disappeared again, the door slamming behind him.

I exhaled, bringing my head down to the granite. I worried every time he went on a call. And despite the fury I felt toward him in that moment, I whispered a prayer for his safety.

Cleaning the house was what I did best, especially when I was antsy, and this was about as antsy as it got. I got out my grout toothbrush and started scraping through every in-between space I could find while I rinsed the surfaces with my tears. Then I scrubbed the toilets and screamed hateful things into them. Finally, I went outside despite the cold weather and began yanking up anything with roots, upsetting their lives as much as I felt mine had been upset.

My mind was still working overtime, and I decided it was time for action. I would leave him before he had a chance to leave me. While he was gone on this call. I went to our joint bedroom and pulled out my luggage. Clothes were thrown into one bag, shoes into another. I sat them beside my bedroom door. I poured my toiletries into an old backpack and zipped it up.

As I flew into the kitchen to grab my cookbooks and beloved utensils, my heart beat wildly. How could Will do this to me? I thought he had been my second chance at love.

If Adam were here, he would have put Will in his place. Of course, if Adam were here, I would have never met Will Worthy.

My phone ringing startled me and made me jump. When I looked at the caller, I realized it was the number of Will's captain, Pete Henry. Pete never called me. My pulse began to race for a different reason as I answered the call.

"Roxie, it's Pete." His voice was strained and sounded spent. "We've just come back from a bad fire in town, and they wound up taking Will to the hospital for smoke inhalation. Thought you might want to head down there."

I tucked all my packed belongings into the bedroom closet and was in the car in an instant, dialing Valerie on the way. "Will is headed to the hospital for smoke inhalation. I don't want to alarm you or Sadie, but I wanted to let you know in case they need to keep him overnight or something."

The response I got was a heavy sigh. "I knew he would hurt himself one day doing this. It worked my nerves so bad when I was married to him," she said. I couldn't tell if she was alarmed or not.

"Well, would you be willing to bring Sadie down tomorrow or something if they keep him? Seeing her always cheers him up. Hopefully he'll be out tonight." I tried to be as nice and chipper as I could manage.

I fought the urge to ask her what had been so funny at the bakery. This was not the time.

"Yeah, let me know," Valerie said, her voice shaky. "Please keep me updated."

"I'll be in touch. Thank you, Valerie."

I quickly dialed Will's parents and spoke to his father. They would come immediately to the hospital. We hung up as I found a parking spot. I took a moment in the car, breathing in and out as deeply as I could. I was still fuming at Will, but I certainly did not want him to be physically hurt. I whispered a prayer that he would come out okay, so I could finally confront him and find out the truth.

I walked inside, chanting the mantra Will had taught me. "Life is more important than stuff." I recalled his story about the pregnant girl and how there was no use for the things if the person was gone. He would never put someone's possessions over his own life.

Pete, still in some of his gear, pulled me aside before I got to the room. "Roxie, I'm sorry this happened."

"What did happen, Pete? How did he inhale so much smoke?" I wrapped my arms around myself, as if that would protect me from the truth.

"I'm not entirely sure. One of the buildings downtown caught fire, we responded." He wiped his brow with a bandana. "Will went in, but there was some unstable roofing above. As best as I can tell, a piece of timber fell and hit Will. It knocked the wind out of him and his mask off his face. It was a few minutes before Grady found him and got him out. He was rushed right here."

I shook my head. There was still so much I did not understand about fire safety. "Why was he in there if the building was so weak?"

"We don't always know that going in. Once we realized the structure was unsafe, we called for everyone to come out. When Will didn't come, we had to rescue him," Pete said as he combed through his scraggly beard with his soot-covered fingers.

"Grady is okay, though?"

Pete nodded. We both turned to the window to see what was going on with Will.

A doctor came out, his white coat smeared black with ash from Will's clothes. "Are you his wife?"

Pete's arm went protectively around me as I nodded. "I am Roxie Worthy."

"He's inhaled a lot of smoke. Enough to do a good bit of damage to his lungs. Do you know his wishes?" The doctor looked at me expectantly.

"Wishes?" I didn't understand.

From behind me, the voice of Susan Worthy called out. "He has a living will and a DNR."

I turned to see Will's parents racing down the hall. Susan's eyes were already tear-stained, and Bill's forehead was furrowed. "Those are his parents," I explained to the doctor. "He has a daughter ..."

Before I could finish my sentence, lights and alarms were going off in the room behind the doctor. Will's room. In a flash, a medical team rushed into the room, leaving us standing on the other side of the door.

My father-in-law stood next to me, one arm wrapped around his wife. As we watched through the window, he put his other arm around me. I allowed myself to lean into him as we prayed Will would survive. The minutes ticked by and felt like hours. We all held our breath, waiting for word on Will's condition.

In my head, I screamed at Will, "*You cannot leave me. I have been left too many times already. You can't leave me by dying or by going back to Valerie.*"

When the doctor came out only minutes later, I assessed his white coat. It was clean of any blood. I sighed with relief. I remembered all too well what it had looked like when Adam died.

He extended his hand to me, and I took it. But then he

looked into my eyes and said, "I'm so sorry, Mrs. Worthy. We did all we could."

"What?" But there had been no blood. His coat was clean. So Will could not have died. Could he?

Beside me, Susan collapsed, and Bill released me to catch her. Pete Henry took me by the arm and led me to a chair. He spoke to me, his voice calm, but my mind didn't register what he said.

Will was dead? I didn't get a chance to say goodbye. I didn't get a chance to ask him what was going on with Valerie. I didn't get a chance to do so many things. In my anguish, my ire was renewed. How dare he die before I could confront him? How dare he leave me both in life and now in death?

As I sat in the chair in the hospital waiting area, I lifted my head, looked to the ceiling, and screamed.

I never got to confront Will. I never had the chance to find out the truth from him. That's something that will be missing from my life forever.

Minutes after he died, Valerie and Sadie showed up. Tears streamed down Sadie's face, while Valerie's expression was stoic. But upon hearing from Bill that Will had not survived, Valerie crumbled to her daughter, clung to her, and wept.

That was all I needed to see. That was the truth of the matter. Regardless, Valerie had still loved Will. I would never know if he returned her love, and it didn't matter. I knew what it was to have your one true love die. I knew the look of despair. I knew the sound of anguish. And Valerie was full of both.

Their marriage may have failed, but their love had not.

❧

*A*t the funeral, I played the part of grieving widow. And I was grieving, don't get me wrong. I was devastated.

But I wasn't grieving the death of my husband. I was grieving the loss of my marriage. I was mourning the death of yet another romance I thought might last the test of time. I would miss Will, the Will I had known prior to the night he came home smelling like his ex-wife.

The one thing I knew I wanted to keep in my life was Sadie. I asked Valerie if I could see Sadie soon. I understood that it might be a while before she was ready, but I said I would wait.

"Why would you need to see Sadie again?" Valerie asked as she lit a cigarette.

"Why wouldn't I?" I asked, baffled. "I'm her stepmother. I love her more than I could ever explain."

Valerie stepped closer to me and poked me in the shoulder. "You're not her stepmother anymore. Will is gone. So is your relationship with my daughter."

I stood dumbfounded. Valerie walked away, pulling Sadie along with her. Sadie turned and looked back at me, her eyes brimming with tears. But there was nothing I could do but watch as another family was ripped from my grasp.

I collapsed against the wall as any and all willpower I had left bled dry and circled the drain.

I found myself alone yet again. I put Will's house on the market and moved back into the house I had shared with Adam. I had rented it out, but had given my tenants a sixty-day eviction notice. When the house Will and I had shared sold, I put the money into the bank for Sadie and handed the paperwork to Will's parents. I also gave them all of Sadie's things, and once again, my home was childless.

Chapter Twenty-One

JARS OF CLAY

"*W*atch out for that one, Nick, she's a maneater!" A trio of men laughed at the far end of the bar at Greene's. Their loosened ties and balding heads showed them to be businessmen, most likely from downtown Columbia.

I glanced around the restaurant to see who they were calling a maneater but didn't notice anyone fitting the bill. A pair of women sat at a table a few feet away, but the men didn't notice them. Everyone else seemed to be part of a couple.

"I hear she's had two husbands die in the act. She practically killed 'em," one of the men said, his baritone voice not lowered at all.

"No, Dan, I heard three. Don't forget about that French one that magically disappeared."

"Well, she's a knock-out merry widow, maybe it's worth the risk." They erupted into laughter.

All the air in my lungs rushed out. I was the maneater? How did these businessmen know who I was and that two of my husbands had died? Was there really a rumor that Remi had disappeared? What was going on?

I saw spots before my eyes as I had not taken a breath in at least a minute. Gina came to me, grabbed my arm, and led it to the back office where she made me sit.

"I'm a ... a maneater? Is that what they think of me?"

Gina sighed. "You know how the rumor mill can be, girl. Just ignore them."

"You don't understand. I don't know those men. How would they know about me? Am I the brunt of jokes all across the state now?"

My life was ruined, I thought. I had no hope left. I might as well accept my place and relish it. They thought I was a merry widow? That I dance on the graves of men I had loved? No matter that I had nothing to do with the deaths of Will or Adam. And Remi had sent me pictures of his kids the day before. But that was what everyone in the world thought of me. I could certainly fulfill my end of the rumors.

After that, I went back to the style of clothes I had worn when I started working at Greene's some eighteen years before. My skirts got shorter, my tops tighter. I ran every morning, ate less, and I lost twenty pounds. I dyed my hair a shocking red and wore heavier makeup than ever before.

When the staff and regulars at Greene's asked what was going on, I told them I was finally living up to my end of the bargain. I didn't explain further than that and didn't need to. They were soon witness to my new persona, the one that hid many years of pain behind a flash of splendor.

Now when men would ask for my number at the restaurant, I would give it readily along with a wink and a shake of my backside. And if any of those guys actually called, I was more than willing to go out. I had dates at least twice a week after that. I went out, I had a blast, and I stopped worrying about what everyone else thought.

I didn't care about anything but taking care of me for once. No man, no looming responsibility, I was going to have the youth Josh Keene had stolen from me all those years ago. Speaking of Josh, he had finally hit it big. He made his way out to Los Angeles and became a songwriter – for television theme songs. I laughed when I heard that tidbit. At least he had gotten out of town, though. I was still stuck working at the same place where he had left me.

I guessed it was my choice, though. I could work somewhere else, but Greene's was familiar, and the only family I had left in the world. Gina had been the only constant person in my life for eighteen years. I wasn't going to walk away like everyone else in my life had.

My reputation as town minx got worse as I went out with several different guys. I was never one to date around, and remembering all the names and what we had done together was a little dizzying at first. But I adjusted. And when I called someone by the wrong name, I just laughed it off. Isn't that what the most notorious woman in town was supposed to do?

At night I curled up in my bed and cried. I knew it was not who I truly wanted to be. But putting on the act was so much easier than dealing with the pain of three failed marriages and burying the two men I thought I could love forever. Not to mention losing Liam and then having Sadie yanked from my life. I missed them all so much. Any time I saw a crowd of children, I looked to see if Sadie was among them. I just wanted a glimpse to make sure she was okay.

I admit, the night of her piano recital, I hid in the hallway. I sat in the back of the high school auditorium and when her name was called, I slipped out the door. I didn't want her to see me, but I wanted to hear her play. I closed my eyes and listened as her hands went over the keys, and I hoped she had been practicing on the keyboard I had sent to her mother's house. She played beautifully through the song and hardly struggled over the chords. I cried when she finished and rushed out the door, but I left a rose on Valerie's car for her.

❧

*O*ver time I started to spend my days off with a regular at the restaurant named David Sechman. I never considered myself as dating him, though in hindsight, that's exactly what it was. David was average height and quite thin. His hair was the same mousy brown mine had been in my youth, and his grayed at the temples just as I imagined mine would be doing if I didn't dye it regularly. His brown eyes held a level of sadness in them. I learned that he had grown up in a military family, and he had never measured up to his father's expectations. Because of that, he never felt like he belonged anywhere specific. He was twice divorced, and his only son was grown.

It began simply enough. After my shift, he asked me where a certain store was. Having nothing else to do, and not wanting to return home, I accompanied him. It was a pleasant enough evening with no expectations. A few nights later, he again asked me for directions, this time to a movie theater. As I was explaining where it was, he asked if I wanted to join him.

Within a few weeks, we were going out regularly. Again, I never saw it as dating, he was just David, someone I spent time with.

Until, that is, mid-June when a woman showed up at

Greene's and sought me out. She asked the hostess for me by name. I was informed that an extremely bad-tempered woman was at the bar waiting for me. I wiped my hands and made my way from the kitchen to the front of the house.

"I'm Roxie Worthy. Can I help you?"

The woman looked at me, sized me up, and slapped me across the face. "How dare you!"

I was stunned, to be sure. I was also thankful it was a slow Tuesday night in the restaurant. All I could manage to croak out to this woman was one word, "What?"

"David Sechman is my husband, and you are the vixen who is stealing him away from me," she cried.

My heart dropped as I crossed my arms in front of my body. This was my biggest fear. I had become what I never wanted to be, a man stealer. "He told me he was divorced. And he's just a friend, I promise. I have no romantic interest in him."

The woman shifted her weight. "Right. Well, we are divorced, but we've been working on reconciling. And he showed up to our therapy session last night saying it was over for good, because he had fallen in love with you, you homewrecker."

David came through the door at that moment and rushed to us. "Tammy, what are you doing here? I told you to leave Roxie and me alone. I'm with her now," he pleaded.

I backed away. "Listen, David, you're a nice guy, but I am not in love with you. At all. I think you need to leave. I'm so sorry, Tammy. I had no idea."

David turned his sad eyes to me. "But Roxie, haven't we had fun together?"

"I think you need to figure out what's going on between you and Tammy," I told him.

For her part, Tammy looked triumphantly at me. "Ha! I

won. I knew you were spineless, just like everyone says. You dig your claws in where they're not wanted, and then you back off at the first sign of trouble."

"I'm so sorry," I murmured. I blinked several times, wondering if the scene before me was really happening.

Tammy took a step back, but then approached me again. She hissed through her teeth. "I remember you. I heard all about your family dying. I felt so bad for you then, but now I think maybe a woman like you deserved it."

It felt like a punch in the gut. All the air left me, and I doubled over, gasping for breath. Aside from the slap, she had not touched me, but her words cut far deeper than anything else. Tears ran down my cheeks as I sank my head onto the cool counter.

Tammy turned to David and grabbed his collar. "Come on, David. We're leaving. Never come here again," she warned.

The bartender, Chad, came over to me then with a rag filled with ice. "Roxie, you are the most drama-filled person I have ever met." I took it and placed it on my burning cheek.

Tears stung my eyes. "I don't know why. Drama follows me everywhere. All my life, I wanted to blend in and be loved. And it seems I will never have either."

I thought back to when I was first noticed by Josh. I had always been a wallflower. But he made me feel beautiful and exciting for a short time. Remi had loved me, though platonically. That had never bothered me, of course.

Ray noticed me for all the wrong reasons. He thought I had money to hand over to him, then he used me as his punching bag.

Then Adam noticed me. He had noticed me long before

I realized. Why had I not met him before I met Josh Keene? We could have had so many more years together. If only …

And Will. He noticed me, too. Until he had noticed his ex-wife again. We had been a family, but the pull of his old family had been too strong.

I took off my apron and left. I didn't say a word to anyone. I couldn't cope anymore and didn't know what to do. I went back home and began looking up realtors. I would sell the house and leave Columbia for good. There was nothing for me here.

Chapter Twenty-Two

THE PALM OF HIS HAND

*W*ithin two days, I had the house listed for sale. I told Linda what I was doing, and she told me to go live my life to the fullest. I put in my two weeks notice with Gina, who seemed a little more than relieved to see me moving on. I worked half-heartedly to end my time as chef and manager at Greene's.

One night, a particularly suave older man came into the restaurant. He came straight to the bar and sat down, staring at me intently. I did not meet his gaze, instead I began to wipe down an area of the counter.

"What can I get you, sir?" I asked without looking up.

"I think the question is really what can I get for you?" he replied.

I was in no mood to listen to this man's riddles. I looked at him and saw a man who looked kind but weathered. He was probably much younger than he looked, which was about sixty. His hair was almost a yellow color, but beginning to gray, and it hung loose around his shoulders. His eyes were deep-set and dark. I almost felt compelled to sit down and really ask this man why he thought he could get me something. Almost.

"Listen, sir, do you want a drink or not?" I said with more force than necessary.

"Do you have Sprite?" he asked with a warm smile.

I gave a halfhearted smile in return. "Sure, be right back."

I got his Sprite from behind the bar and set it in front of him. "Anything else?"

My back was starting to hurt, and my fashionable but senseless shoes were not helping. I was getting too old to play this part.

"Can you have a seat?" He patted the table next to him.

Letting out a sigh, I looked around. The place was almost empty, and I knew Gina wouldn't mind if I sat down for a few minutes. Reluctantly, I perched on the chair opposite him.

"My name is Linus," he said. Then he slowly picked up his drink and took a long swallow. "What might your name be?"

Glad to be off my feet even for a moment, I replied, "I'm Roxie. Did you want anything off the menu? I designed it myself."

"The actual menu or the food?"

"The food. I made the menu. I actually have a culinary degree," I said with half a laugh.

"Well, then bring me your favorite thing off the menu," he said. His eyes twinkled. I found myself staring at him momentarily.

I had to think. What was my favorite? Of course, Adam's favorite. It had even been named after him on the menu. The Adam's Apple Scallops. And I actually had it made that afternoon. "That would be our scallops," I told him.

"They're pan seared with an apple glaze. I know it sounds crazy, but just try it."

Linus nodded, and I disappeared to make his meal. Tender broccolini finished the plate. I brought it out to him with a more genuine smile. The thought of Adam and Liam warmed me.

When he finished – and he finished all of it – he handed me his card.

PASTOR LINUS CHRISTER

PASTOR AT LARGE, FINDING REFUGE CHURCH

803-555-1921

PASTORCHRISTER@RBCHURCH.ORG

"You're a pastor?" I asked. My view on Christianity lately was lacking favor. In fact, I had not felt the Spirit move within me in years. The Holy Spirit left me when God so brutally disrupted my life.

"I take it you are not impressed with that," he said.

"Honestly, I'm not," I told him. I put my hand on my hip. "I went to church, I believed in your God, Pastor Christer. And then God brutally ripped my family away from me. Twice." Bitterness welled inside me, and I allowed it to bubble over.

"Call me Linus, or Pastor Linus," he said, the smile still across his face. "Would you be willing to meet me tomorrow? I have a message for you."

"A message? Who are you? What do you want with me?" I hissed. I was skeptical. I didn't know who was sending me messages through some hippie pastor, but I didn't want it.

"What if I said it was from Adam?"

My heart stopped. Adam? How did he know Adam? Tears automatically welled in my eyes. I tried in vain to blink them back, but they spilled over onto my cheeks. I could only nod, I was too choked up to speak.

"Please, come to the address on the back. I'll meet you outside if you like. We have a little park. It's supposed to be a beautiful morning." He stood and laid money on the table before him. "Come by around nine? And thank you for the meal. It was truly delicious."

Again, I could only nod. Nine o'clock. I could do that. I flipped the card over and looked at the address. I knew exactly where it was.

࿔

The entire evening and well into the night, I debated not going to see the pastor. I had even called Remi in the middle of the night to ask him what he thought.

"*Cherie*, maybe this man can help you get out of your slump. What will it hurt? Even if he can't help, you are not any worse off than before," he said.

"I know. But I'm scared," I admitted.

"Of what? Of getting your confidence back? Of finally living again? Don't be silly, Roxie," he reprimanded. "What else do you have to lose?"

I shed tears. "Nothing. I have nothing left to lose. You should hear what people say about me, Remi, it's ugly."

Like a mother hen, Remi tut-tutted me and spoke firmly. "Listen. Ugly it may be, but true it is not. Stand up for yourself, Roxie. Stop being a floor mat!"

"Doormat," I corrected with a half-hearted smile.

"Come on, *Cherie*. What is the American saying? 'Put on your panties and just do it!'"

"Close enough," I said, smiling a little more. "Thanks,

Remi. Say hi to Becca for me, and kiss those beautiful children."

So that morning, I quickly dressed in a modest shirt with blue jeans and headed out the door. I made my way to the church addressed on the back of Linus' business card. I sat in my car, feeling numb for about five minutes before getting out. I only went a few steps before seeing Linus on a bench by the front door.

"I knew you would come, Roxie," he said. "You want to make things better, I know. Walk with me."

My heels clacked against the concrete, a sound that always reminded me of my mother. Momma always said when you remembered a person who was gone, it was their way of saying hello. I sighed. Too many people I loved were gone.

Linus led me to a little garden around the side of the building. The flowers were beginning to unfold their blooms as the spring sunshine hit them. In the center of the garden was what looked like a little stone wishing well. Linus peered in and tossed a penny into the opening.

"Yesterday, you said you had a message for me," I reminded him. A slight breeze blew my hair into my face and made me shiver. I wrapped my arms around myself.

"I know you have been married five times, Roxanne. And I know that you are not married now to a man you have been seen with around town."

I glared at him. "How do you know that? Actually, who doesn't know that? What does this have to do with Adam? You mentioned Adam."

"I did," he replied. Nothing more.

Frustrated, I asked, "Did you know him?"

Shaking his head he said, "Not well, I'm afraid. But I met

him once. And his kindness allowed me to become a man of God."

"I don't understand." I shifted my weight nervously. Why did he always seem to talk in riddles?

"Years ago, I was out of work, homeless actually, when a young man with red hair gave me a chance. He helped me find a job, and that changed my entire life. It led to my going into ministry and helping others in tough situations. I learned his name from the fellow he got me a job with, and I followed Adam's progress over time. I was so distraught when I heard he had passed away with your son. And I wanted to do something for you afterward, but I never knew what, and I never wanted to overstep my bounds. I admit that over time, I forgot about you."

Linus looked at me with kind, weathered eyes. "I wish I had done something sooner because I can see what a pickle your life has become. I heard your name on the tongue of some of my congregants recently. Not in mean-spirited gossip, mind you, but concern that you were on a path of self-destruction. It took me some time, but I found you." He paused and took a deep breath. "And when I did, I still wondered what I was supposed to do. But then it was like God was telling me that He had your family with Him, your little boy, and He wanted to make sure you would get to heaven as well one day."

Tears sprang to my eyes. "What? Liam?" I whispered. I pulled his edge-worn picture from my purse and showed it to the man.

I could see his eyes grow moist. "Yes, God assured me Adam and your son are waiting for you in paradise." His voice choked up, and he handed the picture back. "I need to reintroduce you to God, Roxanne. And here you are."

It took me several moments before I could speak. "You're

saying God spoke to you directly and wants me to have faith again?"

"Yes."

I spoke harshly, "But God took them away. God is a family killer." Was this man playing with me? Anger wrestled its way to the surface. "That sweet baby, my Liam, and my Adam, they were killed in a stupid, senseless accident. How could a God who is good do that? And Will? What a mess that ended up being."

Linus looked at me, "God is always good, all the time."

I paced back and forth in front of him. How could he say that, knowing what had happened to my family? "Why would a good and fair God allow that to happen, Linus? What God would take away my husband and son?"

He shook his head and briefly closed his eyes. When he opened them he said, "I won't pretend that I have the answer to that, Roxie, because I don't. I just trust that God knew what He was doing." He rubbed his hands over his face, then posed the question, "Do you know the hardest part of my job, Roxie?"

I looked at him, exasperated. "Trying to explain how good God is to people who don't believe you?"

He chuckled. "No. It's trust. The hardest part for any pastor – any believer, really – is trust. Trusting that no matter how crummy things get, how desperate we feel, that we can trust in God and know that His plan is a perfect one. Even if we don't understand it. Especially if we don't understand it."

Linus leaned against the well while I moved restlessly around the garden. How could he be so calm? It infuriated me. I wanted what he had, this sense of peace within him. "Where do you find that trust?"

He tapped his chest. "Right here. Much like being in

love, truly being in love, it's easier to do with the heart than the head. The head wants logic and reason to prevail. But the heart – it believes because it wants to."

"I want to believe again." And I did. I really did. I wanted to believe in love again. I wanted to believe that life was worth living. I wanted to turn back to the God I had loved alongside my husband. I stood in front of the pastor, feeling weighed down, almost as if I were drowning. Part of me wanted to give in and see my family again. But then part of me knew I needed to hang on where I was.

"And you will believe again, Roxie. Have you heard of living water?"

"No, what is it? Some new fancy electrolyte drink? Holy water you want me to drink?" What was he talking about? First talking about believing and trusting in God and now he was talking about water? I could tell Linus was a strange hippie-type, but this was just odd.

Laughing, Linus's eyes crinkled, and the creases on his forehead multiplied. He had what I dubbed as 'happy wrinkles.' "No, hardly. It's never thirsting for anything again. Never wondering if you will survive the day, the year, your life, because you know you will with Christ. That's living water."

Again he was talking in riddles. This was something he seemed to do often. "Where do I get it? I'll take some of that." Anything that would help me survive sounded good right now.

He straightened, crossed to me, and laid his hands on my shoulders. "Ah, Roxie, you are thinking of an actual drink. I'm talking about the living water of the Holy Spirit."

"The what?"

"'Whoever drinks the water I give them will never thirst.

Indeed, the water I give them will become in them a spring of water welling up to eternal life.'"

I eyed him, skeptical. "Listen, I went to church my whole childhood. I was involved when Adam was alive. And I have no idea what you're talking about."

"That's because you went to church to hear about Jesus. You didn't have a relationship with him. There's a difference. You need to develop the relationship. But it is simple if you just have the faith of a child."

I looked into the fountain as his words washed over me. I saw my reflection in the wavy water. "The faith of a child ..." I repeated.

"Your step-daughter had complete faith in you. Adam and Liam had faith in you. What would they think of you now?"

My head snapped up. How did he know all this? "How—"

His face wrinkled slightly as he smiled. "Does it matter? What would Sadie think of the life you're living now?"

Sighing, I closed my eyes. "Oh, Sadie. I'm so sorry. Liam. Oh, babies." Tears spilled down my cheeks as I looked back at the man before me. He was right. "Can you help me?"

Linus clapped his hands together, "Oh, no, I can't help you. But you can help yourself, and Jesus will be with you. And I will, too."

"I want to be someone they would be proud of," I said with determination. "I need to clean myself up."

"Atta girl," Linus said as he took my arm and led me away from the fountain.

Chapter Twenty-Three

THE ROAD LESS TRAVELED

ithin six months, I had changed my life completely around. I sold Adam's house that held far too many memories and bought a small three-bedroom bungalow in a nice neighborhood thirty minutes away in a town called Prosperity. I had adopted a pair of orange kittens to keep me company and named them Garfield and Morris. They kept a smile on my face.

I held true to my notice at Greene's and left after my two weeks were up. Alcohol had ruined my life more than once, and I realized I did not want to see the stuff again. Ray had been an alcoholic, Adam and Liam killed by a drunk driver. Nothing good had ever come from the people around me drinking. I refused to serve it anymore.

I lived modestly off the trust Adam has set up for me while I figured out what I needed to do with my life. I even changed my name back to Roxanne Joyce.

All the clothing I had been wearing were thrown into the trash. I traded a millennial girl's clothing for something more age appropriate. Low and behold, high-waisted jeans were coming back into fashion, and I discovered the ability to cover my bottom end with a tunic shirt over leggings. I ditched the wild hair color for a rich chestnut brown.

I threw myself into ministry at Linus's church, Finding Refuge. It was a growing church with just under five hundred members in just over two years of existence. I began baking breakfast casseroles for the staff and service teams. Then I expanded into providing breakfast items for the church attendees every week. And I loved it.

A few people eyed me. A few people avoided me like the plague. Some spoke to me, but nobody seemed ready to allow me into their inner circle. But they did, however, ask me to cater events for them.

Suddenly I was catering birthday parties, anniversaries, business luncheons, and more. I was blown away. People were trusting me with their food. I made the Adam's Apple Scallops and added Remi's French Dip and even a Keene Burger. Desserts were Liam's Lemon Tarte and Sadie's Chocolate Cake. I had perfected a recipe for cookies-and-cream truffles that made people swoon.

⚜

*I*t was then I realized what I should do with the money Remi had given me. It had sat unused in the bank for all these years, waiting for something marvelous. I had toyed with ideas over the years, but nothing had seemed right. This idea was the one I was waiting on.

I decided to open up a small cafe and coffee shop with the money Remi had gifted me. I called it Living Water. Anyone could come in and get coffee, a sandwich, and a hug. The cafe was down the street from my new house, and it was an instant hit with the working crowd. We were open five days a week, and I had two employees to help me out. Both were from a local ministry that aided women who had fled domestic abuse.

Pastor Linus took credit for the name of the cafe, of course, and I was happy to give it to him. He had saved me. Or rather, Jesus had saved me through him.

Linda Joyce and Susan Worthy were my first customers. I had really lucked out in the mother-in-law department and had two amazing women come back into my life and support me. Susan had even brought Sadie in to see me one day, and that was the best day of my life in a very long time.

Living Water served coffee and tea, as well as freshly baked goods like muffins, cakes, truffles, and fresh sandwiches. Gina and even Chef Tallant came to see me and often ordered cakes and pies for their restaurants. Chef adored my cookies and cream truffles. I was happy, I had new regulars, and life was becoming a new normal.

One day, Pastor Linus came into the cafe with an interesting proposition. "Roxie, I want you to give your testimony and lead worship for us," he said.

"Excuse me? You can't be serious," I laughed as I wiped down the kitchen counter after breakfast.

"I'm serious. You have an amazing testimony. You have come full circle from the pits of hell to basking at the foot of the Lord," he said.

"Gee, thanks," I teased. He wasn't wrong, though. I had experienced the pits of hell for sure.

"You want people to know you're changed? That God has worked in your life? Tell them yourself. The only way to combat the rumor mill is to actively fight against it," Linus argued.

"Okay. I'll do it," I agreed.

I questioned my sanity when I agreed to speak, but I

supposed following my own plan wasn't working out too well. I would give following someone else's a try.

§

*T*wo weeks later, I was in my usual spot, but instead of sitting quietly, I was sweaty, my knee bouncing, my hands fidgeting. I was sure everybody was staring at me, even though nobody knew I was going to be sharing that morning. I had invited everyone who was family to me at that point, my three sisters, my in-laws, Chef Tallant, and Gina. Chef and Gina were the only ones who came, and I was not surprised. They did not sit with me, but sat in the back of the church separately.

Linus quickly went up the steps onto the church stage. He was much different from my childhood pastor, and even the one from the church Adam and I had attended. Linus was casual, relaxed, and stayed on the same level as his parishioners.

"This morning we're going to shake things up a bit. Many of you have met Roxie or have heard of her. This morning, I have asked her to come and share a few words with you. Please give her your undivided attention."

He motioned for me. I stood on shaky legs, glad I had worn ballet flats and not heels. I made my way to where Linus stood with his arm outstretched. He shook my hand and pulled me into a hug.

"You can do this, Roxanne," he assured me. Then he pulled away and took a seat.

I stood before the crowd, all eyes on me. At eighteen I had been the most unnoticed person in all of South Carolina, and now here I was, standing before hundreds of people with the purpose of being noticed. How had this happened? A halted breath left my lips.

"Good morning. My name is Roxie Joyce," I said with an unsteady waver in my voice. My palms were sweaty, and my heart was racing. "You may remember me as Roxie DePrivé, Roxie Keene, Roxie Bonhomme, Roxie O'Toole, or Roxie Worthy. No, I'm not kidding. But now, now I hope you will remember me as Roxie, the child of God."

I spent the next thirty minutes talking about my story and the redemption of Christ in my life. My voice went from weak to strong, my knees from wobbly to steady. It seemed I had inherited something from my father after all – the ability to speak in public.

When the service was over, Linus stood next to me as person after person came to me, and shook my hand and thanked me for telling my story.

One woman with short blonde curls on her head approached me and shook my hand. "Roxie, do you remember me at all?" Sadly, I had to tell her I did not. "I'm Jessica Jones, well, Jessica Pinner. The goth you stayed with the night before you married Josh Keene."

I was amazed. I had not seen Jessica since that night. What a terrible friend I had been then and now, not even to remember her. "Jessica! Oh, I am so sorry for not recognizing you. You look marvelous. How are you?"

She had a smile that was warm and inviting. "I am great. Actually, Mr. Linus called me up and invited me to come hear you. When I told him I knew you, he said it was God's plan, and I have to agree."

My gaze shifted to Linus. "What are you talking about?"

"I'm a publicist now, and I would like to talk to you about maybe writing a book and getting on the Christian public speaking circuit," she told me. "Can we have lunch or coffee tomorrow?"

I was astounded. Me? Write a book and take up public speaking? I shook my head. "Surely, you are joking."

Jessica looked at me. Her formerly ink-colored hair was now platinum, and she wore a smart dress suit and three-inch heels. She took me by the shoulders and looked directly into my eyes. "You have a story to tell. One of redemption. One of not giving up. Do you want to share your story?"

"Absolutely. Why don't you come to my place and I'll cook lunch for you?" I gave her the address, and she said she would see me the next day.

♣.

*N*ervous didn't define my feelings the next day when Jessica Pinner Jones rang my doorbell. I hadn't seen her in more years than I could remember, and I wanted to impress. The house, of course, was scrubbed from top to bottom. The kittens were loose in the living room, and, thankfully, I had trained them to stay out of the kitchen, though Garfield liked to press his luck from time to time.

I checked myself in the mirror one more time. I wore a flowy, sleeveless, knee-length dress in my favorite shade of green. It reminded me of Adam. The color had looked so good on him. I was barefoot, in hopes that I would convey a sense of casualty and comfort. My hair was pulled back into a low ponytail, and I wore almost no makeup aside from a little mascara and lip gloss. How different I was from the eighteen-year-old version of me. Or even the thirty-five-year-old version.

I opened the door to see Jessica dressed immaculately in a crisp white shirt and red trousers. She hugged me tight. "Oh, Roxie, had I known all those years ago you were going to spend the night, then marry Josh Keene, I would have done something."

I laughed. "What would you have done?"

She shook her platinum hair. "I'm not sure. But I would have done something. I probably would have thought it was so romantic at that age. Now I can see how it was a cry for attention."

I showed her to the living room, and we sat down. "I wish I had known then it was a cry for attention. But you're right. I was so shocked someone saw me and knew my name, I mistook it for love."

She leaned forward and took my hand. "Oh, Roxie, I am so sorry. But it looks like God has not let your heartache be wasted. So many women out there are widows or formerly abused, and they need someone to tell them it will turn out okay."

I thought for a moment, my life up to that point flashing in my mind, and the tears in my eyes threatened to spill over. "You know, Jess, every day I struggle with trying to be 'okay.' Some days I fail miserably. But some days I do fine. I take each day as it comes. I allow myself some grief for Adam and Liam, even Will. But I also try to create good in the world as well."

"That's why I'm here. Let's get you creating good," she said with a smile.

Chapter Twenty-Four

HALLELUJAH CHORUS

I closed my eyes and when I reopened them, it was three months later, and I was in front of my first true audience who had come specifically to see me. They had listened to my entire story, though it was far from over. I took a deep breath.

"And that, friends, is the story of my redemption. I did write a book. It will be coming out soon, called Living While Drowning. And while I am excited to share my story here with you, I'm even more excited to share the gospel and the truth with the people who walk into Living Water. The people who just need a bit of kindness in their day, the people who need to hear good news. My employees are women getting back on their feet after their own rough go. Everyone who comes in can get a free hug and a sympathetic ear.

"Before you ask, I will tell you a few things. Ray is still in prison, and I do feel safe from him. He will never hurt me again. Remi and Becca are still happily married with four children to keep them on their toes. They came stateside last year, and I was thrilled to catch up with them. Josh was still in Los Angeles last I heard, and I wish him nothing but the best."

I stepped forward on the stage. "I don't see Sadie as much as I would like, but knowing that she's safe and happy is the top priority."

I looked around, as my eyes had adjusted to the lights. So many women looked up at me, some looked bored, but most looked like they had been on an emotional roller-coaster with me. A few looked like they knew exactly what I was talking about in some way or another.

"I thank you so much for coming out today. I believe it's time for the supper break, and when you come back, author Liza Higgins will be speaking to you. Please allow me to pray for you, and you'll be dismissed."

I delivered a quick prayer and the house lights came up. I stepped down from the platform, and Jessica stepped to me quickly. "That was perfect, Roxie. Just amazing. Not a dry eye in the house, I tell you."

I raised my eyebrows. "Seriously? Oh, no!"

"No, Rox, it's a good thing. They connected with you. The Spirit moved them," she explained.

I tucked my hair behind my ears and fought the urge to wrap my arms around myself. I realized it was a defense mechanism I had adapted early in life. Of course, it never worked, but I had tried.

Several people walked past me and thanked me for shar-ing. A few people asked for selfies with me, which I thought was silly, because a year before I had been the pariah of South Carolina. Jessica reminded them to tag me on social media.

"Tag me?"

She slipped her phone from her pocket and showed me the Instagram page she had set up for me. There was my photo and name, dubbed as "Roxie Joyce, life encourager." There were already several photos shared to the page.

"People can tag you or use your hashtag," she explained, and she hit a button on her smartphone. Already, a few photos were posted under the tag '#roxieisliving.'

"That's amazing, Jess. Thank you so much," I told her. I would have to check it out later when I was at home.

I ate the meal brought to me and sat backstage to listen to the next speaker. When I found out I would be followed by the amazingly famous Liza Higgins, I was honored and humbled. I had read several of her books over the years and always enjoyed them. It was encouraging to know I was being counted among her peers.

At the end of the night, a young woman approached me timidly. "Excuse me," she said in a meek voice. I welcomed her over to me and invited her to lean against the stage next to me. "My name is Julia."

She refused to look at me as she spoke, but she poured her soul out to me. Julia had been married for a year and a half to a man who beat her. She was sure her family knew about it and did nothing. And up until this point, she thought it was their job to help her. However, she said, she realized that it was her job to help herself. She said she planned to go home and pack her bags.

I pulled Julia close to me as she cried. I felt like she was crying in relief, and I could feel her body relaxing. I began to pray for her, quietly but clearly. I prayed she would be able to leave, that God would protect her from retaliation, that her husband would see the error of his ways. I prayed that God would use this trial in her life to glorify Him.

After a minute she pulled back. "I'm so sorry," she said. She looked frightened and fragile. Her eyes darted side to side, and her chin quivered slightly.

I lifted her chin with my hand, so she was looking at me. I peered into her chocolate brown eyes and saw the smattering of freckles over her olive skin. "Never be sorry, Julia. God will help you, and you will be set free." She smiled at me. "Do you have somewhere you can go?"

She nodded and squared her shoulders. "My grandma said I can come to her. She's in Florida."

I grabbed my bag and pulled out my business card. Handing it to her, I told her to call me if she needed someone to talk to, and that she was welcome at the cafe any time. She thanked me and rushed away.

Amazement filled me that so many women had come to hear my story, and that they had stayed. God had truly put a testimony in me, and I knew it was worth it just to be able to help a girl like Julia. I shook my head in wonder. Could I help others as well? Me?

The lack of ambition I was accused of as a child came back to me. The years of being put down, of not measuring up, all welled up inside me. It wasn't that I didn't have ambition, it just did not fit into my family's mold. I didn't want to be a politician or something grand. I could make an impact in my own way. Feeding people, loving on them, giving encouragement – that was my ambition.

With a small smile on my lips, I began to pack up my things to head home. The realization that I was somebody and somebody worthy at that, was a new concept for little Roxie DePrivé.

Liza Higgins stopped me and gave me her card with her personal email and phone number on it. "You know what you're doing up there, darlin'. You are the epitome of the saying 'God doesn't call the equipped, he equips the called.'"

My cheeks flushed as she patted my arm. "Thank you, Ms. Higgins."

Her round eyes squinted as she grinned. "Don't thank me, sugar, I didn't do nothing. You have a story and a gift. Use them both."

The motherly advice from her deep Southern accent reminded me of my momma. And Momma always said to mind my elders, so I decided Liza Higgins was right. I would use my gift. I told her as much, and she went off with a laugh, reminding me to keep in touch.

Jessica had booked this as my first speaking engagement, and I had three more in the coming months. I told her I wasn't interested in touring the country, but I would be happy to go a few hours from home on occasion. The cafe was my top priority.

I finally felt like things were falling into place, and my life had a nice rhythm. Some days, the ache of missing Liam and Adam was almost unbearable, but I forced myself to get up and get moving. I had people counting on me and Living Water. I had Bible study groups meet there a few times a week from different churches and denominations. I had a few lost souls come in looking for prayer and a place to unload.

I wasn't sure what the future might hold for me, but I was sure that I would be ready for it. I hoped that Momma was looking down on me from heaven and proud of the woman I had become. I was still more than happy to blend into the crowd, but I also knew that I was one chosen to stand out thanks to the deliverance of Living Water.

*E*ight years had passed since I had opened Living Water with the seed money from Remi. Now I had four cafes in South Carolina—Columbia, Charleston, Greenville, and Myrtle Beach. They were all fully staffed by women who had needed a hand up in life. Single mothers, formerly abused women, women who had been living out of their car with their two children, they all poured themselves into Living Water, and I poured myself into them. I had been made godmother of four of my employees' children.

Lori came into Living Water one day a few weeks after my first speaking engagement. She cried as she told me how proud she was of me. She said our parents would have been thrilled that I was doing something so amazing with my life. Apologies for how she had treated me flew from her, and I was quick with my own as well. It was so healing to finally have my sister back after so many years.

My sister, Shelly, had called me up one day from New York, where she had gotten a job with The Today Show. I was flown to Rockefeller Center and interviewed for a piece on my life, the cafe, and my newfound career as a public speaker and encourager. The best part of that, however, was reconciling with my sister.

From there, Jenny, who was now the mayor of Lexington, had me do a ribbon cutting on a battered women's shelter and also made a proclamation that July 18th would from then on be known as "Pledge Sober for Liam" day in the city. We kissed and made amends, but Jenny and I still didn't talk much.

I was given the opportunity to speak at a parole hearing for Ray O'Toole. Misty also came and spoke. We supported one another as we told the review board of the horrors inflicted on us and how it had set a course for the rest of our lives. He saw no wrongdoing on his part and was denied the chance to get out of prison. Misty and I celebrated with lunch at the cafe. After chatting, we decided she would go to Myrtle Beach and be the manager of the Living Water there and counsel women as well.

I still went to Finding Refuge Church where I led a Bible Study. Linus had become something of a father figure for me. But this time, one full of love and compassion instead of judgement. I joined him and his children for holiday meals and was accepted into the folds of the Christer family.

Public speaking had begun to take up more and more of my time. Jessica now had me travelling up and down the east coast, sharing the story of love and redemption, hope and encouragement. I spoke at churches, retreats, even a college graduation. Each time, a young widow or a woman in an abusive relationship approached me and thanked me for sharing my story. All they wanted was to know that they're not alone. Isn't that all any of us want?

But I still loved waking up before the sun, going to my very first Living Water location, and baking bread, preparing for the day, smelling the aroma of freshly brewed coffee. I would greet my employees with a hug and smile at the children coming in with their parents for a fresh scone.

And my real miracle happened that summer, eight years after I opened my doors. I looked up from rolling truffles in my hands and saw a familiar young woman come through the door. She approached me cautiously and took a deep breath.

"Roxie? Do you remember me? It's Sadie." And she collapsed into my arms, tears flowing.

I held the child I had fallen so in love with, now a woman in her own right. When the tears abated, I led her to a table, sat her down, and let her tell me her story.

ACKNOWLEDGMENTS

I would be remiss if I didn't start off thanking my husband, to whom I dedicated this book. Roxie was married five times, but once is enough for me. Marshall, you have been a constant source of encouragement for me since we were thirteen. Now at forty—I love you more than ever. Thank you.

Major shout outs to the team at Monster Ivy Publishing. Mary and Cammie for believing in this story and pushing me to make it better. And to Lydia for knowing all the 90s references. I groaned through each set of edits, but I truly believe you three have made this book as amazing as it is and I am forever thankful. Each of you has been an amazing cheerleader for me and I can never say enough just how much it means to me!

Many friends have also been amazing cheerleaders for me, urging me to keep on writing, to finish the editing, and just being part of my tribe. Sarah, Sallie, Bethany, Marissa, Kim, Michelle—you all are wonderful and I love you!

Lastly, I want to thank you, the reader. Without you, I

have no reason to write. I hope you enjoy this book, reading about Roxie and her journey. Thank you for journeying with her.

Roxie's five husbands are all imaginary. I never dated a French aristocrat or an abusive redneck. But Josh was certainly a mix of every boy I went to high school with. 90s music forever!

This book was written about the woman at the well from John 4 in the New Testament. She meets Jesus, a scorned and lonely woman. He tells her she has been married five times and she is astonished. He offers her living water and she doesn't get it—much like Roxie thinking it's a "fancy electrolyte drink." But eventually, it dawns on them both that Living Water is not actual water but something that will quench the soul. What could be more enthralling?

I knew I needed to write this unnamed woman's story. What had led her to the point of being such an outcast? Why on earth was she married five times? Despite all that, Jesus chose her to become the Bible's first evangelist (A sinful woman no less!).

"The woman left her water jar and ran back into town. She said to the people, 'Come and see a man who told me everything I have ever done! Could he be the Messiah?'" John 4:28-29 CEV.

I love that in this version she "ran" back into town, leaving her water jug behind. She was in a hurry. She went back to tell all the people who had shunned her and treated her poorly about Christ. This is why Roxie ends up becoming a public speaker in the book, sharing her story and the redemptive love of Jesus.

I write what I call "gritty Christian." Just because you believe in God doesn't make you immune to hard times and heartache and I want to convey that in my books. Just like with Job, God allows those hard times so we draw closer to Him and lean on Him. It can be an incredibly difficult lesson to learn, but it's an important one.

God bless you all.

ABOUT THE AUTHOR

Allison Wells is an author, avid reader, and sweet tea addict. She graduated from Clemson University and began writing books as a way to escape the doldrums of newspaper reporting. Allison is married to a wonderful man and they are raising one red-headed teen daughter and three wild boys in the foothills of the Blue Ridge Mountains. Check out her daily adventures on social media. Her motto is, "Life is Short, Eat the Oreos."

ALSO BY ALLISON WELLS

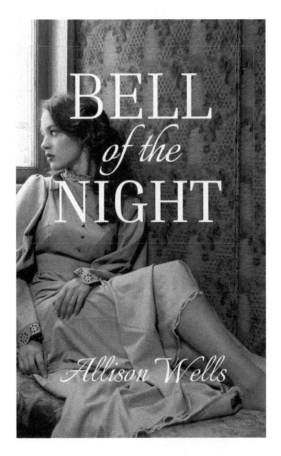

Bell is trying to find her way out of a famed brothel in New Orleans' red-light district when an unknown preacher walks into the parlor, intent on saving the sinful souls of the South.

BELL OF THE NIGHT

Chapter 1

"You go in that room, and you do whatever it is you do that makes you so popular." Madam Knight wagged a chubby finger while her other hand rested on the soft pillow of hip that jutted out to the left. The bracelets she wore on her wrist pinched her skin, and the charms jingled as her finger shook. Madam stank of cigarette smoke and roses. The neckline of her black dress plunged deep, revealing her large chest – an asset she insisted on showing off at all times. Even the apron worn by the madam seemed designed to aid her gaudy display.

She wondered if she would end up like Madam Knight in her old age. The thought disgusted her, and she absently ran her hand down the curve of her slim body.

"Do you hear me?"

Attention returned to the woman who controlled her every move. "Yes, ma'am." She kept her eyes low, her voice soft and submissive.

She knew how to play the game. She had learned at an early age. Girls who didn't obey went hungry and were worked harder. It wasn't a position she wanted to return to.

Girls who did as they were told were favored, they were treated and fed well and had nice beds to sleep in.

Madam Knight raised an eyebrow and pressed past, her ample rear swishing down the hallway. She disappeared into the parlor of the spa, her shrill voice greeting another client who patiently waited his turn.

New Orleans, Storyville, to be exact, wasn't the place for proper young women. But she had not been proper since setting foot in Madam's brothel years earlier. She had learned quickly and become a master at what she did, paying the price when she didn't do as she was expected.

She turned toward the closed door before her – the room was called The Parisian, mainly for its lavish gold walls and deep red furnishings. A little statue of what Madam called the Eiffel Tower was inside. With a deep breath, she heaved the door open. It wasn't heavy, but the weight of her life was, and it forced her to push harder. Her step was cautious, her eyes kept low. Some girls entered a room with gusto. She had learned that being demure, shy even, was the way to act with most. The customer always wanted to be in charge.

This was a new client – a first-timer. She had been with several boys for their first experience in the brothel. A few of them were unable to go through with it, but most did. The majority were nice, very few treated her poorly. Out of this one, however, she expected the latter.

Madam had said his name was Jimmy Arnold, the heir to the Arnold Hotel dynasty. Like many others, his father had brought him to the spa for his grand entrance into manhood. Madam had recommended her for this particular client because of her gentle nature. She wondered why one of the other more pliable girls hadn't been sent to this room, as they were meek. She wasn't meek, she only acted that way.

She entered the room and gave a cautious glance toward the hotel heir through her lowered lashes. From about five feet away, she guessed he stood more than a head above her with short hair the color of corn silk. He looked neither nervous nor aggressive. In fact, he almost looked bored. Perhaps this was not his first time, and his father had no clue. That would make things easier, but he was hard to read. She gave a small curtsy and stood in the center of the room, awaiting his first move.

He took a step toward her, his soft heel soundless on the carpet. He reached a hand to her chin and lifted her face with a single finger. She met his gaze but did not smile. Smiling was saved for saying thank you or for her regular clients who often gave her cash personally so she could hide it away. His stormy blue eyes examined her while his other hand rubbed the fabric of her dress between his fingers.

The dress was the color of the sky, made of silk. Despite her social status, she was always well clothed. Madam made sure every one of her dresses was blue, the color chosen for her. It was a good color for her, the coolness playing off the warmth of her dark curls. Her hair, almost black in color, wound in tight ringlets down her back, though she usually wore her hair pinned to the top of her head to keep it under control. Her eyes were also nearly black in color, but her skin was as pale and smooth as milk. She had overheard Madam once saying she was the most beautiful of all her girls, but she figured all the girls were told that if they brought in enough money every night.

The young Mr. Arnold released her chin and stepped back. "How does this work?" he asked. "Do you do as I tell you?" Disdain was in his voice, but he was curious. That she could tell.

"Yes, sir," she replied, her voice low and soft. "Or I can help ... things ... if you desire."

"I think I know what I would like." The hotel heir pulled his shirt off over his head, revealing a well-toned chest. She used to flinch and look away when men would expose their chest, but it no longer held any emotion for her.

He went around to her back and quietly undid her dress. She closed her eyes and prayed to a God she wasn't sure existed for someone to rescue her – but nobody ever came. It was ritual for her now; the clothes came off, and she prayed for a miracle that never happened. Then she did her job for the few pennies Madam allowed her to keep.

When it was over, she helped Jimmy Arnold dress, as it was her personal custom. She always helped her clients look just as sharp going out as they did coming in, as if they had not just used her body for pleasure. She spoke as little as possible, especially to clients who turned out like Mr. Arnold. Even though she could tell he was inexperienced, that hadn't stopped him from treating her like dirt. Worse than dirt.

Dressed, the hotel heir tossed a penny to her. "I suppose I should tip you for making sure I look respectable leaving this place. I might just come back to see you again."

The girl did not want to look desperate for the coin, but she had precious few to call her own. She tucked the penny into a hidden pocket along her collar and followed him out of the room. Once they were in the parlor, the younger Mr. Arnold was met by his father, who promptly slapped him on the back and handed him a lit cigar.

"Happy sixteenth birthday, my boy," he bellowed. The boy looked at her and nodded his head. His father's gaze followed. "Ain't she a ripe one? I may have to come see you myself, darlin'! Just don't tell your mother, Jimmy."

She stared ahead. When Madam shot her a sideways glance, she curtsied a little and batted her eyelashes the way Madam liked. To not flirt back with clients was to risk losing dinner for the night, and they received so little as it was. Madam showed the men out the door with a wave and a smile, her chest leading the way.

"Well done, my pet, well done!" Madam exclaimed as she came back into the parlor. "Mr. Arnold paid a small fortune for his son's sixteenth birthday. And the young Mr. Arnold surely wasn't bad to be with, was he? Quite a handsome boy. I trust you showed him the ropes."

"He didn't seem to need much showing, Madam. I did as expected, though," she replied, her voice still as timid as she could make it.

Madam snickered. "Good girl. Now, he didn't give you any extra money, did he?"

Madam made sure there were no pockets on any girl's dress so they could not keep money on them. She regularly checked in their underclothes drawers or rifled through their things for hidden coins or bills they might hide from her.

"No, Madam," she lied.

She hated lying, but it was the only way she would be able to save some money for when she was kicked out on her twenty-first birthday for being too old for Madam's clients. She had stitched tiny pockets into the collar for coins, completely undetectable from Madam's random searches. She had made a larger space along her hemline for bills, though those were fewer and farther between.

"Of course not," Madam cooed, pinching her cheek until it hurt. "You are one of my best girls, aren't you? Now, if you don't mind, a Mister Smith is waiting for you in The Magnolia Room. He asked specifically for you and didn't mind waiting when I told him you had ... ah ... run on an errand for me. We do want our clients to feel like they are the most important one, you know."

"Yes, Madam." She curtsied and turned to the mirror.

Taking extra care, she straightened her hair and adjusted a few pins. A fresh coat of lipstick ran smoothly across her lips. She didn't care what color it was, just that it went over her lips and protected them from the onslaught they experienced nightly. Fluffing a few wrinkles from her dress, she was ready for the next one. She knew several Mr. Smiths and wasn't sure which one was waiting for her.

She walked down a different hallway and knocked on the third door on the left. All the doors were worn, the handles smooth from use. Glancing down the dimly lit hall, she could hear laughter come from one of the other rooms. There was no gaiety for her once the sun went down.

When a deep voice bade her to enter, she did. It had not been ten minutes since she had left the company of Mr. Arnold, and when Mr. Smith – the one with the mustache and body odor – practically ripped her dress off, she knew it would be a long night.

New Orleans was exactly as Teddy Sullivan expected. Brightly colored and jubilant on the outside – teeming with depressed sinners and the downtrodden on the inside. He had just moved to the Southern port city from rural Maryland on his journey to save the wicked souls of the world. His home parish was full of those already saved, boring folks whose worst sins were gossip and gluttony. Christ had called his followers to reach the ends of the earth, and by golly, this was it.

Colors popped out at him everywhere he looked. Some buildings were bright yellow, others green or blue. He even passed a pink house. Never in his life had he seen a pink house. Teddy was lured into the opulence he saw. But that opulence had been bought with the devil's money, he knew. And he was determined to change the city for the better. He would paint New Orleans for the Lord instead of the enemy.

His mentor, Billy Sunday, would be so proud of him, Teddy thought. Once he got a church up and running, he would write to Reverend Sunday, the so-called "baseball evangelist," and let him know all about his success. There was no room for failure in Teddy's mind. New Orleans would be a city won for Christ.

Teddy turned around, suitcase in hand, and surveyed the damage the devil had caused. He knew he could save lives here if he could get a foothold. His first order of business was to find a room to sleep in. His second order of business was to find a place to preach.

As he strolled along Basin Street, he came to the Night and Day Spa for Men. It was a cheery yellow house, three stories tall with feminine lace curtains in all the windows. Deciding it looked clean, Teddy entered in hopes that they could direct him toward a cheap place to rest his weary head.

A large woman with too much cleavage protruding forth to be in good taste greeted him warmly as he stepped into a plush parlor.

"Hello, Sir! Welcome to the Spa. How may I assist you this evening?"

"Hi, yes, ma'am. I'm sorry to bother you. I'm new in town and am looking for a cheap room to rent. I figure as you probably see a lot of new arrivals you could recommend a place?"

The heavyset woman frowned, probably upset that he wasn't giving her business, but perhaps once he had settled in, he could come in to witness to her employees and customers. Plus, Teddy had heard all about spas and their healing qualities before and thought some time in a steam room sounded good.

"Well, I happen to know Mr. Arnold of Arnold's Hotels. He has several across New Orleans. Will you be here long, Mr. –?"

"Sullivan," he answered with a smile. "And yes, I'm moving to the area, but I don't mind holing up in a hotel for a bit so I can get settled."

Teddy looked around the room a little more. The furniture was near opulent – the most luxurious he had ever seen. Everything decorated in rich reds, greens, and golds. From the corner of his eye, he saw two young girls enter the room. The abundant hostess took up most of his view, but Teddy could almost swear that the taller of the girls, the one with red hair, was wearing a nightgown. The other girl, smaller with dark curly hair, wore a blue dress with a neckline that sunk nearly as low as that of the woman before him, though her chest wasn't nearly as abundant. Teddy hoped his eyes were simply playing tricks on him in the low lighting. He knew maids could hike up their hems for tips, but this was outrageous. What kind of spa was being run in by this grotesque woman? The sin in this city was worse than he thought.

The smaller girl looked up and met his gaze briefly. She lowered her lashes in a move Teddy might have thought was flirtatious, but the pain he saw behind her eyes outweighed the allure of a pretty face. She wasn't playing coy with him; she was hiding the windows to her soul.

"Wonderful, Mr. Sullivan," the woman said, drawing his attention back to her and her ample bosom. "We love new residents here at the spa. Go down this road here three blocks and make a left onto Canal. The Arnold Arms will be on your right. You can't miss it, and Mr. Arnold welcomes people who want to stay long term. Just tell him Victoria Knight sent you."

She gave a hearty chuckle, though Teddy didn't know what the joke had been. The woman ran her hands down her sides and swayed her hips a little. Teddy did his best to look anywhere but at her.

"Thank you, Mrs. Knight. I appreciate your kindness," he said, trying to block the girls from his mind and remember the directions.

"Any time, Mr. Sullivan. Next time you come in, remind me, and we'll give you the newcomer's discount."

"Thank you," Teddy said as he slipped out the door.

He surveyed the windows again and noticed what a large spa Mrs. Knight ran. He wondered at the services they offered. As far as he knew, spas offered steam rooms, hot baths, and other aquatic therapies. This spa's offerings must be vast to use such a large building, he mused.

As he tried to make sense of the directions given to him, Teddy's mind was drawn back to the curly-haired girl with the pain in her eyes. Despite the poor lighting and the near blackness of her eyes, he could still see the hurt that lingered there. He would definitely have to return to that spa and gauge their receptiveness to attending church services.

The Arnold Arms Hotel soon sprawled out before him a good eight stories high, its grandeur and presence foreboding. The building had at one time been white, but the paint was now yellowed with age and salty air. However, that didn't diminish the majesty of the place. Teddy wasn't sure he had the cash to afford a room in such a locale, but he walked through the front door to see. Maybe they would take pity on a poor minister from the North.

"Excuse me, sir. I am in need of a room for at least a week, if not several weeks," he said to the suited lad behind the counter. "But I'm not entirely sure I can afford such a swanky place."

The boy gave a lazy smile in return. "I'm sure we can work something out, sir. I'm the owner's son, so I can help you with anything you need. What brings you to our fine city?"

"I'm a minister, come to find a flock for the Lord here in New Orleans," Teddy exclaimed with a smile, his enthusiasm shining through.

The blond-headed teen did not return his smile. "There's plenty of people here, Reverend," he said with tightness in his Southern drawl. "Since you're a man of the cloth, I can give you a generous discount on a small room on our top floor. We even have an elevator."

"Praise God! I tell you this is the friendliest town I have ever encountered," Teddy said as he stamped his hand down on the counter. "I'll take what you got, my good man!"

Teddy was shown to an eighth-floor room that was sparsely decorated. A simple single bed was neatly made against the far wall; behind it, a three-legged nightstand with a small lamp sat waiting for a patron's wallet and glasses. The single window opposite the bed let in the only natural light. But it was clean. Teddy loved it.

"This is not our best room, Reverend, but it's affordable, and I can guarantee you'll have peace and quiet up here.

And you can stay here as long as you like; we'll bill you weekly. Just tell us when you're ready to check out. We do serve supper downstairs at seven p.m. sharp."

"It's just what I need, my boy. What did you say your name was?"

The teen looked at him, taken aback. It seemed he expected everybody to know who he was. "I'm Jimmy Arnold. Son of James Arnold."

"Thank you so much, Mr. Arnold. A certain woman, Mrs. Knight, she said, assured me I would find it hospitable here. I look forward to staying here and getting to know your fine town," Teddy said as he set his bag down.

The boy raised an eyebrow to him. "Mrs. Knight?"

"Yes," Teddy said with a smile.

"Another one goes down," he said with a scowl on his face.

Not understanding, Teddy asked the boy to repeat himself.

"Nothing. Nothing at all, Reverend," Jimmy said. The scowl turned into a well-practiced smile. He nodded and left the room.

Alone, Teddy stretched out onto the small bed. He set his wire glasses down on the nightstand and rubbed his eyes. He had about thirty minutes before the hotel dinner was served, and he wanted to rest his eyes after all the colors and sounds he had experienced walking through the city streets. After he ate, he would hit the streets again, looking for the right place to use as his makeshift church. He also hoped to meet more locals.

After a filling dinner, Teddy set out again. The French Quarter was exactly like he had heard. People spoke a mix of English and French, the melodious voices floated in the air along with the sounds of a distant piano being played.

Teddy smiled at the songful ruckus. Babies cried, and mothers shushed them while children played in the streets. One group played kick the can, the can landing at Teddy's feet. He eagerly kicked the can back into the game, a smile breaking out onto his face. The entire city was alive, Teddy thought. It lived and breathed all on its own.

Teddy turned left onto another street, and while the scenery wasn't vastly different, the atmosphere certainly was. Jazz music blared, and the sound of a live trumpet blasted through an open doorway. Teddy had heard about jazz music from others. It was the music of sin, they had said. The music of loose women with no morals – let alone questionable morals – and the men who kept them in business. While he had never heard jazz music before, he wasn't sure why it was so objectionable. It was different, soulful, and catchy. It didn't seem to be harmful the way others had told him.

Bistros and music houses behind wrought iron gates were abruptly replaced with propped up garish gates welcoming in anyone who dared. Now that it was night, he realized he had wandered into Storyville. The red-light district of New Orleans was where legal brothels stood grandly, and nickel hookers littered the alleys behind them. The very street he walked earlier that afternoon without a clue in the world.

A swallow stuck in his throat as he turned a circle, realizing just what kind of buildings stood before him. Teddy was sure his face blanched, and he had to cough a few times to unlodge the lump in his throat. He had intentionally walked into one of these dens of sin to ask for directions. The girls he thought had looked questionable really were questionable – they were prostitutes!

The brightly colored, appealing buildings he had

admired that afternoon now looked grotesque in the lamplight. The gingerbread eaves cast foreboding shadows like prison bars. An eerie blood-red glow came from several windows, beckoning men like a siren in the ocean.

As he looked around, a woman called out to him, inviting him inside. His heart thudded in his chest, and he saw spots before his eyes. He hurried past the woman whose tittering echoed after him, confusion and humiliation filling his heart.

Teddy wasn't sure how to feel. He was a preacher, a man after God's heart. He was supposed to avoid people of doubtful repute. Yet, Christ had called him to minister to people such as these. Sinners. People who wouldn't know Him otherwise. Maybe this was where God had called him, a man of the cloth sent to witness to those who made a living taking their clothing off.

He could feel it in his heart. Yes, this is what he was to do. God was calling him to help save the ones the rest of the world had given up on. That was what Reverend Sunday had taught him and encouraged him to do. Was this not what he had been preparing for all along? And he would do it, one sinful soul, at a time. Teddy walked down the block to the Day and Night Spa and stood before the open doorway.

He was greeted once again by the flashy large woman with the near-exposed bosom. The finery of her dress was diminished by the gaudy jewelry and obscene amount of cleavage.

"Mr. Sullivan! You came back to us," she gushed. "I'm so glad. Are you ready for your newcomer discount? Tell me what you're interested in, and I'll help you find what you are looking for." Again, her hands ran down her body from waist to hips. Thick fingers covered in rings tried to draw attention to the woman's curves.

Teddy blushed madly. Single women of his parish back home had flirted with him, but none had outright offered themselves to him. It was completely indecent. But of course, the indecency of it was what made this woman rich.

She sensed his hesitation and nervousness. "Not sure just yet? No, of course not! You've only just arrived." She waved her arm in a circle. "All my girls are well trained in entertainment and relaxation. Maybe a trip to the steam room would help you relax to start? A mere fifty cents for a steam. Make it a dollar, and we will throw in a massage for you. I'm sure you're tired after traveling so far. Did you take the train?"

"The train? Yes," he stammered. He took a deep breath. A steam bath did sound good. But was it a sin to consider a steam in such a place? If he was going to introduce these women to God, he needed to get in their good graces. Time in a steam bath sounded safe, didn't it?

"Yes, Mrs. Knight, I think a steam sounds … heavenly." He smiled.

"It certainly is, sir," she said with a husky chuckle.

She turned and quietly lifted her hand. Immediately, the young brunette girl he had spotted earlier quickly approached and gave a brief curtsy. Her tightly wound curls bounced as she moved. The Madam whispered into her ear, her words curt but breathy.

"Now, Mr. Sullivan, that will be one dollar," she said, assuming he wanted the massage. Without arguing, Teddy pulled a dollar out of his pocket and handed it to Mrs. Knight, who promptly stuffed it between her breasts. "This girl will show you to the steam room. There are dressing rooms for your personal items. Enjoy yourself."

With that, she sauntered off with a wink and left Teddy standing with the petite brunette. She curtsied to him and turned without a word. He obligingly followed, praying the whole way that he would figure out just what to say that might bring this girl closer to the God he loved.

She sighed as she led the way to the steam rooms. At least it was a steam room and not a bedroom, she thought. The tall man with the clean-cut look followed her apprehensively. She was used to that, though. Men came from other cities, places where brothels were illegal, to see what Storyville was all about. They would return home to brag about their time in the district, she just knew it.

Madam had called this man Mr. Sullivan. He looked nice, sincere almost. Not like many of her other customers who looked nothing but lustfully at her. Mr. Sullivan did not seem to have that devious streak she was used to seeing. He kept his distance from her and refused to look her in the eye. With dark hair cut short and his face clean-shaven, his bright green eyes stood out behind the glasses he wore. They reminded her of young magnolia leaves. His face and hands were tanned but were not dark and wrinkled like those who labored outside. She guessed he was close to thirty, a good ten years older than she was, but there was no way to know, and she really didn't much care.

Outside the steam room, she turned a small knob, then opened a dressing room door. "You may leave your clothes in here, sir. There's a robe you may put on if you wish. I will meet you inside."

The man nodded and disappeared behind the door. She heard fumbling but decided he would ask for help if he required it. Many men she assisted in the steam room requested that she undress them personally, an act she found to be more intimate than the job she was paid for. A sigh of relief escaped her lips as she closed the door behind him.

She quickly went into her own dressing room and disrobed, putting on a short gown cinched loosely at her waist. She checked the mirror and pulled a few loose tendrils from her bound hair; she arranged the gown so that it exposed her shoulder and a bit of décolletage. Her training had taught her to always show as much skin as possible. She slipped out of the dressing room and into the steam room.

The room was warm, and she immediately felt the dampness on her skin. Despite the heat, she enjoyed the steam room. It was relaxing, and she didn't usually have to give of herself, though she was instructed to offer and give the price. The steam rooms were like a sanctuary since the men could hardly see her, and she could hardly see them. The men usually just wanted to talk and maybe touch a little. She sat on the wooden bench behind the steam and pulled the collar of her gown open a little. Her patron came in slowly, unsure of his step in the dark, misty room.

"This way," she called softly to guide him. He found her and sat on the opposite end of the bench a good four feet away from her. "Do you want your massage right away, or would you like a minute to take in the steam first?" She kept her voice low and soft. She looked at him, his green eyes still piercing despite the lack of bright lighting.

"Um, just a minute, please, if you don't mind," he said. "I just need a minute to collect my thoughts."

She shrugged a little, but he didn't notice. "That's just fine, sir. Let me know how I can assist you. What was your name?"

"Theodore Sullivan, but my friends call me Teddy," he

said as he pulled the terry cloth robe closer to his chin. Like every other patron, he didn't bother to ask her name.

"Mr. Sullivan," she said, testing out the name. "What brought you to our fair city?" She scooted a few inches closer to him. She went through all the words and moves by rote, just as she had been trained.

He cleared his throat. "Actually, Miss, I'm a preacher. I just came here from Maryland to start a new church." He looked away from her, embarrassed.

"Oh," she said quietly. Another man supposedly devoted to God, who was more interested in worshipping skin. Sensing his embarrassment, she quietly said, "Don't feel bad, Mr. Sullivan. We get all kinds here, even preachers."

He sat up straight as an arrow and quickly retorted, "I'm not here for that! I can't imagine any man who has dedicated his life to Christ frequenting a ... a ... bawdy house!" He stood and shook his fist in the air.

"I'm sorry, sir, but you've got to admit ... you are here," she said quietly. The outburst didn't surprise her, the embarrassed ones always seemed to get irate.

He looked around the room and at her, his voice calmed. "Yes, I am here. But I'm here to try to save you all from your sin. One person at a time," he said, stepping toward her.

"You don't have to worry about that, Reverend." She laughed. "The priests come weekly to hear our confessions."

"They do?" He seemed shocked.

She giggled again. "They do. They hear our confessions, and then they get the week of sin started again. The priests of New Orleans are some of our best patrons."

The pain and distress were obvious on the man's face. Apparently, there were no corrupt clergymen in Maryland. At least not ones he knew of. She knew that those who proclaimed righteousness were usually the biggest hypocrites.

"That's terrible. I can't believe that. I'm not here for that. I don't even want the massage. I came here so I could talk to you girls, one by one, and tell you about Christ and how he died for you. I want to help you all get away from these brothels. These legal houses of sin and debauchery." The man paced the floor in front of her, clearly upset.

"Mr. Sullivan, I would love to get out of here," she said breathlessly, knowing she shouldn't speak at all on the subject. But for some reason, she felt like she could open up to this man.

The man stood, dumbstruck. "Wait – you don't want to be here? Truly?"

She choked back a chortle. "Who would choose this life? Madam Knight owns us. I hear slavery isn't legal anymore, but she bought each of the girls here. I don't know about the others, but I want to leave."

"I'm baffled," he said, scratching his head.

"Clearly."

"Why not just leave then? Why do you stay?" He sat again and peered into her eyes. He wanted to see her, not just view her for his own merriment. It made her heart race.

"Did you not hear me? She owns us. The only way out of this life is to run and risk getting caught or get married. And last I heard, there's not many men beating down doors of whore houses to marry us. If you have somewhere for me to go where Madam won't come after me, and I won't starve to death, I'm all ears!"

"That woman out there, she owns you? How old are you?" The notion was still registering in his head. She could see the confusion in his eyes.

"I'm nineteen now, but she bought me from my uncle

when I was eleven." Looking down, she shared some of her story. "My parents died, and the town preacher gave me to my uncle because he was the only relation they could find. He brought me here and sold me to Madam for two dollars. I saw her give it to him. Then Madam gave me a new name and set me to work."

"That's terribly sad," he said. He looked as though he might cry, but perhaps it was just the moisture from the room.

"That's my life, mister."

"And you ... you sleep with these men?"

"We don't sleep much, Mr. Sullivan," she said honestly.

"Oh, Jesus, help her," he exclaimed. "Since you were eleven?"

"Yes, sir."

"And you had no say in the matter at all?"

"Of course not. None of us did," she said. "Well, most of us, at least. We were bought into it, or forced into it because of circumstances."

"I need to get out of here," he said, rushing for the door and loosening the material around his throat. He grasped for the door, and she followed him, afraid he might faint any moment.

Once out in the cooler air, Teddy Sullivan got his breath back. She fanned him off and offered him a chair, her robe falling open in her haste.

"Please cover yourself," he pleaded, shielding his eyes.

She did as he requested, haphazardly pulling the robe together and cinching it. Men looked at her body all the time, so she thought nothing of the exposure.

"I'm sorry. I guess I had the wrong notion about these places," he said. "I thought my mission was to come here and save all of you from this life. I thought you all had chosen it with gusto. Never did it enter my mind that you were forced to do ..." He stopped talking and took a deep breath. "Well, I'm sorry."

"It's okay, Mr. Sullivan." She tried to reassure him. "We're used to it. I'm used to it. This is my life. And I like most of the other girls here. We are family."

He went into his dressing room without speaking. She waited for him outside the door, not bothering to change herself.

When Teddy came out, he pressed a coin into her hand. "Please take this," he whispered.

"But I did nothing to earn it," she said with a quizzical look on her face.

"You talked to me. That is all I want. Goodnight, Miss—" He stopped. "I didn't catch your name."

"I never told you. Most men don't ask."

He took a step closer to her and took her hand in his. Her heart beat loudly in her chest with the intimate gesture.

"What is your name, miss?" His gaze changed, and he smiled at her genuinely as his green eyes gazed into hers.

She returned the smile. Her brown eyes welled with tears at his tenderness. "My name is Bluebell," she said, breathless. "But my friends call me Bell."

CPSIA information can be obtained
at www.ICGtesting.com
Printed in the USA
FSHW020216010221
78087FS